Prism

"Nikki Soarde shows the love, tenderness and sexiness this type of ménage can bring when the people involved truly care for each other." ~ *EuroReviews*

"...a terrific story. Ms. Soarde is a talented author, with a knack for creating very sexy and totally believable characters." ~ *Coffee Time Romance*

"...these sex scenes are hot, hot, hot! Reading these scenes reminded me of sitting in the corner with my first, hot paperback and gorging myself on each and every sexual scene. ...I was left breathless with anticipation." ~ *Just Erotic Romance Reviews*

Twilight

"As fans of Ms. Bast know, she writes stories that have an element of suspense, the paranormal, and steamy lovemaking. Twilight delivers all three, along with characters that the readers will come to care about." ~ *Romance Reviews Today*

"Bast has written a tantalizing treat in which two men find ultimate pleasure in satisfying the needs of one woman. The ending is exciting and tense." ~ *Romantic Times BOOKclub*

Pirates Booty

AND LADY MAKES *Three*

Nikki Soarde
Anya Bast
Ashley Ladd

ELLORA'S CAVE
ROMANTICA PUBLISHING

An Ellora's Cave Romantica Publication

www.ellorascave.com

And Lady Makes Three

ISBN #1419953443
ALL RIGHTS RESERVED.
Prism Copyright© 2005 Nikki Soarde
Twilight Copyright© 2005 Anya Bast
Pirates Booty Copyright© 2005 Ashley Ladd

Edited by Sue-Ellen Gower, Briana St. James and Linda Carroll-Bradd.
Cover art by Syneca

Electronic book Publication July 2005
Trade paperback Publication March 2006

Warning:

The following material contains graphic sexual content meant for mature readers. *And Lady Makes Three* has been rated E–rotic by a minimum of three independent reviewers.

Ellora's Cave Publishing offers three levels of Romantica™ reading entertainment: S (S-ensuous), E (E-rotic), and X (X-treme).

S-*ensuous* love scenes are explicit and leave nothing to the imagination.

E-*rotic* love scenes are explicit, leave nothing to the imagination, and are high in volume per the overall word count. In addition, some E-rated titles might contain fantasy material that some readers find objectionable, such as bondage, submission, same sex encounters, forced seductions, and so forth. E-rated titles are the most graphic titles we carry; it is common, for instance, for an author to use words such as "fucking", "cock", "pussy", and such within their work of literature.

X-*treme* titles differ from E-rated titles only in plot premise and storyline execution. Unlike E-rated titles, stories designated with the letter X tend to contain controversial subject matter not for the faint of heart.

Contents

~

About the Author

෨

Nikki lives in a small town in Ontario, Canada. In the midst of the chaos that comes with raising three small boys, working part-time as a lab tech in a hospital blood bank, and caring for her ever-adoring husband, she dreams up her stories. Nikki's work is an eclectic combination of romance, mystery, suspense and humor with characters that have plenty of room to grow. To learn more about her and her work visit her at www.nikkisoarde.com.

Nikki welcomes mail from readers. You can write to her c/o Ellora's Cave Publishing at 1056 Home Avenue, Akron OH 44310-3502.

Also by Nikki Soarde

෨

Balance of Power

Duplicity

Ellora's Cavemen: Legendary Tails III (*anthology*)

Jagged Gift

Phobia

Prism

By
Nikki Soarde

෴

Trademarks Acknowledgement

~

The author acknowledges the trademarked status and trademark owners of the following wordmarks mentioned in this work of fiction:

Audi: Audi AG

Formica: Formica Corporation

L'Oreal: L'Oreal Société Anonyme France

Tylenol: McNeilab, Inc

Nautilus: Jones, Arthur DBA Nautilus Sports/Medical Industries

Armani: GA Modefine S.A.

Chapter One

ॐ

Dax rolled over and slapped the snooze button, but Shania Twain wasn't silenced so easily.

"Jesus," he muttered, as she continued to glory in her femininity. He didn't care how wonderful it was to be a woman, didn't know — didn't *want* to know.

He hit the button again. But her voice still filled the room, her sugary twang almost as irritating as her irrepressible cheerfulness.

"What does it take—"

Smack.

" —to get you—"

Splat.

" —to shut the fuck—"

Swack.

" —up!"

He rolled out of bed, crouched on the floor, reached for the plug and yanked it out of the wall.

Silence. Blissful, rapturous, blessed *silence*.

Dax dragged himself back up to sit on the edge of the bed. He dropped his head into his hands and groaned. "Tequila," he moaned. "I remember tequila." Actually, he remembered a *lot* of tequila. He also remembered an enormous platter of very spicy nachos, loud music and...karaoke. Did he really sing along to Robert Palmer's *Addicted to Love*?

Suddenly he lifted his head and sniffed the air. Coffee.

Naked and running solely on caffeine fumes he trudged down the hall into the kitchen. He grabbed a mug from the cupboard, doped it up with sugar and had downed his first scalding sip by the time he felt the presence behind him. Very slowly he turned around.

"Hangover?" asked Clay, his voice as silky and lustrous as the amber tie knotted loosely at his throat.

Another dose of caffeine fortified Dax to face Clay's laser-blue gaze. Those eyes had blinded lesser men. And more than a few women.

Dax gulped down another mouthful and raised his gaze. "This isn't a hangover."

Clay crossed his arms over his chest and leaned his rangy frame against the doorjamb.

Damn, he looked good. But then again, Clay always looked good. Whether, like today, he sported pleated chinos and a draped rayon button-up or ass-hugging jeans and a skintight muscle shirt, Clay always looked put together. With that spiked blond hair, gold earring and half-day's worth of stubble, the guy screamed out *style*. He fuckin' dripped with it. If he were anybody else, Dax would have resented the hell out of him for it.

"No?" asked Clay. "If it's not a hangover, then what is it?"

"It's a manifestation of God's wrath, visited directly on my skull."

"You don't believe in God."

Dax took another sip, savoring the heat as it drained down his throat. "Call in the priests. I'm about to recant."

Clay rolled his eyes, but didn't smile. Something was wrong.

But then Clay held out his hand and opened his fingers. "How about drugs? Do you believe in drugs?"

Dax hesitated. "Drugs?"

"Uh-huh."

"Good drugs?"

"The best."

"Tylenol?"

"With codeine."

Dax snatched them up and popped them in his mouth. "You're an angel."

"Huh." Clay turned away. "If I'm an angel, what does that make you?"

Dax swallowed the pills with the last of the coffee, tossed the mug in the sink and followed his partner into the living room.

As usual, the place was a mess. Newspapers and textbooks littered the coffee table, and a half-eaten bowl of popcorn sat on top of the television. Several stray socks had huddled beneath the state-of-the-art stereo and a stack of unpaid bills waited patiently on the armchair. The futon, at least, was free of clutter, but only because all the crap got kicked off of it whenever one of them decided to nap there.

Dax leaned against the back of the futon for support. "Huh? What the hell does that mean?"

Clay stood before the CD rack, hands jammed in his pockets, scanning titles. "You were drunk last night."

"Yeah? So? I seem to recall that happening before." He brushed a few strands of his long chestnut mane out of his eyes. "On occasion."

"Yeah, well you were *really* drunk."

Already feeling more himself, Dax hopped over the back of the futon and sat down. He leaned forward, bracing his elbows on his knees. "I seem to recall spending half of my time at college being 'really' drunk. You didn't mind then."

"That's because I was 'really drunk', too. I didn't know the difference."

"*Aha.*" Dax leaned back and spread his arms wide. "There's the problem. You didn't drink *enough* last night. If you had, then maybe you would have had some fun."

Clay pulled out a CD, examined it, stuck it back in the slot. "Somebody needed to stay sober so they could drive you home and carry you into bed."

"You didn't carry me," said Dax, feeling defensive, "and since when is this a problem, anyway? I lost count of the times I had to clean you up and put *you* to bed."

Suddenly Clay whirled on him. "I was fucking *bored* last night, okay? The crowd was dull, the service was slow, the food was bad, and—" He growled something unintelligible and stalked over to the sliding glass doors. He unlocked the door and tugged it open a few inches, allowing a fragrant spring breeze to flirt with his hair.

Dax was feeling disoriented. This wasn't like Clay at all. "And what? What else?"

"Come on, Dax. *Karaoke*? I mean, how desperate is that?"

"I just wanted to try something different. If you didn't want to go, you should have said so."

"I did. But you were already too drunk to listen to me. Too drunk to care."

"You're just mad because I dragged you onstage with me."

"I don't even want to *talk* about that."

Dax sprang from the futon. "So, what? I embarrass you now?"

"Only when you imitate Robert Palmer and dance like…like…Ginger Rogers."

Dax's mouth hung open. *Ginger Rogers?* Before he could come up with a response, Clay added, "And for God's sake put some clothes on."

Dax glared at him for a moment before swaggering over to the balcony doors of their third-floor apartment. He leaned against the glass, facing Clay. "My being naked never bothered you before, either."

Clay tossed a nervous glance outside, at the three-story walk-up on the other side of the street. "Maybe not, but the neighbors might have a problem with it."

"I don't know. I think I look pretty good."

Clay's eyes roamed over him, the attempt quick but thorough, and not nearly as discreet as he probably thought. He swallowed thickly, his gaze resting in the general area of Dax's groin. "You know you do."

Dax smiled. Hours of squash, cycling and swimming kept him toned and fit, and he refused to be ashamed of what he'd worked so hard to attain. "Well, then, let 'em enjoy the view."

Dax glanced at the front of Clay's chinos and added, "*You* certainly are."

Clay's gaze snapped to his. "Don't change the subject. If the neighbors see you, they—"

"Oh for God's sake, who the hell cares about the neighbors?"

"We care."

Dax stepped closer. "Do we?"

Clay didn't retreat. "Of course we do. It took us a year to get the landlords to accept our…arrangement."

"Fuck the landlords."

"You don't mean that."

Dax grabbed Clay by the tie and dragged him back into the living room. "Okay, okay, you've got a point."

They stood there, in the middle of the living room, nose to nose, chest to chest, breath mingling, blood pumping.

Dax released Clay's tie and allowed his hands to drift. Through the light fabric of Clay's shirt, Dax traced the outline of Clay's pecs, skimmed the ridges of his abs. Unlike Dax, Clay preferred to get his exercise indoors on treadmills and Nautilus equipment. He worked out four times a week and it showed.

His hands resting on Clay's belt, Dax whispered, "I don't wanna fuck the *landlords*. You know full well who I wanna fuck."

"Is that your answer to everything, Dax?" His body remained stiff, but the objection was halfhearted, and he didn't move away.

"It works for me."

"Maybe I don't want to."

Dax's hand roamed lower, until he brushed across Clay's fly. He pressed his palm against the enticing bulge and grinned. "Oh yeah? Tell me another one."

Clay leaned forward and Dax caught a whiff of exotic spices and heavy musk. "I'm due down at the dealership, Dax."

"Not for three hours, you're not. That's lots of time."

Clay's hands were on him now. Strong fingers gripped Dax's waist, and pulled him closer. The silky fabric of Clay's shirt brushed Dax's chest, cotton chinos rubbed against his cock. His already substantial erection hardened still more.

Clay's whiskers grazed Dax's ear. "You know," he said, his breath as hot as the blood that pumped through Dax's veins. Into his cock. "I lied before. You didn't dance like Ginger Rogers."

Dax sneaked his hand beneath the waistband of Clay's pants and felt the other man's fingers dig more deeply into his skin. Dax touched the base of Clay's penis and Clay groaned.

"I knew it," said Dax, as he stroked and teased. "I knew you were making it up."

Clay's breathing accelerated, his chest heaving rapidly as Dax drew a line with his tongue down Clay's throat.

"Actually I was being kind," said Clay, his voice surprisingly even. "You looked more like an epileptic monkey."

"What?" Dax's head snapped up and he tugged his hand free, but before he could land a punch Clay had slammed him back onto the futon, and pinned his wrists down.

"Hey!" protested Dax, too surprised to put up a decent fight. "You can't say something like that to me and get away with it."

Clay waggled his eyebrows. "Watch me." And then he bent his head and took Dax's cock deeply into his mouth.

Dax's head fell back against the futon. "Oh Jesus." He writhed and groaned but Clay's grip on his wrists only tightened. Physically the two men were a pretty even match, a trait that came in handy for the occasional wrestling match. Or sex game. If Dax had really wanted to, he probably could have dislodged Clay's hands and freed himself. But why the hell would he want to?

Clay didn't bother with niceties. His mouth was rough, hard, his tongue eager. Sweat broke out on Dax's chest, trickled down his belly. Apparently Clay noticed. Suddenly, he broke off to lave Dax's stomach with his tongue. He lapped up the beads of sweat that had pooled in Dax's navel, and then dragged his tongue back over the flat plane of Dax's belly toward his cock. The action was slow and torturous, the anticipation agonizingly sweet.

"Jesus, man," groaned Dax as his stomach muscles twitched and quivered. "Get on with it already."

"Patience," said Clay, "you're always in such a rush." His tongue reached the base of Dax's penis and drew a languid line along its length.

He reached the tip, licked away the bead of cum and then, very slowly, took him deep again. He sucked slowly at first, and Dax relaxed, giving himself over to the sensations. But the respite was brief.

Within moments Clay had resumed his hard, rapid strokes, and Dax's fists were clenched as he fought a climax that threatened to come too soon.

Abruptly Clay released his wrists, reached around, dug his fingers into Dax's ass and that was all it took. Dax came, arching his back and pumping himself dry as the ecstasy poured through him, and out through his loins. Clay's grip on his buttocks never relaxed. He held Dax firmly, taking him far back in his throat until, drained and spent, Dax collapsed back onto the futon.

Clay sat back on his haunches and watched him. His blue eyes danced with mischief and unsated desire. He swiped his sleeve across his mouth and grinned. "You taste like tequila."

"Tequila. Right. Of course I do." Dax sucked in a deep breath and studied his lover. "You can't wear that shirt to work now."

Clay glanced down at himself and shrugged. "Oh well. What's another cleaning bill? I—"

Dax leaned forward, grabbed the shirt in both hands and wrenched it apart, sending buttons flying and exposing the flesh that he so desperately needed to see.

"Hey!" shouted Clay. "This thing's designer. Do you know how much it cost? I—"

Dax leaned forward, grabbed Clay by the legs and arms and swung him up in a fireman's hold. He headed down the hall toward the bedroom.

"What the hell do you think you're doing?" shouted Clay, the irritation in his voice overshadowed by laughter.

"What does it look like I'm doing?"

"But why not in the living room?" Clay's hands found Dax's ass and squeezed.

"I've got an idea."

"An idea?"

They reached the bedroom and Dax threw the other man onto the bed. Clay just lay there, panting, his broad chest glistening with sweat, his cock straining at his fly.

Dax crawled onto the bed, sat between Clay's legs and grabbed his tie. He wrapped it once around his palm and pulled until Clay was sitting up and their mouths were but a breath apart.

"How many ties do you own?" asked Dax, his eyes focused on Clay's.

"I dunno. Fifteen, maybe?"

"That's what I thought."

"Why?"

Dax waggled his eyebrows. "I think it's time we put them to good use."

"What does that mean?"

"Pick out four you think you can part with and I'll show you."

* * * * *

Clay sat bolt upright in bed and cast a worried glance at the clock. A discarded tie covered the digital display and Clay had to fling it aside to see the time.

He breathed a sigh of relief, and flopped back on the pillows. He hadn't slept as long as he thought, and still had an hour before he was due down at the Audi dealership. He was just mulling over the clients he was scheduled to see that afternoon when a loud snort from the other side of the bed demanded his attention.

He propped himself up on his elbow and looked down at the man beside him. He smiled and shook his head. Dax slept like he did everything—with gusto. His long wavy hair was fanned out across the pillow, his arms and legs flung wide. He had a knack for taking up almost three-quarters of the available space on the bed, and his snores could rattle the windows at fifty paces. He worked hard, and played harder, his rugged physique and deeply bronzed skin, attesting to just how much time and energy he devoted to his passions. He gave his all in every situation, and he never turned his back on trouble. Or on a friend.

Barring the occasional forgivable one-night stand, and one catastrophic stab at the suburban, white picket fence myth, Dax and Clay had been together almost since graduation and Clay had never once regretted his decision. They were good together. They were good friends, and God knew the sex was great.

So what was going wrong?

Clay knew he'd overreacted the night before, but he didn't know why. He also didn't know why they'd been arguing more lately, picking fights over everything from which brand of coffee they should buy, to escalating long-distance bills.

He lay back on the pillow and stared at the ceiling as he considered the events of the past few months. Had something changed and they just couldn't see it? If so, how did they figure out what *it* was, and when they did, what did they do about it?

But the more he thought about it, the more certain he was that *nothing* had changed.

Everything in their relationship was exactly the same as it had been a year ago. Two years ago. *Five* years ago.

And then it hit him. At last he knew exactly what was wrong. How could they have missed it? How could they have been so blind?

He closed his eyes and groaned. Now, if only he could figure out what to do about it.

Chapter Two

ဢ

Sidney stared out the airplane window and watched the approaching Toronto skyline. The CN tower speared the sky like a giant needle and the waters of Lake Ontario glittered in the early afternoon sun. It had been three years since she'd been here, three years since she'd seen the faces of her family and friends. Three years was too long to be away from home.

"Ms. Poirot?"

"Yes?" answered Sidney, turning to face the stewardess who crouched beside her. She was a cute little thing, with curly blonde hair and guileless blue eyes. She seemed so innocent, so young.

Sidney shuddered. Just when did someone in their twenties start looking *young*?

"We're on approach," said the girl with a solicitous smile, "and I need you to do up your seat belt."

"Right." Sidney reached for the belt and snapped it together. "Of course."

The girl nodded toward the empty seat beside Sidney. "Your husband has been in the washroom for quite a while. Do you think I should check on him?"

Sidney blinked. "Husband?" And then she realized the mistake and laughed. "Oh God, no. That man's not my husband. I don't even know his name. We just got to talking and realized we had some business interests in common."

The stewardess straightened and Sidney followed her glance toward the first-class washroom stall.

22

"I think he'll be fine," offered Sidney. "He just had a little too much to drink."

The stewardess nodded. "I see. Well, I'll check on him anyway." She turned to go and then seemed to think better of it. "Is there anything I can get you before we land, Ms. Poirot? A glass of water, perhaps? It's been a long flight and we left Paris very early."

"No, thank you," said Sidney, turning back to the window. "I'm fine." And then she shook her head in self-deprecation.

Who was she kidding? She wasn't fine. Hadn't been fine for almost two years now. She'd descended into hell two years ago, and had been struggling to fight her way out of it ever since. Her husband had betrayed her, had lied to her and used her, and it had taken her too long to figure out the full scope of his offenses. She'd wanted to believe in him, had wanted to believe in their marriage vows and the sanctity of that trust, but in the end all her illusions had been shattered.

The divorce had been final three months ago, and it had taken her almost that long to figure out that it wasn't enough. She'd hoped that the finality of the divorce would help her put the whole revolting experience behind her, help her get on with her life. But in the end she'd realized it *wasn't* enough. She needed love and support, needed someone to talk to and laugh with. She needed to share her experiences, and she needed to forget about them and have fun. And thanks to a frantic work schedule and antisocial husband, she hadn't made many new friends in the city she had tried to call home. She'd decided to come back to Toronto. Permanently.

As the city grew closer she considered all those she'd left behind and wondered who would still be here waiting for her. She thought of her sister, married now with four children and a life that Sidney could barely dream of, let alone identify with. She thought of her parents who had grown old and now battled physical infirmities. And then she thought of all the people she'd met in college. Her years at the University of Toronto had been some of the best days of her life, and she had sworn to keep in contact with many of those she'd come to call friends. Of course, she hadn't kept that promise. Who did?

Her seatmate staggered back down the aisle and flopped into his seat. She tossed a wary glance his way to assure herself that he wasn't going to throw up or do something equally offensive.

And then, as her gaze roamed over his mussed up hair and disheveled Armani suit, it hit her.

She knew exactly who she should call. She smiled.

She would look him up immediately. Or maybe she'd wait until she checked into her hotel, showered, did her hair, and fortified herself with a snifter or two of forty-year-old cognac.

This man was not someone to be taken lightly.

* * * * *

Clay tapped his pen on the blotter and stared outside at the sun-washed landscape. The two French lilac bushes that grew on either side of his window framed the view with pale lavender and virginal white. The car dealership was perched on a hilltop, affording him a breathtaking view of the town of Orangeville on one side, and the hills of Caledon on the other. The velvety green carpet rolled away into the distance, dotted with stands of birch and maple trees, pristine white fences and glittering blue ponds.

A flash of brown caught his eye, and he managed to make out a thoroughbred streaking across his paddock, a study in grace, strength and beauty. Not only were

Orangeville and Caledon favorite bedroom communities for the megalopolis of Toronto, but they provided an ideal location for the breeding and raising of horses. Clay sighed. Too bad he was allergic to the things.

"Hey, boss," said a voice from the doorway.

"Yeah, Rick?" he asked, tamping down his irritation. Richard was one of Clay's most successful salesmen, but Clay wished the guy would refrain from calling him "boss". Technically, of course it was true. As sales manager, Clay was in fact his boss, but Clay thought that title should be reserved for the owner.

"You finished with the Watsons?"

Clay frowned, and glanced around his office. "Do you *see* them here?"

"Did they drop a wad?"

Clay's grip on the pen tightened. Good salesman or not, Rick was young and in need of a few lessons in etiquette. What if a customer were outside the door and heard him talk like that? Clay opened his mouth to speak but the ring of his telephone interrupted the reprimand.

He held up his hand. "Hang on a second, Rick. After I take this, I'd like to talk to you."

He picked up the phone. "Clay Masters, Sales Manager."

The other end was silent for a moment, and then a very tentative female voice asked, "Clay? Jeez, I can't believe I actually found you."

Clay blinked. That voice. There was something familiar about it, but... "Uh...I'm afraid you have me at a disadvantage. Should I know you?"

"Oh, I'm sorry..." She laughed then, a light breathy laugh that tripped over the phone line and tipped his tummy on its side. He knew that laugh. "Sidney? Sidney Jennings?"

The laughter stopped. "It's not Jennings anymore, it's—" She hesitated. "Wow. You're good. How did you know?"

He leaned back in his chair and smiled. "It was that laugh of yours. I never met anyone else who laughed like you."

"That's right," she said softly. "I'd almost forgotten. You used to say I sounded like the creek behind your parents' house."

"Uh-huh." He tapped the pen on the blotter again. "Your laugh. Like water bubbling over stones. It was one of your best features."

"Oh Clay, you always did have a way of making me feel special."

Suddenly Clay noticed Rick waving frantically from the doorway. Clay shook his head and waved the man away. He hadn't heard from Sidney for years and a call from a long-lost friend definitely deserved his full attention. He could deal with Rick any time.

"You were special, Sid. Still are, as a matter of fact. Didn't I hear that you made it big with one of the cosmetic firms over in France?"

"My, my, you have good sources."

"Just keep my ear to the ground, that's all. I like to keep up."

"Mmm. I wish I could say the same. I had no idea where you were, and I was just lucky enough to catch your mother on her way out the door. She told me where to find you."

"I didn't go far, did I? I wasn't as brave as you, venturing out into the big exciting world."

"I don't know, Clay." Her sigh was laced with pain. "Sometimes home is the best place to be, after all."

Clay hesitated to break the silence that followed. "So, what's up, Sid? What brings you back to the land of hockey and snowmobiles?"

"It's a long story."

"I've got the rest of my life."

She laughed again, and he was glad. "Well, it's too long to discuss over the phone. How about we meet for coffee or something?"

"I've got a better idea. How about I take you out to dinner? Are you staying in Toronto?"

"Yeah, I have a hotel here."

"Good. I could take you out to Il Fournello. They have the best—"

"Actually, I'd kind of like to get out of the city. Why don't I come up there? I don't need anything fancy. Burgers down at Sammy's would do me just fine."

He smiled. He would have loved to treat her to something special, but knew better than to argue. This was one woman who knew what she wanted and didn't make any bones about saying so. "Okay. It's a date. I could meet you there, say at seven?"

"Great."

"Good, I—"

"Oh, and Clay?"

He glanced at his calendar and realized he had another appointment in five minutes. "Yeah, Sid?"

"Did you happen to keep in contact with Dax?"

Clay swallowed. "Uh...Dax?"

"Yeah. You know...Dax Redmond. I seem to recall some pretty wild nights with you two. You guys were pretty tight, and I was hoping maybe you stayed in touch."

Clay tossed a glance at Dax's picture perched discreetly on a shelf in the corner. The dealership staff knew of their living arrangement, but he didn't like to advertise it too overtly to the customers. "Uh…yeah. I think I could find him. Maybe he could even join us…if you like."

"Oh, that would be wonderful. The two of you together were a blast, and I could really use a lift."

"You've got it."

They said their goodbyes and Clay hung up the phone, but for several moments he didn't move. He just stared at the phone and remembered.

Sidney Jennings. Tall, raven-haired, exotic, with legs to her throat, eyes the size of silver dollars and a keen mind for business. She was beautiful, self-assured and ambitious. And damn if she couldn't party harder than anyone Clay had ever met. Including Dax.

He could already imagine Dax's reaction to the news. A huge smile would spread across his face and his jaw would drop open. And then he would say one little word.

And that word was "Wow"!

Chapter Three

ട

Sidney took a deep breath and pulled open the door to Sammy's Burger Joint. She'd only ever been here once, and it had been almost ten years ago, but she remembered it vividly. It hadn't changed a bit. Chrome and stainless steel, Formica, red vinyl and a little juke box at every table. It smelled of barbecue sauce and hot grease, and the waitresses wore pink uniforms with white aprons. It was the quintessential '50s diner, and was so far removed from anything French, it refreshed her soul.

She stepped inside and scanned the restaurant. Her tummy was hopping and her palms were sweating and she had no idea why. It was just Clay, after all. Clay and Dax were the closest to brothers she'd ever had. She cringed. She'd never even kissed either of them, but for some reason thinking of them as relatives seemed somehow…incestuous.

She stuffed her clammy hands into her jean pockets and spotted a dark chestnut head peeking out from above a booth way in the back. Smiling, she wove her way through the restaurant.

Dax saw her and his face lit up.

"Sidney!" He sprang from the table and enclosed her in a hug that should have, by all rights, crushed at least three of her ribs.

She wrapped her arms around him and hugged him back, savoring the feel of sinew and muscle beneath a layer of well-worn cotton. He smelled like the outdoors, like wind and sun and rain. She caught sight of Clay who had slid out of the booth and now stood beside them.

He looked down at her and shook his head. He tapped his friend on the shoulder. "Jesus, Dax, let the poor thing breathe."

Dax relaxed his embrace but kept one arm wrapped firmly around her waist. "Are you kidding? Sidney here's a regular amazon. I bet she could take us both with one arm tied behind her back." He frowned down at her. "Right? I wasn't hurting you, was I?"

She shook her head. "No, not at all. I needed a really good hug." On the last word her voice cracked and she was mortified to realize she was fighting tears.

"Hey," whispered Clay, reaching for her. "What's wrong?" Then he put an arm around her shoulders, and that was all it took.

The dam burst and tears flooded her eyes. A moment later she found herself compressed between two warm, firm bodies, sobbing against Clay's shoulder while Dax stroked her back and whispered soothing words in her ear.

She continued to cry, long and hard, far past what she'd imagined herself capable of. Or perhaps she just hadn't realized just how deeply her husband had cut her, how lonely she had actually been.

The more she tried to stop it the harder she cried. She was beginning to think the well would never run dry when she heard Clay say over her head. "See? See what you did?"

"What? What the hell do *I* have to do with this?"

"Are you kidding? Every woman you've ever touched has ended up in tears at some point."

"You are so full of it, Clay."

"Face it, buddy. You're cursed."

"You bet I'm cursed. Cursed to have to put up with someone like you for a friend."

"Oh yeah. Here we go…"

In unison they said, "With friends like you, who the fuck needs *enemies*?"

Sidney laughed, and gave them both a mighty shove. They moved back, but not far.

"See?" said Dax, his grin a poor mask for the concern that haunted his eyes. "I told you she was an Amazon."

"You guys…" She shook her head and was startled to feel Clay's thumbs on her cheeks, brushing away the last of her tears.

"Better?" he asked.

Feeling more than a little self-conscious she pushed his hand away and tried her best to smile. "Yeah, yeah. Other than the fact that I'm so hungry I could eat a whole cow, I'm fine."

Dax clapped his hands and rubbed them together. "Good. That's what I like to hear. So what do you say? Enriched white bread, greasy red meat and cheap beer all around?"

Feeling better than she had in months, Sidney smiled. "Sounds better than caviar and champagne to me."

The two men nodded agreement as they motioned for her to snuggle back in the corner of the booth and waved down a pink-frocked waitress.

* * * * *

Dax sat back in his bench and watched her. She was smiling and laughing now, no doubt thanks to his and Clay's banter and antics. They'd very deliberately not asked her about the outburst, focusing instead on more happy topics. They'd reminisced about college days—everything from pub crawls and dorm raids to absent-minded professors and disastrous lab experiments.

Clay dropped his head on the table and moaned. "Oh God, please. Please don't bring that up again. The explosion blew out half the windows and they had to replace two microscopes."

"Look at the bright side," teased Sidney, laying a comforting hand on his shoulder. "They didn't sue."

"They threw me out of the course!" He turned his head to face her. "It was all very humiliating."

Dax drained the last of his beer. "Humiliating perhaps, but it ended up being the best thing that ever happened to you."

Clay sat up and glared at him. "Oh? How the hell do you figure that?"

"If it hadn't been for that fiasco you never would have switched to business."

"Mmm."

Sidney squeezed his shoulder. "Come on, Clay, admit it. You're much better with debits and credits than you are with flasks and microscopes."

"Maybe, but still…"

Sidney leaned closer, put her head on his shoulder and batted her long, dark eyelashes at him. "And if you hadn't switched to business I never would have met you."

"Okay," he conceded. "You got me." Then he turned and planted a kiss on her forehead.

Dax smiled. Those two had always been closer. Clay and Sid had met first through a shared economics course, and Dax had stumbled into the group later—quite literally. He'd been late for class and in his mad dash across campus, had mowed the other two down, knocking textbooks to the ground and scattering notes to the wind. The rest, as they say, was history.

"Or you," said Sidney, her gaze now trained on Dax.

"Yeah. Or me."

Sidney leaned forward, reached across the table and grasped Dax's hands. That little touch sent tiny shivers skittering up his arm. "So, Dax. I know what Clay ended up doing, but what about you? Are you teaching rock climbing? Or maybe a guide for white-water rafting tours?"

Dax smiled. He understood why she would make those kinds of assumptions. In university he'd been a goof-off where academics were concerned. He'd been studying kinesiology, but while it applied very directly to the things he loved to do, he'd had a hard time sitting down and actually reading the texts.

"Actually," he said slowly, "I'm working at the Royal Ontario Museum designing displays while I work toward my PhD in anthropology."

Sidney's eyes couldn't possibly have gotten any bigger. She just stared at him, eyes wide and unblinking and as dark and hypnotic as the midnight sky. Dax felt himself being drawn to her in a way that he hadn't thought possible. He'd always thought she was one of the most beautiful women he knew, but had never really felt attracted to her in any sexual sense of the word. The new sensation surprised him, threw him off balance and he had to fight to ignore it.

He reached out and touched a finger to her chin. "Close your mouth, Sid. I don't want the poor waitress to have to wipe up your drool."

She shook her head and sat back. "Wow, Dax. I mean…" She laughed. "Wow. I don't think you could ever tell me anything that would surprise me more."

Dax and Clay's eyes met before returning their attention to Sid.

"So, what about you, Sid?" asked Clay, his voice soft and compelling. "What happened in Paris that has you so tied up in knots?"

Sid stared at her beer, lifted it to her lips and then set it back on the table. "My husband screwed me over."

"You mean he screwed *around*?" asked Clay.

"No. I mean he screwed me over. Emotionally, intellectually, financially, you name it, he did it. He did everything *except* screw around." She laughed but it was edgy, nervous. "Hell, at least *that* I would have known how to deal with."

Dax and Clay remained silent, waiting for her to finish the story in her own time.

She took a large swallow of beer and, her eyes trained on the bottle, continued. "In case you didn't know, we worked together for L'Oreal. We'd both moved up in the company quite rapidly. I was in product development and marketing and he was into distribution and finances. We'd gotten to know the business so well, we started talking about starting up our own company. We started to save with that in mind, and soon we had several investors lined up. We left L'Oreal on good terms and set the whole thing in motion. The investors signed the contracts, added their money to what Ned and I had already saved and the morning before we were scheduled to finalize everything and begin production of our first product line..." she met Dax's gaze, "he disappeared."

Dax blinked. "What?"

"He took off. He withdrew our money, emptied the bank account and left."

"Jesus," muttered Clay. "Did they catch him?"

She nodded. "Yeah. He was a smart businessman, but a stupid crook. They caught up with him in Venezuela a month later. Luckily he hadn't spent much of the money, and we were able to pay the investors back in full, as well as recoup much of my savings. But I had lost interest in starting up a business." She shrugged. "And of course the marriage."

"Did he go to prison?" asked Clay.

"He'll be out in two years."

"Shit."

"Yeah," she muttered. "Shit."

Dax leaned forward. "I know people," he whispered. "You know…on the *inside*."

Clay leaned in and joined the conspiracy. "Yeah. You know…" he shot a covert glance at the table next to them, "*people*."

Dax waggled his eyebrows. "We could have somebody take care of him for you."

"Yeah," mimicked Clay. "Take *care* of him."

Sidney laughed and the mood instantly lightened. "You guys are so full of shit."

"Maybe," said Dax through a grin. "But we're cute as hell."

Sid looked at him, and then shifted her gaze to Clay. "Yeah. I've gotta agree with you there. You two look great." Her gaze shifted back to Dax. "Really, really great."

Dax preened. "You hear that, Clay? She wants me."

"Actually," said Clay. "I think she wants *me*."

Sid grinned. "I want both of you. Always have, you know. Always will." She grabbed the check. "But I guess I'll just have to satisfy myself with buying you dinner."

"Hey!" Clay tried to snatch the check out of her fingers, but she held it close.

"My treat," she insisted. "The least a maid in distress can do is feed her white knights."

"Well," said Dax. "When you put it that way…"

A few moments later the trio stepped out into a balmy spring evening. A thousand stars glittered in the sky and a soft breeze toyed with their hair. Sidney looked so beautiful, her face lit by moonlight and her eyes brimming with something that Dax hoped was happiness.

They walked her to her rental car and for a moment the conversation lagged.

"Are you okay to drive back to Toronto?" asked Dax. "Because if not—"

"Can I stay with one of you?" Sid clapped her hands across her mouth and took a step back. "Oh shit. I can't believe I just came out with that. I'm so sorry."

"Sid—"

"It's just that when I walked into that hotel room it felt so cold and empty and I am so tired of being alone. Even when we were married I felt alone, you know? Somehow over the years he just got so cold and distant, and I didn't know what to do about it. I just gave up and after a while we even stopped having sex and—" Tears brimmed in her eyes again. "Oh God. I can't believe I told you guys that."

"Sid, it's okay," said Clay, reaching for her.

She took a step back. "No, it's not. I shouldn't have asked."

"Yes you should have." Clay glanced at Dax. "It's just…"

Dax finished for him. "We're just not sure…uh…who you should stay with."

"I should go back to the hotel."

"No," insisted Clay, his voice more forceful than Dax had ever heard it. "No, you shouldn't. We'd just like a minute to talk it over, okay?"

She took a deep breath, glanced from Clay to Dax and nodded. "O…okay. I…I should go back in and use the bathroom anyway. I've got a bladder the size of a walnut, you know. So…" She nodded again. "Yeah. I'll be right back." And with that she struck off across the parking lot.

Only when the restaurant door had closed did the two men relax.

"Christ," said Clay.

"Ditto."

"So what do you think?"

"I think she needs us."

"I know *that*, you jerk. And I want to help but…" Clay leaned back against her car, drummed his fingers on the hood. "But if she stays with us she's gonna have to know the truth. And I'm afraid…with all she's been through…if we tell her this now it'll be too much for her."

"Come on, Clay. You've always treated her like china, and that woman is made of steel. She's stronger than you think."

"And she's more vulnerable than *you* think."

"She can handle it."

Clay glanced toward the restaurant. "Maybe she can." He looked back at Dax. "But can we?"

Dax licked his lips. "What do you mean?"

"You know exactly what I mean. She wasn't kidding when she said she wants us." He leaned in close and whispered, "And the thing is we want her too."

Dax closed his eyes and leaned against the car beside his lover. "I know. I felt it, but I wasn't sure if you did."

"Oh yeah. I did."

"Oh."

Suddenly Clay shifted closer, his body brushing up against Dax's in a way that had Dax's heart hammering inside his chest. His lips very close to Dax's ear, he whispered, "The thing is, I'm wondering if this is such a bad thing."

Dax hooked a thumb inside the waistband of Clay's jeans, breathed in his cologne. "What do you mean?"

"We're bored, Dax. We need some shaking up. Don't tell me you haven't noticed it, haven't felt it."

He hadn't. Not really. But now, hearing Clay say it, he knew it was true. "Yeah," he admitted. "Yeah, I guess I did."

Clay pulled back a little, just far enough to meet Dax's gaze. "And maybe this is exactly the kind of shaking up we need."

"Are you suggesting what I think you're suggesting?"

"You know I am."

"What if it's not what *she* needs?"

"I think it is."

"But what if it's *not*?"

"All we can do is ask."

"But first we have to tell her."

Something flickered in Clay's eyes. "I think I have a way around that." And then he kissed him.

* * * * *

Sidney stepped out of the restaurant and started across the lot. She could see Dax and Clay standing together. They were leaning against her car, deeply absorbed in conversation. They stood close, very close. Almost too close. There was something about them. Something about the way—

She stopped. She stopped dead in her tracks and watched in stunned silence as Clay moved in closer to Dax and did the unthinkable. He kissed him.

He leaned in and covered Dax's mouth with his own. He kissed him hard. Deep. Open-mouthed, their lips melded together broke apart, came together again. Tongues warred and teeth clashed. Clay held him firmly by the shoulders, and Dax's hands had fisted in Clay's T-shirt.

It was a provocative sight. To see two men, silhouetted in moonlight—two broad-shouldered, narrow-waisted men in tight-ass jeans and muscle shirts, locked in such a passionate exchange was— She stumbled backward. This was *Clay* and *Dax*! These were her friends. Two men she had known for years, had shared so much with and now…now *this*?

She took a step forward and screamed, "You bastards!" And then, her cheeks damp with tears once again—she turned and fled.

* * * * *

"Shit."

Dax slammed a hand against Clay's chest. "Nice going, genius."

"*You're* the one who said she was made of steel."

"Made of steel, you jerk. Not solid fucking stone."

"I just thought—" He growled. "Shouldn't we go after her?"

"Way ahead of you, buddy." And with that Dax sprinted off down the street.

Clay waited only a heartbeat before taking off after them.

Chapter Four

&

Sidney ran until her lungs burned. She ran past quaint boutiques and antique shops, darted beneath wrought iron streetlamps and swerved around strolling pedestrians. Her thighs began to tighten and a cramp took root in her side, but still she pushed on. Rage was a powerful motivator.

"Sid! For God's sake, stop!" It was Dax and she had no doubt he was gaining on her. She pushed harder.

Her legs pumped like slender pistons, but she knew it was no use. Dax used to run marathons in college. She heard his feet pounding the pavement behind her and knew she didn't have a prayer. She needed a plan. A goal.

Suddenly she veered off the sidewalk and sprinted through a dimly lit parking lot. If she remembered correctly—*yes*. She crossed a neatly manicured backyard and, with Dax hot on her heals, vaulted over a four-foot cedar fence. She landed on the other side, turned, took a step, stumbled over something in the dark and fell headlong into water.

A pool? she thought, her mind strangely calm despite the situation. *When did Clay's mom put in a pool?*

Stunned by the presence of a pool, as well as by the bracing temperature of the water it took her a moment to get her bearings. Her jeans and running shoes weighed her down and had her sinking to the bottom in record time. When her feet touched cement, however, she planted them solidly and pushed off. Her head had barely broken the surface when she felt strong hands latch around her arms and drag her toward the side.

"Let go of me!" she shouted.

Dax ignored her. He heaved her to the edge of the pool where Clay crouched, waiting to grab her. He grasped her under the arms and despite her vigorous protests and struggles, lifted her, dripping jeans and all, clean out of the pool.

He swung her up in his arms and proceeded to carry her away.

"Put me down!" she screamed.

He kept walking.

She pummeled him with her fists. "I said, put me *down*!"

He climbed a set of stairs that led to a large cedar deck and at last set her down in a lounge chair. He pointed a stern finger at her. "Stay." And with no more explanation than that, he stalked off.

Something dripped on her head. She looked up to see Dax standing over her. The first thing she noticed was his shirt. Sopping wet, it clung to his chest in ways that she didn't want to think about, so she shifted her attention upward. The view there was no less disturbing. Judging from his expression she was surprised the water wasn't boiling off his skin.

She swatted at a hank of long chestnut hair that was dripping copious amounts of water onto her head.

"Get away from me," she growled. "You're getting me all wet."

Dax closed his eyes and shook his head. And then he turned and walked toward a small enclosure in the corner. He swung open the door and stepped through.

She began to shiver and a moment later felt a warm, fluffy towel being draped around her shoulders. "Thanks," she said grudgingly as she pulled it in tight.

Clay stood and looked like he was about to say something to her when a sound from the enclosure on the other side of the deck startled them both. They looked over to see Dax folding up a large plastic sheet.

"What the hell are you doing?" asked Clay.

"What does it look like I'm doing?" He hit a switch on the wall and a motor somewhere ground to life. It was then she noticed the steam.

"I hardly think this is the time."

Dax turned a bored glance on Clay. "I'm cold and wet and thanks to that mad dash through town, my nerves are shot to hell. It's the perfect time." He stripped off his shirt. "You can't tell me your mother will care."

Clay frowned. He looked at Sidney, and then he looked at Dax. And then he shrugged. He stood and moved to strip off his shirt as well.

The entire situation had left Sidney feeling off balance and disoriented. When both men started peeling off their jeans she felt the need to protest. "I can't believe this. Don't you think we should—"

Dax reached for his underwear.

"Dax David Redmond," she warned.

He stopped, turned to look at her.

"Don't. You. Dare."

The briefs slipped to his ankles. Naked and gloriously uninhibited by it, he stepped into the swirling water of the hot tub. Clay, standing right beside her, shrugged resignedly, and followed suit. The briefs fell to the ground and she watched him walk away. Muscles strained beneath smooth bronzed skin, rippling and shifting with each long stride. His shoulders were broad, his buttocks small and tight and she couldn't deny the truth.

God, he was beautiful. They both were.

She had to work at rekindling her outrage, but by the time he stepped into the water she was ready. She leapt from her chair, stepped over the towel that had fallen at her feet, marched over to the tub and glowered at them. "What the hell do you two think you're doing?"

The water bubbled around Clay as he leaned his head back on the cushions that surrounded the tub. "I believe the term is 'hot tubbing'. Isn't that right, Dax?"

"I believe so." His eyes were closed. "This is a tub and the water's hot. Sounds right to me."

"I can't believe you two are taking this so lightly. We have things to talk about."

"So talk."

"Not with me up here and you two…down there."

Clay opened his eyes and motioned to a seat across from them. "So join us."

She opened her mouth and sputtered, "I…I don't have a bathing suit."

"Neither do we."

"B-but what about your mother?"

"It's her bingo night. She'll be gone for hours."

"As long as you're stripping," said Dax, "why don't you throw your clothes in the dryer? There's one just inside the back door."

She sneered. "Should I take yours, too?"

"Nah, that's okay. I've got a couple of spare sets here."

She looked at Clay. "You mean your mother *knows*, and she didn't tell me when I called?"

"Good God," said Clay, "of course she knows. And what was she supposed to say? 'Here's Clay's work number, and by the way, he likes to fuck other men?'"

She opened her mouth to reply, realized how ridiculous she sounded and snapped it shut again. "Fine." She whirled around and stomped off toward the back door, grabbing her towel off the deck on her way by.

Two minutes later she stood beside the hot tub, wrapped in a towel, and feeling more exposed than she ever remembered. She glanced at the door to the enclosure that was still standing open. She kicked it shut with her bare foot.

Clay tapped the water. "Come on in. We won't bite."

Dax winked. "Unless you want us to."

They were baiting her, but she refused to let them see how uncomfortable she was. In one swift motion she dropped the towel and stepped into the water. She sat down on the bench and instantly felt herself relax. The intense heat seeped into her skin, through to her muscles, right down to her bones. She closed her eyes and allowed the bubbles to do the rest.

* * * * *

Clay had intended to give her several minutes to settle in, but Dax wasn't nearly so patient. "Okay, you've had a minute to get yourself together. So now tell us what the hell that whole scene was about."

Her eyes flew open. "What whole scene?"

"Calling us 'bastards'? And then taking off like a bat outta hell? I never would've pegged you as a phobe, Sidney. I thought you were bigger than that."

Clay put a hand on his shoulder and could feel the tension humming through him. "Take it easy, Dax."

Sid sat up a little straighter. "You think I ran off because I was offended by what I saw?"

"What other reason could there be?" asked Clay.

"I...I was angry because you hadn't told me! We were best friends in college, and I thought we were still friends. I can't believe—"

Incredulous, Clay held up his hands. "Hold on just a second. We haven't seen you for, what? It's been at least six years, since you called or wrote. If I recall we weren't even invited to your wedding, and yet, we were supposed to make a special effort to *notify* you when we hooked up?"

She crossed her arms over her breasts. "What do you mean by 'hooked up'? I figured you were together since college."

"Not quite," said Dax slowly, "We stayed in touch after graduation, but it took a couple of years of muddling around with other people before we figured out who we really were and what we really wanted."

Sidney's self-righteous demeanor slipped a notch. "You mean to tell me that when we were in college you two never...?"

They exchanged an uncomfortable glance and she pounced. "*Aha!* You did!"

"Once," admitted Clay. "At the time we thought it was an aberration. That was why we never told you. We thought it was a mistake."

Dax whistled. "And what a mistake it was. That was some of the best sex of my life."

Clay couldn't help but grin. "Yeah. I wish all my 'mistakes' felt that good."

When he turned back to Sidney he could swear she was squirming inside her skin. It was his turn to pounce. "Come on, Sid, 'fess up. You weren't angry because we kept something from you. You were embarrassed and upset by what you saw."

She looked down at herself and Clay found himself wishing the hot tub timer would run out. He'd caught such a fleeting glimpse before she stepped into the water, but what he'd seen had been most...illuminating. Small firm breasts, slight waist, well-defined quads. Sid had obviously taken care of herself and he wished like hell he hadn't noticed.

"No," she said, her voice tight. "Really. I wasn't embarrassed. It wasn't that at all."

Clay frowned. "Look. If it makes you uncomfortable it's okay to say so. Everybody has their own unique preferences, and we can hardly judge you for—"

"No." She almost shouted the word, and then she said more softly, "No, you don't understand."

They waited.

"I...uh..." She took a deep breath. "I didn't want to admit it to myself, let alone to you, but now that I think about it..." She squared her shoulders. "If I really, *really* think about it I have to admit that..."

"Sid?"

"When I saw you two kiss it kind of turned me on, and my own reaction shocked me so badly that I didn't know how to deal with it. That was why I ran."

Clay blinked. He looked at Sid, and then he looked at Dax. They both smiled, but Sid didn't seem to notice.

"It was so strange," she was saying. "I've never experienced anything like that before, and I've certainly never fantasized about it. So I figure it was, like you said, an...aberration. A...mistake. And I covered my confusion with anger."

Clay cast her a sidelong glance. "Would you like to make sure?"

She licked her lips. "What do you mean?"

"Would you like to check whether or not it was an aberration? Or if it was the real thing?"

She swallowed. "How would I do that?"

"We could do it again, and you could see how you…feel about it."

Color crept into her cheeks and he was sure it wasn't just from the heat of the water. "I…uh…no thanks. That's okay."

"Come on, Sid." Dax floated over to her, sat beside her on the bench. "Give it a try. You never know what kind of new adventures await you if you never step out the door."

Her gaze flitted between the two of them. "What does that mean?"

Clay followed his partner's lead and floated over to sit on the other side of her. He curbed the intense urge to touch her. "It means we've fallen into a rut, and we've been looking for something to snap us out of it."

Dax moved in closer. Close enough that his breath must have washed over her skin. "We're thinking you might be just what we're looking for."

"We like you, Sid," said Clay. "In fact I think I could say that we love you. And we're both very attracted to you, so—"

"I didn't think that was supposed to happen," said Sid. "You know…being attracted to women."

"There's a whole spectrum of sexuality. Surely you know that."

"I suppose."

Dax shrugged. "Why not just give it one more try? You know. Look through the prism and see how you like the colors." He brushed a damp strand of hair off her cheek. "Watch us and if you don't like it tell us to stop."

"But if you *like* it," added Clay, "then let us know that too."

"What, exactly, are you suggesting?"

"Do we really have to spell it out?"

She licked her upper lip, wiping away the sweat that had beaded there. "Yeah. I think maybe you should."

Clay leaned in and dropped his voice suggestively. "The three of us, Sid. Together."

"A *ménage à trois*?" Her eyes were wide, but her accent perfect. Of course.

He nodded.

"Oh."

She fell silent, looking from one to the other, the wheels in her brain obviously turning furiously as she considered the possibilities.

Clay and Dax sat back and hoped.

Chapter Five

ഇ

Sidney studied the men who sat on either side of her. One blond, the other dark, one with long hair the other short and spiked, one spontaneous and hotheaded, the other cooler, more reserved. Both tall and tanned and sexy as hell. They wanted each other and — *oh God* — they wanted her.

She was on the rebound. She was coming out of a bad marriage, and she was very vulnerable. But she knew these men — knew them and trusted them. They weren't looking to hurt her, weren't asking her for any more than what she was willing to give. And they wanted to give back, too. Of that she was sure.

Dammit, it had been so long since she'd had a satisfying sexual relationship and even when she and her husband had been sexually active it had lacked passion. Their lovemaking had been tame at best, and dull at worst. This adventure promised to be anything but.

If, as Dax suggested, she was willing to open the door and step outside her comfort zone.

She held her head high and said, "Okay."

Dax's eyebrows arched. "Okay?"

"Okay, I'll watch you and…" she shrugged. "I'll let you know."

Dax and Clay exchanged a glance and then, to her surprise, instead of moving around her and sitting together on the bench, they floated off their seats and met in the middle. They knelt on the floor of the tub, their bodies just inches from her knees, and just inches from each other.

She found herself wishing the bubbles would stop so she could have a better view of what lay beneath the surface and, as if it had read her mind, the timer cut out. The water calmed and she was able to see them—every inch of them. From head to shoulders to chiseled pecs, to sculpted abs to— she swallowed.

"Like what you see?" asked Dax, his eyes as mischievous as his voice.

"Just get on with it," she goaded, dragging her eyes away from the pair of impressive erections before her. They must be magnified by the water. It was the only explanation. "Gimme your best shot."

"You heard the lady," said Clay. "Get on—"

Dax framed Clay's face with his hands and sealed their mouths together. Their lips joined, but to her surprise it wasn't a wanton kiss. It was slow and thorough, languorous yet laced with passion. She caught a glimpse of tongues playing and felt an unmistakable heaviness grow in her center. It was no mistake. Seeing them together aroused her.

She noticed Clay's hand resting on Dax's chest and acted on impulse.

Without thought for the implications, she placed her hand over his and felt the pounding of Dax's heart in synchrony with Clay's own pulse. His hand was wide, heavily veined and, she knew intuitively it would be very strong.

She felt Dax's hand slip around her waist, and allowed him to draw her off the bench. Clay's arm hooked around her as well and then she realized they had stopped kissing and were looking at her, the question obvious in their eyes.

She said nothing. She cupped Clay's jaw in her palm, brushed her thumb across the day's worth of stubble and, very slowly, drew him in for a kiss. His lips met hers, warm and firm and, although they'd never done this before, strangely familiar. He didn't push, allowing her to take the initiative. But when her tongue eased past his lips he returned it with fervor. His grip on her waist tightened and he drew her closer. Close enough that his cock, hard and engorged with blood, was pressed firmly against her cleft.

Her hands slipped beneath the water and explored his chest, his ribs, his back. Muscles rippled and twitched beneath her fingers and she wondered that she'd never felt the urge to touch him like this before.

She felt Dax move in behind her. He moved in tight until his chest was pressed against her back and his cock was nested in the crease of her ass. He pushed her damp hair to one side and began nibbling on her neck. One hand cruised over her rib cage to cradle a breast. He tweaked a nipple and she sucked in her breath with pleasure and surprise.

Her head fell back, breaking off the kiss with Clay, but granting Dax better access to her throat. Clay took the opportunity to bend down and take her other breast in his mouth. Her breasts were small and his mouth seemed so large. He devoured it whole. His tongue caressed and sucked and his little moans of pleasure sent even more blood coursing to her clit.

He broke away and straightened. His eyes inches from hers he said, "It's been a while. I'd almost forgotten how good a woman's breasts can taste."

At that Dax ceased feasting on her neck long enough to give his lover a quick, hard kiss and she felt her desire build. She grabbed Dax's hand that was still resting on her breast and urged it lower. Clay noticed what was happening and covered her hand, sandwiching it between Dax's and his own.

Their fingers reached the apex of her thighs and brushed through the tiny triangle of hair. She withdrew her hand, allowing them to explore on their own, savoring the sensation of two hands, two sets of fingers toying with her sex.

"Nice," murmured Dax against her shoulder, "I've never sampled shaved pussy." Sid left a small wedge of hair at the top of her vulva, but other than that was clean-shaven.

"I have," said Clay his vivid blue eyes glazed with desire, "but it's been a helluva long time."

Fingers parted the lips of her sex and smoothed over her clit. One set of fingers eased inside her, and then another. She couldn't identify what fingers belonged to whom. Didn't need to, didn't care. She parted her legs and Clay moved between them. He withdrew his hand and cupped her thighs, parting them further, lifting them so that she floated near the surface, her legs hooked around him.

She turned her head and kissed Dax's neck, flicked out her tongue and licked him. He tasted hot and sticky, salty from sweat. He tasted wonderful.

"Would you like a taste?" she murmured.

"Of what?" asked Clay, his hands now cupping her bottom and a thumb nudging inside her.

"That shaved pussy you're so fond of."

He grinned, lifted her higher, until her bottom just broke the surface and her legs floated on either side of his shoulders. Her shoulders were still supported against Dax, but he braced a hand in the small of her back to steady her further. She lifted her head and watched as Clay, still on his knees, bent his head and sampled her. From anus to apex he licked her, his tongue pausing only briefly to dart inside her before it continued on its way, exploring the folds, fondling her clit.

Dax was watching too, his breathing rapid and ragged. The hand that wasn't supporting her was splayed across her flat belly, his fingers holding apart the lips of her sex, allowing Clay better access, and himself a better view. Clay's tongue toyed with her clit and dipped inside her, all the while he was making soft rumbling sounds in the back of his throat. The sound of a hungry man gorging on ice cream.

His pleasure accentuated her own. It built and she fought the urge to squirm in their arms. Her breathing had become ragged, and her blood bubbled, as hot and vigorous as the water that had been fizzing around her just moments ago.

When Clay reached the small triangle of pubic hair, he licked Dax's fingers, drawing one into his mouth to suck briefly before returning to his task.

Without warning Dax's fingers moved lower and ground against her clit, sending a sudden and unexpected orgasm spiraling through her. She went stiff, arching her back and digging her fingers into the muscles of Dax's thighs.

Clay gripped her ass hard and thrust his tongue inside her, sucking her, lapping her up, as the pleasure pulsed through her.

"Hey," grumbled Dax, as the orgasm faded. "No fair. I thought we were gonna share."

Clay looked at him from beneath hooded eyes. "You want a taste?"

"You know I do."

Abruptly Clay straightened and, with Sid still between them, awarded Dax a hungry kiss. Sid's face was so close to them she could smell her own scent that lingered on Clay's lips.

"Mmm," said Dax when they broke apart. He grinned down at Sid, slid his tongue across his upper lip. "You're delicious."

Impossibly, her cheeks grew hotter. She blew out a long, slow breath, wondering if her heart would ever settle back into a normal rhythm. "This isn't fair. I feel like I had all the fun."

"Don't worry about that." Dax bracketed her waist in his hands. "We're just barely getting started." And then he twirled her around so she was facing him. He moved back to sit on the bench and drew her in to straddle him. She grasped his cock and sheathed herself on him. He speared so deep she felt a nudge against her womb. She drew back, descended again, began to pump her hips.

"Damn," said Dax, his voice low and breathless.

Suddenly the motor beneath the floor, ground to life and the water began to churn. She heard a splash as Clay jumped back into the tub and moved in behind her. He laid his hands on her shoulders, his cock pressing against her back.

The water lapped at her chest, buoying her breasts. The bubbles massaged her muscles and the heat lulled her. She leaned back against Clay and murmured softly as his hands cruised down to her breasts. He cupped them, offering them to Dax who leaned over and took them into his mouth, laving and sucking each in turn until she was writhing between the two men, hungry, eager for something she couldn't quite identify.

Dax gripped her hips and took control. With her back braced against Clay, Dax thrust himself into her, pummeling her with his body repeatedly until she was gasping for breath. She felt off balance and her arms flailed, but only for a moment. Clay grasped her hands, held them tight.

She gripped him hard, using him for leverage and matching Dax thrust for thrust as the pressure built.

On the brink of another orgasm, she made a soft whimpering sound and clenched her fingers around Clay's hands.

"Dax," said Clay, the word a command that she didn't understand.

Perhaps she didn't, but Dax did. He wrapped his arms around her, drew her in tight and crushed her mouth beneath his own. He thrust deep, impaling her on his cock and ravaging her with his tongue. With Dax buried inside her she climaxed again, surrendering to Dax's assault, squeezing Clay's hands in sync with the rhythm of her orgasm.

Dax tensed, went very still, and then let out a soft, low moan before relinquishing his claim on her mouth.

"Christ," he whispered. "I've never—"

"Clay!"

They all went still, tensed at the sound of the voice that reached them from the other side of the enclosure.

Clay glanced at Dax who just mouthed, "Oh shit."

"Yeah, Mom?" replied Clay.

"Oh good," she said. "I just wanted to make sure it was you."

They heard the sound of the latch and Clay moved so fast he was little more than a blond blur. He erupted from the water and dashed for the door. He held it shut and engaged the hook before his mother realized what was happening.

The door jiggled on its hinges. "Oh," said his mother. "Is Dax in there with you?"

Clay leaned his forehead against the door, obviously exhausted by his mad dash. "Yeah, Mom. Sorry about that. It was kind of an impromptu visit."

"No problem. It's just that I brought someone home with me from bingo, and I'd rather…uh…"

Clay turned his head and grinned. "No problem, Mom. Just keep him in the kitchen. We'll get our clothes and slip out the back gate. He'll never know we were here."

"Great." Even Sid could hear the relief in her voice. "Thanks, hon." They heard the sound of footsteps, and then abruptly they stopped. "Dax?"

"Yeah, Lil?"

"Good," she called back. "Just checking."

A moment later they heard the slam of the screen door.

Sid gave Dax a questioning look. "What was that about?"

"We'll explain later," said Clay, the door to the enclosure already open a crack. "Right now we've got to make good our escape." He glanced through the crack. "The coast is clear. You two wait here while I get the clothes."

She turned back to find Dax grinning at her. "And you thought Paris was exciting."

Sid leaned her forehead against his and laughed.

Chapter Six

ಐ

The trio tumbled through the door of the apartment and landed on the futon in a heap of laughter and giggles.

Clay had landed on the bottom with both Dax and Sid heaped on top of him. Sid's breasts were pressed against his chest, her still-damp T-shirt clinging to them in ways that sent a fresh wash of blood coursing to his groin. Dax lay on top of her, laughing like a goon.

"Jeez," wheezed Sid, her lips inches from his. "I've been spending too much time trapped between two hunky men. A girl could suffocate this way."

"Ah." Clay framed her face in his hands. "But what a way to go."

Sid smiled, her eyes locked to his. "I've never told you this, but I love your eyes. Drowning in them, now *that* would be the way to go."

Dax rolled off and plopped down on the futon beside Clay. "Cut it out, you two. I've had too much beer and hot tubbing to put up with this mushy stuff."

Sid tossed Dax a withering look as she sat up and straddled Clay. She ran a finger down Clay's cheek, traced his throat, and explored his pectoral muscle. "So what was that all about, boys?"

They both stared at her, confused.

"Come on. Spill the beans. What's the deal with your mother, Clay?"

Clay cleared his throat, frowned. "What do you mean? She brought a man home and didn't want to advertise her son's sexual preferences. That's all there is to it."

"No, no, that's not what I mean." She leaned forward, propping her elbows on Clay's chest. "Why did she call Dax's name? What did she mean when she said she was just 'checking'?"

A tiny knot formed in Clay's gut. He put his hands around Sid's insubstantial waist and picked her up, setting her feet firmly on the floor.

"Hey! What's wrong?" she grumbled as he stood and walked to the kitchen.

"Clay's a little touchy about this," said Dax, the laughter in his voice irritating beyond words.

Clay opened the fridge and pulled out a bottle of water. He stalked back into the living room and leaned against the patio doors. He twisted off the cap, took a long swig, all the while aware of the other two watching him.

"Can you blame me?" he said at last.

"I don't get it," said Sid. "I thought your mother was okay with…everything."

"*Okay* is a pretty strong word," offered Dax. "She's accepted it, but—"

"She loves me and she tries to understand, but she worries constantly that I'm going to take other lovers. You know…start hanging out in men's washrooms? Dress in drag? Get a disease?"

Sid groaned.

"It doesn't help that she caught you that time with Mike Hardy."

Clay pressed the cool water bottle against his forehead. "God, what a night that was."

Sid sat up a little straighter. "Were you and Dax together at the time?"

"Yeah," confessed Clay. "We were."

"Don't get him wrong," said Dax, tossing an impatient look at Clay. "We've both done some experimenting on the side from time to time. Always safely, of course," he added quickly, no doubt to reassure Sid. "We always take precautions outside this relationship. We may live together but we've never demanded exclusive rights."

Clay shrugged. "It's just usually worked out that way, is all. There aren't many people either of us are interested in getting intimate with. It doesn't help that the few times we have looked elsewhere, it's usually turned out badly."

"Oh?" Sid drew her legs up and sat cross-legged on the futon. Clay was pretty sure she hadn't bothered to put on her bra, and yet her breasts straining against the wet T-shirt were full and firm. Clay felt something inside him stir, but tamped it down.

"How badly?" asked Sid. "Any juicy stories for me?"

"No, no," said Clay a little too quickly. "Nothing that you'd be interested in."

Dax chuckled. "Except of course—"

"Dax!" warned Clay.

"—for the time Clay got engaged."

Clay hung his head and groaned. Dax had no sense of discretion or propriety. Count on him to let it all hang out.

Clay sensed a presence close by. Sid traced a finger down his cheek. "Engaged, Clay? To a woman?"

"Yes," he said tightly. "It was a mistake."

"Don't hold out. Tell me everything."

"I don't think—"

"Clay met her just after he and I slept together for the second time. He'd finally figured out the truth, but was heavy into denial and latched onto the first pair of breasts that ventured along."

"Jesus, Dax, do you *know* when to shut up?"

"Not generally." Dax grinned. "But you know you love me for my candor."

Clay rolled his eyes.

"It's okay," said Sid, her arms latching firmly around Clay's waist. "It's an understandable mistake. We all make them."

"Maybe. But most of us don't leave a bride crying at the altar while they run off with the best man."

She grimaced. "Oh. I see. That's…uh…"

"Very nineties," quipped Dax.

"It wasn't funny," said Clay. "It was horrible. Ugly. Despicable. I hurt her and embarrassed her, and I'll never forgive myself."

Sid shuddered visibly. "Did she throw things?"

"Yeah." Clay felt the mood lighten. He grinned at Dax. "But, ironically, not at me."

It was Dax's turn to look pained. "She took it out on me. She said it was all my fault, claimed I'd brainwashed him, stolen him from her. Blah, blah, blah. To this day she can't walk past me without sneering."

"You see her a lot?" asked Sid, eyebrows raised.

"Too much." Suddenly Dax launched himself off the futon. "Enough of this depressing Amy-shit." He swaggered over to Clay and breathed in his ear, "I think we have other things to attend to."

"That's right," said Sid, trailing a finger up Clay's arm as Dax began to massage his shoulders. "We have some unfinished business."

Clay fought down his instinctive reaction to their touch. "What do you mean?"

"She means that you didn't get sufficient attention tonight in the hot tub." His fingers dug into Clay's deltoids and Clay fought the urge to let his eyes roll back in his head. "Right, Sid? Isn't that what you meant?"

Sid caressed his chest. "Uh-huh. That's exactly what I meant."

Suddenly Clay pushed himself away from the doors and distanced himself from the other two. "I got plenty, thanks," he argued, uncertain why he was fighting this, and unsure why his mood had suddenly shifted so dramatically. "Right now I just need sleep."

Sid's eyes went wide. Was he reading disappointment there? Jeez, he just couldn't seem to get it right.

"But Clay…"

"Later," said Clay, whirling around and stalking off toward the bedroom. "Right now I'm just really tired." He opened the door and hesitated. "You can get Sid set up in the spare room, right Dax?" And with that he stepped inside, closed the door behind him and threw himself on the bed.

Maybe sleep would cure whatever it was that ailed him. He just knew, at that moment, he didn't deserve to feel good.

* * * * *

Sid gaped at Clay's retreating back, and jerked back at the slam of the door. He'd turned down sex because he was too *tired*? Obviously there was more to it. Had to be.

She whirled on Dax. "What the hell was that? What's gotten into him?"

"My fault," said Dax on a sigh. "I should know better than to bring up Amy. He didn't deal well with her at the time and he still doesn't." He walked away and disappeared into the kitchen.

Sid followed him, leaned against the wall and watched him open the refrigerator and rummage through the drawers.

"Want an apple?"

Sid glanced back toward the bedrooms. "Shouldn't we go after him? Talk to him?" She took the shiny red piece of fruit that Dax offered her. "Or something?"

Dax shook his head. "There's no talking to him when he gets like this. He's like a tough old steak. He has to simmer in his own juices, stew in his own guilt for a while before he's done. Only then is there a hope in hell of snapping him out of it." He bit into the apple. "But don't worry. I know just what to do."

Sid bit into the sweet crispy fruit. "You do?"

"Uh-huh."

"Oh? And what's that?"

"We'll let him fall asleep, and then…" He chewed and swallowed, waggled his eyebrows.

"And then what?"

"And then we'll just have to put him on a plate, stick a fork in him and see if he's done."

* * * * *

Clay tried to roll over. And then he tried again. He tugged on his left arm, and then on his right, but they seemed leaden. Immovable.

His eyes flickered and he glimpsed glimmering candlelight, caught a whiff of jasmine and vanilla. He tugged on his hands again, to no avail. And then he felt the pressure on his wrists.

His eyes flew open. "What the hell?"

"Oh," said Dax, his voice very close to Clay's ear. "Awake at last."

"You sleep like the dead, Clay." It was Sid. She spoke into his other ear all the while tracing intricate patterns through the hair on his chest. "I was beginning to wonder if you'd ever wake up."

He turned his head one way, and then the other. He was sandwiched between Dax and Sid, their naked bodies pressed up against either side of him, their hands touching and exploring, tickling and enticing. "Wh–what are you two up to?" he asked. And then he noticed that he couldn't move his legs either. He lifted his head to see and then dropped it back onto the pillow.

"Jesus, Dax. I knew I never should have agreed to the tie thing. You're like a kid with a new toy, aren't you?"

"Mm-hmm." Dax's hand cruised over Clay's belly and brushed across his penis. He couldn't have restrained his reaction if he'd wanted to. "I've always been a fan of new toys. And you wouldn't let me tie your legs before. This is much more fun."

Sid shifted, her breasts grinding against Clay's side as she massaged his calf muscle with her foot. Her thigh rubbed up and down his leg, nudging his cock and making his entire body throb.

"Let me go," he breathed, his heart hammering inside his chest. "Take these things off and I'll cooperate. You can screw me blind, have your way with me." He smiled his most beguiling smile. "Whatever you want. Just let me go."

"I see what you mean, Dax," said Sid. She combed her fingers through Clay's hair, nibbled lightly on his ear. Her thigh rubbed over his hardening cock. "He's not good with submission."

"Submission?" Clay lifted his head and then dropped it back on the pillow when Dax gripped his cock and began to massage it. He groaned. "Dax? What did you tell her?"

"Just that you're a control freak." He played with Clay's balls, fingers inching toward his anus. "Down at the dealership you order people around all day. Here you handle the money, do all the shopping. You're Mister Responsible. Mister I-know-what's-best. You need to loosen up sometimes, lover. Let somebody else call the shots for a change."

"You're full of it, Dax."

Dax sat up and shifted his body so that he sat between Clay's splayed legs. Clay knew he'd regret buying this damn four-poster bed someday.

"Am I?" asked Dax, his long hair brushing Clay's cock. "I don't think so." He leaned down, drew his tongue along the length of Clay's erection.

Clay squirmed, the urge to sit up and do *something*, almost overwhelming.

"He's right, isn't he?" Sid ran her fingers over his lips, touched his cheek, traced his jaw. "This is killing you."

Clay tried to plead with his eyes. "*You* could untie me."

She laughed at him with her eyes. "I don't think so."

Dax took him in his mouth and Clay felt the sweat pop out on his forehead.

"I'm enjoying this far too much." Sid's eyes followed the movement of Dax's mouth.

"You like watching us."

She licked her lips and Clay felt an unexplainable rush of excitement. "Yeah. I guess I do." She grinned. "I won't tell your mother if you don't tell mine."

Suddenly she sat up and straddled his belly. She leaned forward, her dark eyes smoky with desire. "Care for some breast with that?" And then she offered it to him.

He accepted it greedily, suckling and nibbling on her nipple even as Dax's mouth ravished his cock. Sid made soft little mewling sounds of pleasure, and her pussy ground against his belly. The combination of sensations was exhilarating, intoxicating, the sense of helplessness adding to the mix, sending him to the brink of madness.

"God," he groaned when Sid's breasts were momentarily denied him, and the motions of Dax's mouth slowed. "Will somebody please *finish* this?"

"What are you asking for, Clay?" Sid's tongue flicked over his lips as Dax caressed his buttocks. "Say what you mean."

"I want…"

Dax laved his balls, inserted two fingers into Clay's ass. Deep.

"You want what?" asked Sid, her tongue darting out to play with his. She sounded like a dream, tasted like midnight, smelled like sex. She reached up and laced her fingers with his immobile ones. "Tell me, Clay. Tell me what to do."

"Please…" He breathed.

She kissed him hard. Drew away. "Please what?"

"Please *fuck me*!"

The next moment she sheathed herself on his cock, her pussy wet and warm and sweet. He tried to arch against her, but she pressed her hands against his chest. "No. Let me."

She rode him hard, and he lost himself in her. For a fleeting moment he wondered where Dax was and then, as if he'd read his mind, Dax appeared behind Sid.

His body in sync with hers, he splayed his fingers across her belly. Sid grasped his hand and urged it lower until he was toying with her clit.

Sid's movements accelerated and just when Clay thought he was about to explode she came. She ground herself against him, each contraction of her orgasm driving him higher until he thrust up with his hips and arched his back in climax.

He reared up, felt something snap and a moment later collapsed back on the pillows, dragging Sid and Dax with him.

They lay there, panting and sated, all three slick with sweat and wet with cum.

"Damn," he groaned. "I ripped the ties, didn't I?"

"Yup," said Dax. "Tore 'em clean in two."

"Those ties cost me a fortune."

"I'll buy you some new ones," laughed Sid. "Hell. For sex like this, I'll buy you a dozen."

Clay kissed her. "Make it two dozen, and you've got a deal."

Chapter Seven

ॐ

Sid leaned against the car door and propped her feet on Dax's lap. They were in the back seat and Clay was driving. Of course.

She leaned back and closed her eyes, reliving the events of the night before. After releasing Clay from the rest of his bonds she'd intended to move into the guest room and allow the lovers some time alone. But it hadn't quite worked out that way. They'd begun to talk and next thing she knew she'd woken up that morning, nestled in between two warm, firm male bodies. It had been at once comforting and arousing. Just thinking about it made her center grow heavy with desire once again.

She opened her eyes and turned her attention to the scenery flashing past her window. Skyscrapers and gold-tinted office buildings glinted in the afternoon sun. Seagulls rode the warm spring updrafts and airplanes sailed high above. The traffic was heavy for a Sunday, and she wondered if it was due to the uncommonly fine weather.

They'd come to Toronto to pick up her things from the hotel. They'd convinced her to check out and stay with them, at least for a few days. While they were here, Dax had a few things to look after at the museum, and figured he could give her a little tour while they were at it.

Dax laid a hand on her ankle. "Massage?" he asked, already unlacing her cross-trainers. He'd allowed his stubble to grow today, but his hair was pulled back in a neat ponytail, and he'd chosen to wear a crisp, cotton shirt. Not even the folds of material, however, could hide the physique beneath. Of course it helped that Sid now had intimate knowledge of every inch of it.

Damn, what's wrong with me? She wanted to jump the guy right here in the back seat, and the thing of it was, she had a sneaking suspicion he'd go along with it.

She tugged her seatbelt a little tighter. "Massage? Oh, I think I could be bribed. If you agree to suck on a few toes while you're at it."

Dax laughed. "I think we've created a monster, Clay. Don't you?"

"Don't bug me," growled Clay. "This Yonge Street traffic is murder."

Dax leaned over and whispered. "See what I mean? He hates driving downtown. I do this all the time, know the place like the back of my hand, but did he let me drive? Noooo!"

"You're a lunatic behind the wheel, Dax," cried Clay. "A fuckin' maniac."

Dax rolled his eyes. He eased off her shoe and sock, and began to massage the ball of her foot.

"Sometimes he sounds like my father," muttered Dax. "He used to call me a maniac, too."

His thumb dug into the arch of Sid's foot and, eyes closed, she groaned in ecstasy. "Because of your driving?" she asked.

"No. Not exactly."

Something about his voice set her on alert. She opened her eyes to study him. "Why then?"

He shrugged, his gaze trained determinedly on her foot.

Clay glanced toward the back seat. "Dax's parents didn't deal with the big announcement as well as mine did."

She sighed. "Oh."

Dax said nothing, continuing his massage.

"What happened, Dax?" Sid asked. "Was there a big scene?"

He smiled, but his eyes were sad. "No. My family doesn't do 'scenes'. At least they don't do them well. They do silence really well, though."

"Yeah," agreed Clay. "They've got the whole cold shoulder treatment down pat."

"I'm sorry, Dax. Families can be so…complicated."

"Complicated. Man, that's the understatement of the year."

He lifted her foot and nibbled on her big toe, making her giggle despite the somber mood.

He moved on to the next but she steeled herself against the tickling. "Do you ever see your parents?"

His tongue flicked at her baby toe. "Not if they can help it. But maybe that's for the best."

"You had a sister that you were close to, didn't you? She was young and kinda hip. What about her?"

"She lost her 'hipness' the second she married *Chad*." He rolled his eyes. "Mr. President of the Optimist Club couldn't be seen with a sexual deviant." He set down her foot, his heart obviously not in it. "I have a four-year-old niece that I've only seen twice."

Clay swerved around a corner, rammed into a parking spot and slammed on the brakes. "Shit! I spilled my damn coffee."

The car jolted so badly that Sid's forehead almost hit the seat in front of her. "Clay?" she yelped. "What the hell?"

He turned around, and his expression was murderous. "This is *not* a good topic to discuss while I'm driving in downtown Toronto, okay?"

Dax leaned in close and whispered. "Clay's a little protective when it comes to my family."

"Damn right I am." He turned to face the front and grabbed the wheel so tight Sid could see his knuckles whiten. "Your parents I can understand. They're old and they come from a different generation. But your sister?" He slammed an open palm against the wheel and turned back to face Sid again. "Dammit, she knows better. She still loves him, but won't admit it. Lets her goddamn husband rule the roost and refuses to let him know she has a thought in her head."

Sid swallowed, stunned by the vehemence in Clay. "You've talked to her, haven't you?"

"Yeah." He blew out a slow breath and his eyes calmed. "A couple of years ago I met her for coffee. I ended up yelling and storming out of the restaurant. Not that it did any good for Dax, but it sure as hell made me feel better."

Something fluttered deep in Sid's chest. She laid a hand on his arm. "You're a good man, Charlie Brown." She leaned forward and planted a solid kiss on his cheek. "But I'm not used to seeing you like this. All this passion is getting me turned on."

He waggled his eyebrows, and sliced a look at Dax. "You can handle the museum yourself, can't you buddy? We could just…uh…wait here."

Dax grabbed Sid's wrist. "No deal. You're both coming and besides, Sid wants a tour. Don't you, Sid?"

She laughed. "Are you kidding? Miss a chance to see the responsible, academic, working-for-real-money side of the irrepressible Dax Redmond? No way."

Dax pressed a hand to his chest and sniffled. "I think she loves me, Clay."

Clay rolled his eyes. "You see what I have to put up with?" He opened his door. "Now, can we get *on* with this?"

* * * * *

Sid stood in the foyer of the Royal Ontario Museum and marveled. Clay had disappeared into the bathroom to try and rinse the spilled coffee out of his jeans, and Dax had been snagged by a colleague for a mini-meeting. So, for the moment, she'd been left to drink in her surroundings on her own.

She'd been here before but it had been years ago, and she'd been far too young to appreciate its magnificence. Polished marble flooring stretched out before her and ceilings soared. Every footstep, every cough, every whisper echoed, lending an air of grandeur, as if she were standing inside an enormous granite cathedral.

The museum was closing for the day and the thinning stream of people bustled and jostled around her as they made their way to the doors. The ROM's eclectic mix of displays—everything from Egyptian mummies and Roman armor to a simulated bat cave and dinosaur bones—attracted thousands of visitors every year. And Dax was a part of it.

She turned to see him nearby, huddled in conversation with a woman holding a clipboard. Their voices were low, but their expressions earnest. Judging from Dax's demeanor, they must be talking about something very important. Perhaps a new exhibit, or a special shipment of ancient documents. He looked so together, so professional, so...un-Dax-like.

She turned her attention back to the foyer and was studying the two enormous totem poles that were centerpieces for a pair of matching spiral staircases when she heard Dax exclaim, "For God's sake, give it up! It's none of your business."

Her curiosity piqued she moved a little closer.

Dax and the woman were so absorbed they didn't appear to notice.

"Maybe not, but I just can't sit by and let you use him."

"*Use* him?" asked Dax, his voice laced with outrage. "What the hell does that mean?"

"You know perfectly well what that means. You needed a lucrative partner, someone who made enough money to put you through school. But the moment you've got your fancy degree you'll drop him like a hot potato." She leaned in so close to Dax that Sid had to strain to hear. "And I just hope I'll be there to pick up the pieces."

Dax held up his hands like a shield and took a step back. "You're nuts, Amy."

Amy? The fiancée!

Amy lifted her chin. "I notice you're not denying it."

"It's not worth my time, or energy." He took another step back. "And neither are you."

"Admit it, Dax, if it wasn't for Clay you wouldn't be where you are right now. You'd probably be on skid row somewhere, begging for change and—"

"Excuse me." Sid laid a hand on Dax's arm. "I think Clay could use some help with that coffee stain. You know how hopeless he is with that sort of thing."

Dax's jaw worked. "Sidney, this is none of your—"

"*Dax.*" She skewered him with her gaze. Her protective instincts were charged and her temper on slow burn. She had no intention of taking any shit from anybody at that moment. And that included Dax.

He glared at her for a moment, shifted his gaze to Amy and then back to Sid. "Okay." And then he stalked off toward the washroom.

"And you are?" asked Amy when the washroom door had banged shut. She had the clipboard clutched to her chest.

"My name's Sidney." She held out a hand but it was ignored. She retracted it. "Sidney Poirot."

"And that's supposed to mean something to me?"

"I'm a friend of Dax and Clay's."

Amy's bored expression was a poor mask for the irritation she felt beneath. She shrugged. "And?"

"And I don't like people talking to my friends that way."

"I only speak the truth. And I'm only looking out for Clay. If it wasn't for Dax—"

"If it wasn't for Dax, Clay would have wasted five years of his life trying to be something he wasn't, and trying to make a life with someone he didn't love."

"He loved me," she hissed. "But Dax brainwashed him."

Sid's eyebrows arched. Had she really heard that right? "Brainwashed? Are you implying that Dax kidnapped Clay, held him in a tiny room, denied him the basic essentials of life and tortured him, all the while flaunting pictures of naked men in his face to entice him over to the *Dark* side?"

Amy gritted her teeth. "No, of course not. But—"

"But nothing, my dear. Sexual preferences can't be programmed like that, and neither can love and commitment. He's with Dax because that's where he belongs, it's as simple as that."

"Dax is using him."

Sidney's fists clenched but she managed not to deliver the upper cut that was sizzling down her arm. She spoke very slowly. "Dax Redmond is intelligent and exciting and spontaneous, not to mention one of the most gorgeous hunks of male flesh you or I have ever laid eyes on. Clay is damn lucky to have him."

Amy was virtually vibrating with rage. "He can't give Clay what I can give him."

"He can give Clay everything you could have given him and more!" Her voice had edged up a notch, but she couldn't have restrained it if she'd wanted to.

"He can't give him *children*!"

Sidney stared at her, the word echoing in her mind. Part of her wanted to laugh at the ludicrousness of it all. Instead she leaned close and said in a theater whisper that echoed through the hall, "Neither can you if he's not fucking you." She stepped back. "Can you?" She whirled and walked away.

"You bitch!" screamed Amy.

Sidney kept walking.

"You're a stupid bitch." Sidney heard the clipboard clatter to the floor, but she didn't turn around. "And just who are you to preach to me, anyway? What the hell do you know about Clay? Or Dax for that matter?" An angry sob escaped her throat. "What the hell do you know about anything?"

At that Sidney hesitated. She considered her response, figured it was a mistake, and decided to say it anyway.

She turned around and walked back to face the jilted fiancée. "What do I know? What do I *know*? I know that Clay has a tiny mole at the base of his penis and Dax likes to have his nipples sucked." She moved closer, close enough to see the silver fillings in Amy's gaping mouth. "I've been with both of them, *Amy*, and I know things about them you can only dream of."

She turned to walk away, but thanks to the amazing acoustics in the cavernous foyer she heard Amy whisper the word "Slut."

She kept right on walking.

She reached the hallway that led to the washrooms. "Come on out," she called. "I know you're in there."

74

Two heads peeked out from around the door.

Clay looked miserable, but Dax was grinning from ear to ear.

"Remind me never to cross this one," said Dax as he tugged Clay out into the open. "I value my testicles too much."

Sid took her place between them and hooked her arms through theirs. They struck off toward the elevators. "So do I, Dax," she quipped. "So do I."

* * * * *

The elevator moved and Sidney's tummy lifted.

"You introduced them didn't you?" she asked when the silence stretched.

Dax's sigh was heavy. "Not exactly."

"You started working here and that's how Clay and Amy met, right?"

"Close enough." He shrugged. "And now I can't get away from her."

"I've tried talking to her," offered Clay, "but she just won't listen." His gaze flitted to Dax. "It's worse than you told me, isn't it?"

Another shrug. But then he grinned and nudged Sidney in the ribs. "Nothing me and the Terminatrix here can't handle."

Sidney was laughing when they stepped off the elevators. "So, what are we seeing?" she asked Dax as they headed down a long narrow hallway. "Your office?"

Dax had been so eager to show her where he worked, but she'd been hard-pressed to share his excitement. What could be so fascinating about an office, after all? She'd seen more than her share of filing cabinets and computer monitors. She'd much rather take a leisurely stroll through the now-vacant museum.

Dax slid his key-card through the slot beside a small, nondescript door. The lock clicked. "It's not just any office," he said, his hand wrapped around the knob. "This one is special."

"Special." Sidney smiled indulgently. "Okay."

Dax pushed the door open and motioned her through. She took two steps and stopped dead. Eyes wide and mouth gaping she stood there and stared. "Wow," was all she could manage to say.

Clay strolled past her. "I think that's a compliment, Dax."

"High praise, indeed." Dax was still standing beside her, but she couldn't drag her gaze away to look at him.

The room was enormous. Ceilings soared, and twenty feet above her head a skylight let in the slanted rays of a dwindling sun. But that wasn't what had caught her attention. "It's...it's beautiful. It's a full-fledged Indian village." Her eyes raked over vividly decorated tepees, fire pits, animal skins and filleted fish hanging on racks to dry. At last she turned to look at him, and his face glowed. "Did *you* do this?"

He nodded, grinned sheepishly. "I may have misled you. I don't really *have* an office. I do most of my research and design work at home, so that's really more of an office than this is. This is my studio, and the village is my latest display."

"B-but it's so *big*!"

Clay stopped in the center of the room, beside an enormous pile of animal skins. He ran his hand through thick, lustrous fur. "It's a special display that's going to be set up on the CNE grounds in August."

The Canadian National Exhibition was one of the largest 'fall fairs' in the country. It ran for two weeks and was one of Toronto's biggest and most well known tourist attractions.

Dax moved in to stand beside Clay. "We've set it up in cooperation with the western Sioux Nation. They'll be providing the period costumes and the inhabitants of the village."

"It'll be a completely interactive display." Clay dropped a hand around Dax's shoulders and squeezed. "And it was all Dax's brainchild."

Sid's heart was in her throat. "Dax, I… I don't know what to say. I didn't think you could surprise me again, but you did."

Dax turned to survey his creation. "I like learning about different cultures and periods in history, but *this* is what I love. The nitty-gritty of putting it together, the sawing and hammering and cutting and—" He stopped when Sid put her hand on his arm.

He smiled down at her. "I like the physical part of it, but I found out that I also love the creating. I mean, I'm just *copying* things that existed centuries ago, but it still feels like it's mine. Like it's part of me."

She studied him for a moment, considering the wide hazel eyes that smoked with passion and intelligence. She inspected the angular jaw shadowed by stubble, dropped her gaze to the tanned bit of chest that peeked out of the opening at the top of his shirt.

She blew out a slow breath and slid a half-lidded glance at Clay whose arm was still draped around Dax's shoulders. "Good God, he's amazing. How do you keep your hands off him?"

Clay chuckled. "I don't most of the time. I want him almost constantly."

"How about now?" She licked her lips, both unnerved and intrigued by the images that flitted through her mind. "Do you want him now?"

Clay stared at her, obviously trying to decipher what she meant, what she wanted, where she was leading.

Her breathing hastened under his watchful gaze, her heart quickened. She read the desire in his eyes, felt the energy build—an electrical storm that threatened to strike down all three of them.

The hair on the backs of her arms lifted, and slowly—very slowly—Clay turned his head and sealed his mouth to Dax's.

The kiss was deep, thorough, with soft little groans of pleasure that echoed through the cavernous space. Dax's hands fisted in Clay's shirt and Clay began working the hem of Dax's out of the waistband of his jeans.

Sid stepped in behind Dax, laid her head against his back and slid her arms around his waist. Her hands skimmed over taut abs, continuing until she reached the snap at the waist of his jeans. She popped it open and he sucked in his stomach in surprise.

She found Clay's hand, grasped him by the wrist and guided him beneath the soft cotton of Dax's briefs. Dax's soft groan of pleasure told her that Clay was fulfilling his duties and she took the opportunity to complete her own task. She slid her hands beneath the denim, beneath the briefs, caressing smooth, hot skin as she eased his clothing down over his hips and thighs. His jeans dropped to the floor and she couldn't resist cupping and stroking a set of firm, well-rounded buttocks.

Dax's hands came around to grip her arms and urge her to do more but she nipped at his fingers. "Just wait," she chided. "We'll get to that."

She grabbed the hem of his shirt and whipped it over his head, leaving him naked and vulnerable between her and Clay.

Clay had broken off the kiss and was now trailing hungry kisses and provocative licks of his tongue down Dax's chest. He found a nipple, and was sucking hard as Sidney moved around to take up a position behind him. When Clay felt her hands at his belt he stopped and stood straight.

She worked at the clasp. "I could use some help here, Dax."

Dax chuckled and while she worked at the denim he took care of Clay's T-shirt. She worked at the jeans, her hands running over another perfectly proportioned ass, another set of muscular thighs. She took a moment to admire and couldn't help herself. She fell to her knees and kissed one dimpled cheek.

Her lips still pressed against his skin she murmured, "If you ever tell another soul that I kissed your ass, Clay Masters, you're a dead man."

"I'll try and keep a lid on it," said Clay, his voice husky and laced with laughter. "But tell me…is it worth it?"

She moved to the other cheek, pressed her open mouth against it and tasted salt and sex. "Mmm." She dug her fingers into his hips, her tongue drawing lazy circles on his skin. "Gimme a minute. I'll let you know."

Her eyes were closed, and she was so absorbed in what she was doing that she wasn't paying attention to anything else, so was startled when Clay exclaimed, "Dax? What the hell?"

A moment later Clay was wrenched rudely away from her lips and out of her grasp.

Her eyes flew open to see Clay fall away from her and land beside Dax in an expansive carpet of animal pelts. Dax had taken liberties and spread out the stack of skins to make an enormous bed of fur.

The two men lay side by side, arms and legs splayed, cocks erect—naked and irresistible.

They grinned up at her and Dax arched an eyebrow. "She's still got all her clothes on, Clay. What are we going to do about that?"

"I've got an idea or two." Clay moved to get up but she held up a hand in protest. "Allow me."

Apparently intrigued, Clay lay back and stacked his hands behind his head. "Proceed."

Feeling the heat rise to her cheeks at the intense scrutiny of the two lovers, she reached for the top button of her shirt. She popped it open, moved lower and reached for the next.

As they watched her, she could see the desire smolder in their eyes. Dax rolled on his side and laid a hand on Clay's stomach.

Her eyes riveted to the two men, Sidney opened the next button, and felt her blood quicken as Dax's hand moved lower.

Clay hadn't moved, his eyes still trained on Sidney, his pulse however, visible as it pounded at the base of his throat.

Sidney opened the last button and as her shirt fell to the floor Dax wrapped his hand around Clay's cock and began a slow massage. Clay's eyes fluttered but remained open. Every muscle in his body stood out in relief beneath his skin.

Sid opened the clasp on her jeans and lowered the zipper. Leaving her thong in place, she pushed the denim over her hips and watched with mounting excitement as Clay began to stroke Dax's cock, fondle his balls.

She stepped out of the jeans and kicked the puddled denim aside.

"Your bra," breathed Clay as the speed of Dax's caresses increased. "Take off your bra."

She reached for the clasp of her front-close, barely there, black demi bra, grasped the two sides as if she intended to open it, but then she stopped. Tracing a delicate finger along the crest of her cleavage she said, "You guys are boring me. Can't you do better than that?"

"Boring?" asked Clay, his expression incredulous. "If you think—"

Dax had sat up and grabbed him by the wrists. He tugged him up off the furs until they were on their knees facing each other. Dax cupped Clay's sex and smiled suggestively. "Turn around."

Clay tossed a covert glance at Sidney. "Only if she takes off that damn bra."

Intrigued by the implications, Sidney unsnapped the clasp and let the insubstantial piece of lingerie fall to the floor. She cupped her own breasts in her hands and tweaked her nipples until they hardened to rosy points. She felt the wetness seep between her thighs and wondered at herself. She didn't know if she'd ever been this aroused, and she hadn't even touched them. Yet.

Chest heaving, Clay turned around, allowing Dax to draw him in tight against his chest. Dax's hands that were splayed across Clay's belly moved lower to toy with his sex while he nested his cock in the cleft of Clay's ass. Dax moved his hips back and forth, running his cock up and down the crease.

In order to see better and feel more connected to the duo, she moved closer, stopping inches in front of Clay. Her toes sank deeply into the plush fur, and she wondered how it would feel to wrap herself up in such decadence.

Dax turned his gaze on her, and licked his lips. His eyelids heavy with desire, he said, "Touch yourself."

Obediently she slid her hand over her belly and dipped inside the front of her thong. She parted the lips of her sex and massaged her clit, lubricating herself with moisture.

She made no protest when Clay hooked his fingers in the waistband of her panties and tugged them down.

"Jesus," groaned Dax, sinking his teeth into Clay's shoulder.

Clay remained silent. He watched her, his face inches from the apex of her thighs. She felt his gaze, felt every brush of his eyes like little licks of heat across her skin.

Suddenly he reached up, grabbed her ass and pulled her to him, burying his face in her pussy, licking and suckling her clit, and dipping his tongue inside her.

She sank her fingers into his hair, writhed in his grasp. "God," she groaned as an orgasm hovered just out of reach. "Please!"

Clay thrust two fingers inside her and abruptly she came, the orgasm bursting across her senses like a bolt of lightning. She pressed herself against his mouth, reveling in the pressure of his tongue against her clit, and pulsing around his fingers as the pleasure rippled over her.

"Christ, Clay," murmured Dax. "I can't wait any longer."

"Lay down," said Clay, his voice muffled by her body.

Breathing hard, and slick with sweat she dragged herself away from his mouth and fell back, landing in a thick stack of furs. Softness enveloped her, as sumptuous and decadent as the two men who hovered over her.

Her body slightly elevated by the skins. Clay leaned over, stiff-armed, bracketing her body with his hands.

He bent his head and kissed her then. She tasted herself on his lips, on the tip of his tongue. He deepened the kiss and then, abruptly, his body jolted.

He groaned softly, pulled away and Sid knew that Dax had penetrated him.

She watched in fascination as Dax moved his hips, thrusting repeatedly into his lover's body. Clay's face grew flushed, his eyes heavy.

Sid bent her knees and parted her thighs.

It was all the invitation Clay needed. His thrust was so deep and so hard and so unexpected she cried out in stunned surprise. But shock soon melted into pleasure as he cupped her ass, lifted her higher and continued pummeling her body.

Dax's rhythm increased, and Clay's quickened to match it. His fingers gripped her ass tighter and inched inside the crease.

Her breath became ragged and when his fingers touched the rim of her anus she nodded. He inserted a finger inside her, and then another.

He thrust deep, and the added pressure was more than she could take. She arched her back as a fresh orgasm racked her body. She came around him, the pulses strong and rapid, and seemingly endless.

Clay groaned and stiffened, pumping himself into her, and like a set of sexual dominoes, Dax came as well. He let out a loud moan of ecstasy and a moment later the three of them landed in a jumbled heap on the bed of furs.

Sid had barely caught her breath when she noticed Dax kneeling between her thighs.

"Dax?" she asked, unable to believe any of them still had energy to move. "What are you—" Her head fell back and all words were stolen from her throat when Dax gripped her knees, pushed them apart and proceeded to feast on her pussy.

"Oh *God*," she groaned. "I can't—" And then Clay kissed her mouth, thrust his tongue inside her, and she wondered that the human body could survive this kind of excessive stimulation.

She moved her hands to his chest with the intent of pushing him away, but instead found her fingernails digging into his flesh as if to hold him there, draw him closer. Afraid of drawing blood, she let go and wrapped her arms around him, clutching at his back as Dax continued his oral assault on her sex.

"Mmm," he murmured from between her thighs. "This shaved pussy thing is getting me hard again."

Clay withdrew his tongue from her mouth, and pierced her with his laser-blue gaze. "What are we going to do about that?" He palmed her breast, tweaked a nipple.

Sid let out an exhausted laugh. "Since when is Dax's testosterone overload *my* problem?"

Dax lifted his head as if to respond, but the sound of the electronic door lock clicking open ceased all communication beyond a collective, "Oh *shit!*"

They scrambled to cover themselves with the furs, but when Amy stepped inside there was still a disconcerting amount of bare flesh available for her visual inspection. She stopped just inside the door. And stared.

Clay reached down and pulled up one last fur to cover the remaining key parts.

"Hi Amy," ventured Sid, now snuggled between Dax and Clay and a luxurious coyote pelt. "There's a vacant spot. Would you care to join us?"

Amy opened her mouth as if to speak, and then appeared to think better of it. She whirled around and stalked out, slamming the door behind her.

"Good grief," said Sid. "What is it with you two and uninvited interruptions."

Clay groaned. "Damn it. I should probably go after her."

"No," argued Dax. "I should. I'm the one who works here."

Sid snorted. "You'll do nothing of the sort. Either of you. Maybe this was just what she needed to wake her up and make her realize she has no place with Clay."

Dax leaned back, stacking his hands behind his head. "I don't know, Clay. Beautiful, vivacious, feisty, smart and damn good in…" He looked around. "Uh…in bed. I think this one might just be a keeper."

"Yeah." Clay nodded, scrutinizing Sid until she felt the heat rise to her cheeks. "A keeper. Definitely."

She licked her lips. A keeper? What exactly does that mean? Where was all this going, anyway? What did—

"So…" said Dax, interrupting her thoughts. A hand sneaked beneath the fur to touch her breast. Goose bumps skittered across her skin and she shivered despite the warmth of the furs. "What were you going to do about my…problem?"

"Problem?" she said, sitting up and reaching for the beaver pelt that covered Dax's groin. She ripped it away to reveal a renewed, and impressive-as-ever erection. "Oh…*that* problem." She crawled over his thigh and settled herself between his legs.

"You know." She touched the tip of his cock with a provocative finger and toyed with the bead of cum. "When you said this was a completely interactive display, you really weren't kidding, were you?"

Dax grabbed her hand and breathed, "I need to clean up first."

"In a minute."

He made no protest when she bent over and sealed her mouth to his, swallowing his laughter and forgetting everything but the feel of warm male flesh against her body and hot blood pumping through her veins.

* * * * *

"More pasta?" asked Clay, offering the bowl of tiny bow ties and sautéed vegetables to Sidney.

She continued staring at her plate and playing with the same hunk of eggplant she'd had on her fork for the last five minutes.

"Sid?" asked Dax. "You okay?"

She looked up, apparently startled to find that she wasn't alone. "Huh?" She looked from Dax to Clay to the bowl he was holding out to her. "Oh. Yeah. I'm fine." She pushed her plate away. "Just full, that's all." She patted her tummy. "That was amazing, Clay. I had no idea you were such a talented cook."

Clay and Dax exchanged a puzzled glance. Sid was clearly *not* fine. Ever since they'd left the museum she'd been sullen and distracted. She'd turned down a group shower and had spent the time before supper gazing out the window. When asked about it, she had evaded the question by offering to help cut up vegetables for the pasta.

Clay sat back and crossed his arms. "Come on, Sid, out with it."

She tossed him an innocent look. "Out with what?"

"You've barely spoken since we left Toronto, and now you barely touched your dinner, despite the fact that I know it's irresistible."

"Definitely," agreed Dax, stuffing a hunk of roasted pepper into his mouth. "Irresistible."

Clay shot him a reproving look, but Dax was completely unrepentant. "Just trying to keep the mood light. I hate serious shit at the dinner table."

Clay rolled his eyes and turned his attention back to Sidney. "So what is it? What's bothering you?"

She pushed her chair back and stood, walked to the patio doors and looked out over the street dotted with carriage lamps and strolling lovers. "I…I don't know how to put this."

"Did we hurt you?" asked Dax. "Scare you? If this is all too much then—"

"No," she said hastily. "It's nothing like that. I've enjoyed every moment with you—with both of you." She turned back to the window and murmured, "Maybe too much."

The ring of the telephone cut off Clay's response.

"I'll get it," offered Dax. He got up from the table and headed to the kitchen to find the cordless phone.

Clay stood and walked over to join Sidney by the doors. He laid a hand on her shoulder. "You can talk to us, Sid. Jesus, considering what we've shared, you should be able to tell us anything."

She shook her head and before she could say anything they both jumped at the loud whoop that issued from the kitchen. "You're kidding!" exclaimed Dax. "When?"

At last Dax appeared in the doorway, the phone still pressed to his ear and his face glowing.

"What's going on?" asked Sid.

"Damned if I know."

Dax was nodding his head and grinning, muttering a series of mm-hmms and uh-huhs in counterpoint to whoever was on the other end of the phone.

"Okay. We'll talk about it and get back to you."

He blinked. "That soon?"

He nodded. "Okay. The morning." He hung up and turned his beaming face on Clay.

"Well?" asked Clay when he didn't offer anything. "What the hell is it?"

"It's the Foster place. It just went up for sale."

Clay leaned back against the door for support. "You're kidding."

"Funny. Isn't that what I said?"

Clay strode forward and grabbed Dax by the shirt. "If you're fucking with me, I swear—"

"Hold it, you two!" Sid grabbed them both by their shirts. "What's going on? What's this all about?"

Clay took a deep, calming breath. "It's the house we've been wanting to buy for two years now. It's unoccupied, but has been tied up in legal red tape ever since the owner died."

"I guess somebody finally cut the tape," said Dax. "But there's a catch."

Clay felt his chest tighten. "Catch?"

"We have to make an offer before nine o'clock tomorrow morning or it goes on to a real estate agent and onto the open market. They're only giving us this heads-up because we've been so…interested."

Clay laughed. "What he means is we've been pests, nagging the lawyers every couple of weeks, wondering when things might clear up so we can buy the place."

"What's so special about it?" asked Sid.

"Christ." Dax flopped down onto the futon. "It's a century home with stonework and hardwood floors and window wells a foot wide."

Clay sat down beside him. "The structure is in good shape, but it needs a complete decorating overhaul." He nudged Dax. "And Dax is just itching to build a whole new kitchen for the place."

"It's got a little stream through the back yard," said Dax on a sigh. "And it's actually got *fish* in it."

Sid stood before them, and smiled. "Sounds perfect."

"It is."

Suddenly Dax sprang from the couch and grabbed her by the shoulders. "And there's *four* bedrooms. Plenty of room for three of us to live comfortably."

Sid looked shell-shocked. "Move in with you?" she asked. "Permanently?"

Clay was a little irritated with Dax for springing this on her so suddenly, but he couldn't deny he'd been thinking the same thing. "We're not asking you to invest or anything. We can afford it just fine. But…" He stood and kissed her on the cheek. "We'd love to have you. I think it could work out wonderfully for all of us."

"But—"

"Think about it, Sid. Where else have you got to go? Back to Toronto? Back to *Paris*? You can work in Toronto and commute from here, if that's what you want. We love you and we want you with us. What more is there?"

She took a step back, away from the two of them. "It's…it's just that…"

Dax moved forward and Clay put a hand on his arm to hold him back. "That's okay, Sid. You don't have to decide now. Take your time."

She shook her head. "No, I want to explain."

They waited and watched as she clasped her hands and wrung them together.

She swallowed and met Clay's gaze. "I kind of…met someone."

Clay blinked in confusion. "What? Where?"

"B-back in France. He's still there…uh…waiting for me." She turned and began to pace. "Nothing really…*happened* between us yet, but I liked him, you know? A…a lot. But considering all the shit with my husband I wasn't ready to commit to anything. I wanted to come home for a while. Get my bearings again."

"It's okay, Sid," said Dax, but it didn't take a clairvoyant to sense the disappointment in his voice. "We understand."

"No," she stopped, and turned her gaze on the two of them. Clay wasn't sure but he thought he saw tears brimming in her eyes. "No, you don't understand at all."

And with no more warning than that she bolted for the door, and ran out into the hall.

Dax ran after her. "Sid?" he called as she dashed down the stairs. "What's wrong?"

"I just need some air!" They heard the outer door slam shut and she was gone.

Dax turned a confused gaze on Clay. "What the hell was that all about?"

Clay walked to the patio door and watched Sid's mad dash down the street. "I'm not sure, but I do think we need to give her some time alone. Some time to think."

Dax moved in beside him and hooked an arm around his waist. "Okay, but no more than two hours. After that we go hunting for her."

She disappeared around the corner.

"Two hours. You've got it."

Chapter Eight

ഇ

Dax stared down at the dark street dotted with pools of lamplight. High above stars twinkled and a half moon gilded the trees and roof tops in faded silver.

A car pulled over and parked a half-block away but other than that the street was empty.

"Dax!"

Startled, Dax whirled around. "What?"

Clay, his elbows dripping suds and a sopping dish cloth in his hand, stood there looking at once irritated and sympathetic. "I called your name three times."

"Oh." Dax looked down at the plate and dish towel in his hand. "Sorry."

"I think that plate is dry now, and there are others that need your attention."

"Yeah, yeah, I know." Dax nodded and elbowed his way past Clay, heading for the kitchen. He put the plate in the cupboard and reached for another in the drying rack. "When we get the house you need to spring for a dishwasher." They'd already spoken to their lawyer who was drawing up an offer for them to sign at seven the next morning.

"*I* do?" Clay's hands disappeared beneath the mountain of suds. "What about you? You're the one who always whines about doing the dishes."

"Yeah, well…" The witty retort that had formed on his brain evaporated. He let out a heavy sigh. "It's been more than an hour."

"I know." Clay's voice was hushed. "But I'm sure she's fine. Let's just give her a little more—"

A knock on the door startled them both. They exchanged a relieved glance and, without bothering to dry their hands, rushed out of the kitchen.

Dax beat him to the door and wrenched it open. "Sidney, thank God you're—" He hesitated, blinked. "Uh...oh."

Clay moved in beside him and when he spoke his voice betrayed none of the surprise he must be feeling. "Hello. Can we help you?"

The man smiled. Thin lips curled into a wide grin that revealed perfect teeth. His dark hair hung rakishly over his forehead and a small scar on his left cheek completed the effect. Dax thought the trench coat was a bit much, though, considering the balmy spring weather.

"I hope so," said the man, a thick French accent clouding his words. "I got zis address...uh...how you say?" He touched a finger to his lips. "It was the forwarding address that Sidney Poirot gave to her sister." His smile widened as if he'd completed some Herculean task. "*Oui?* Is zat right? Is she here?"

Dax's heart tripped a little faster.

"Not at the moment," Clay was saying, "but we expect her back soon."

The man nodded, apparently relieved. "Good. I was not sure if I had the right place."

Ever the gracious host, Clay stepped aside. "Would you like to wait here for her?"

"Oh yes," said the man as he stepped inside. "Zat would be wonderful. Zank you."

"Make yourself at home," said Clay. "Dax will take your coat."

Dax tried to glare his outrage at Clay but, as usual, Clay ignored him.

"Zank you." The man, smiling like a lunatic, shrugged out of his coat and held it out to Dax.

Dax grumbled to himself but took the garment. He threw it across the armchair.

"Would you like a drink?" asked Clay from the kitchen. "I think we have—"

"What did you say your name was?" growled Dax.

"Red wine would be lovely, zank you." The man had already seated himself on the futon. He crossed his legs before answering Dax. "I don't believe I did." He extended a hand. "Jacques Dubonner."

Dax wanted to ignore the hand but couldn't stomach the thought of Clay's nagging about it. He shook it once and stepped back, hands stuffed in pockets. "You know Sidney from Paris?"

"*Oui.*" He accepted the glass of wine that Clay held out to him. "We were...acquainted there. And when I had opportunity to come to Canada I thought I should...what is it you say? Look her up."

Dax nodded and turned toward the window. He had been so anxious for Sid to come home, but now he wasn't so sure. This was *the guy*. The love interest. The Frenchman. The one she was going to reject them for. Not that they had any right to lay claim on her. It had just been a quick thrill ride, a little excitement to get him and Clay out of their relationship rut. It had all just been for fun.

He shot a glance at Clay. *Hadn't it?*

Clay met his gaze for a moment before returning his attention to their guest. "I'm sure Sid will be thrilled to see you. As a matter of fact we were just talking about you tonight."

The man coughed and almost spilled his wine. "Really?" He seemed surprised. "How sweet. What, exactly, did she say about me?"

* * * * *

Sid rounded the corner and stopped. She stood beneath a carriage lamp and looked up at the third-floor balcony across the street. The lights were on, and she could see a silhouette moving back and forth across the room. She could tell by the way he carried himself that it was Dax. Was he pacing because he was worried about her?

That thought curled through her like warm, fragrant smoke.

She leaned back against the wrought iron lamppost, and allowed the evening breeze to flirt with her hair.

She'd lied to them. Again. The first time she'd lied because her reaction to them had been so intense and unexpected that it had frightened her. She'd turned and fled and lied to cover up her reaction. And this time was no different.

Their offer had appealed to her. Too much. The idea of moving in with Dax and Clay had tempted her, appealed to her in more ways than she cared to admit, and that had scared the wits out of her. So she'd made up the Frenchman to cover her tracks and give her a good reason to turn them down.

She couldn't move in with them. She just couldn't.

She couldn't move in with them because doing that meant giving up something she'd dreamed of all her life—a husband and a home and a family of her own. The great North American dream, the white picket fence stereotype. The happily-ever-after myth.

She hadn't necessarily counted on the minivan and the two-car garage in the suburbs, but she had hoped for a few basic slots in her life to be filled. And moving in with a couple of bisexual buddies just didn't seem to fit any of those slots.

Sure moving in with them didn't have to mean a lifetime commitment. It could just be for a few weeks, a few months, or however long it took for her to find her feet. But she had this sneaking suspicion that it wouldn't work out that way. She had the feeling that once she got settled with those two, she wouldn't want to "unsettle". She had a feeling she'd want to stay right where she was. And she wasn't sure she wanted to take that step.

She closed her eyes, allowed her head to rest against the cool metal. The thing was they made her happy. She'd never been so at ease, so comfortable, or felt so much…*herself* with anyone else. They were intelligent and funny and caring and exciting and…how could she turn her back on all that?

And then there was the sex…

She grinned in spite of herself. There was certainly something to be said for two or three or four orgasms a day. Not that she could keep that up indefinitely, but still it was something to consider.

As was Dax and Clay's relationship. They'd been committed to each other first, had been together for years before she'd waltzed back into their lives. How would she ultimately fit into that? Would they come to resent her for coming between them? For screwing up their perfect life?

Not that it had been perfect. They'd admitted that but—

And what about children? What if they wanted children, too? This kind of relationship didn't exactly rule out that possibility. But did she really want to raise a child in that kind of environment? And what about—

"Aaauuugh!" she screamed into the night. "Okay," she said aloud, pushing herself away from the lamppost and striking off down the street. "The only way to resolve this is to talk about it." She reached the front door of the apartment building and wrenched it open. "If we're going to make this work we gotta set the ground rules now, and the most basic one is honesty."

She took the stairs two at a time.

"Right, boys?"

She reached the third-floor landing and pivoted on one foot to face the door.

"Right."

She knocked smartly and waited.

* * * * *

Clay pinned Dax with a glare and kept him at bay while he walked to the door. This situation needed to be handled coolly and calmly and Clay doubted Dax's ability to do that. In fact he was afraid that if Dax opened the door and found Sidney on the other side he might just scoop her up in his arms and make a run for it.

If she was going to stay she had to stay because she wanted to. And if she was going to leave...

He opened the door and was greeted by a pair of slender arms wrapping themselves firmly around his neck.

"I'm sorry, Clay," she said, her voice muffled by his chest. "I'm sorry I ran away again."

He hugged her back, closed his eyes for a moment and breathed in the scent of her hair. "That's okay, Sid. We understand."

"It's just that I needed to—"

"Sid." He eased himself away from her, and tried to ignore the cauldron of Dax that was simmering on the other side of the room. "Sid, there's someone here."

She sniffled, dragging her gaze up to meet his. "What? Someone?"

He brushed some dark hair off her face. "Yeah. You have a visitor. We thought maybe he was someone you might want to see." She was frowning up at him when he stepped aside to allow her to see *Jacques*.

Slowly she turned her gaze and watched as the Frenchman stood slowly and stepped forward. "Hello, Sidney. I—"

"You?" Her breathing seemed heavy and her face grew pink. "*You?*" She took a step forward, bracing a hand against Clay's arm, as if for support. "What in the *fucking hell* are *you* doing here?"

Jacques took a step backward. "Now, Sid, take it easy." All traces of his accent had disappeared. "I just want to talk."

She took another shaky step forward, her fingers still digging into Clay's arm. Clay noticed Dax move in a little closer, his expression as puzzled and concerned as Clay's.

"You want to *talk*?" asked Sidney, her voice edging up another notch. "*Talk?* How about we talk about *this*?"

What happened next was a blur. He couldn't say for sure what happened in what order, but somewhere along the line Sidney lunged for Jacques, Dax lunged for Sidney, and Clay tried to catch them both without success. Sidney screamed a few foul epithets and by the time Dax reached her, she had managed to land a solid right hook to the Frenchman's face.

Blood sprayed across Dax's chest but at least he got there in time to keep Sidney from landing a few more telling blows and earning herself an assault charge to boot.

Clay jumped in and dragged them both away from the wailing victim.

"Let me *go*," screamed Sidney. "Damn it, let me go!"

Clay held her firm. "Will you be good? Or will you attack him again?"

She stopped struggling. "I won't attack." She batted her eyelashes at Dax. "But if Dax would just hold him down for me—"

"Sid," warned Clay.

"She's a lunatic," screamed Jacques, holding a discarded dishtowel to his nose. "A certifiable nutcase."

"*I'm* crazy?" she yelled back. "You're one to talk, Ned. And what the hell are you doing out of jail, anyway?"

Clay and Dax's eyes met, and in unison their lips mouthed, "Ned?"

Clay released Sid, and so did Dax. They both took a step forward.

Ned took a step back, fear shadowing his eyes.

"What do you think?" growled Dax. "He's kinda scrawny. Shall we snap him like a wishbone?"

"Sure," said Clay, taking a step forward. "You grab one leg and I'll take the other."

They took another step toward their victim but were stopped short by a fine-boned hand placed firmly against each of their chests.

"No," said Sid, her eyes calm now, her voice even. She turned around to face the man who had betrayed and victimized her. "Thanks for the offer, guys, but this one's mine."

* * * * *

Sid studied Ned Poirot and wondered what in the hell she had ever seen in him. "Rat" was written all over his features, as clearly as if it had been spelled out in violet neon.

"Listen, Sid," he whined, his voice distorted by the towel held to his nose.

"No, you listen." Sid stepped forward and rammed a hand against his chest, sending him sprawling back onto the futon. "You sit there while we call the police. I'm sure they'll be happy to send a paddy wagon to pick you up, and then they can send you back to whatever French prison you managed to dig your way out of."

"I didn't break out," he grumbled, studying the dishtowel now spotted with blood. "They let me out."

"You're lying."

"No. I'm not." He sat up a little straighter. "My lawyer found a loophole the size of Paris, and pulled me out through it." He grinned. "Ain't it great when the legal system works the way it's supposed to?"

"You son of a bitch." Clay's firm hand on her arm was all that kept her from leaping onto her ex-husband and pummeling him to within an inch of his life.

He leaned back, apparently aware of his precarious position. "Look, can't we talk about this? I just wanted—"

"What's to talk about? You're a liar and a cheat and a thief, and I'm glad to be rid of you."

He blinked, lowered his eyes. "I wanted to apologize."

If he had slapped her she couldn't have been more stunned. "A-apologize?"

"Yeah. I never meant to hurt you, babe. I just—"

"Don't call me 'babe'," she growled.

"Right. Sorry."

Sid took a step back, away from the foul stench of bullshit. She bumped into Clay who wrapped a protective arm around her waist.

Ned frowned.

"You never meant to *hurt* me?" she continued. "Well, that's a good one, Ned. You stole my money and betrayed me, but you didn't think I'd get *hurt*?"

Ned moved to stand but Dax stepped forward and he seemed to think better of it. He remained seated.

"That didn't come out right."

Sid waited, staring at him and keenly aware of the presence of her two lovers. Protective and comforting, like a suit of armor lined with satin.

"Uh...what I meant was, that I didn't set out in the beginning to steal from you. But things happened, and I got scared and then my greed sort of got away from me." He smiled, as if it would make a difference. "I did care about you, Sid. I guess I just needed you to know that."

"Are you done?" asked Dax.

Ned cast him a wary glance. "I guess."

"Good." Dax looked at Sid. "Can I toss him off the balcony now?"

"Sure."

Dax moved forward and with a little yelp Ned scrambled to get away from him. He vaulted off the couch, but Dax cornered him between the patio doors and the stereo. He held up his hands to ward off his attacker, but Dax stopped a couple of feet away.

Sid walked over and joined Dax, slipping an arm around his waist and giving him a soft kiss on the cheek.

Ned frowned again. "What's with you and these two, anyway? It almost seems like—"

"Get out, Ned."

"But…"

"I'm through listening to you, and I'm through feeling like a victim. Maybe I should thank you for coming back and reminding me of that."

He opened his mouth, hesitated, and then blurted out. "Okay, I'll go. But before I do…" He eyed Dax, and then shifted his gaze to Clay who had moved in behind Sid.

His Adam's apple bobbed. "I just need to ask you one thing."

Sid tamped down her temper. The sooner they finished this, the sooner he'd be gone.

"Yes?"

"Uh…can I have my share of the money back? I know it was only a few thousand but— Hey!"

Dax had grabbed him by the scruff of the neck and was hauling him off toward the door.

"Bye, Ned." Sid waved as Clay opened the door for their guest. "I wish I could say it was nice knowing you."

Dax tossed him into the hall and he hit the opposite wall hard.

The door slammed.

"But I would have been better off marrying a three-horned toad."

And then she was sandwiched between two hard chests and wrapped in four strong arms.

"You okay, babe?"

"Man, you were awesome."

"Yeah. The way you decked him…"

"Like a pro."

"A real trooper."

"An Amazon. Didn't I tell you she was an Amazon?"

Sid laughed, and pressed her face against Dax's chest. "Stop it."

"Why? It's the truth."

She shook her head and looked up into a pair of smoldering hazel eyes. She felt the sting of tears. "I'm sorry."

Dax frowned. "For what?"

She pulled away from them, turned to face them both. "I lied to you." She lifted her chin. "Again."

They stood there, looking at her and waiting and looking so strong and tall and sexy. She melted inside all over again.

"Your offer scared me. It scared me and so, like an idiot, I reacted by making up the story about the guy in France. And then, like usual, I ran."

They moved closer. "Scared you? Why?"

She swallowed. "Because it appealed to me. A lot."

They both touched her. An arm around her waist, a hand on her shoulder.

"Appealed to you? As in, you're thinking about it?"

"Uh...yeah. But..." Warm breath on her ear, heat creeping across her skin. "But we have things to talk about."

"Things?" A brush of lips and whiskers on her neck. "What kinds of things?"

A tongue ran along her collarbone and she struggled to maintain her focus. "Yes. Things like money and household chores. And then there's the future..." A hand had slipped under her T-shirt and cupped her breast. She groaned.

"The future?"

Another hand slipped inside her jeans.

Her mouth had gone dry but she managed to squeak out. "Yeah. You know…how do I fit in with you two? And what about…" she made herself say it, "children."

Her T-shirt was off, and that hand eased aside the cup of her bra at the same time as the other one slipped inside her panties.

She knew she should tell them to stop. This was serious stuff, and they needed to talk about it. But…

"Children…" mumbled Dax, whose tongue had just drawn a lazy circle around her nipple.

"Something to think about." Clay toyed with her clit, and then eased a finger inside her. She felt thick and heavy and wet, and she wanted nothing more than to grind herself against his hand. But she didn't.

"Yeah." Dax's teeth raked across her nipple and she whimpered. "Definitely worth thinking about."

"Guys…" She meant it as a protest, but it came out as more of a plea.

And then Clay's mouth was next to her ear, and he whispered, "We'll talk about all that, Sid. We'll talk about everything, and we'll figure it all out. But right now all that matters is that we love you."

With breath that seemed to burn her lungs she whispered, "You do?"

Dax popped the button on her jeans and proceeded to strip them off her. "Yeah. We do."

She closed her eyes and leaned back against Clay's arm that was now braced against her back. "I love you, too."

He scooped her up and carried her to the bedroom, with Dax close behind.

Clay laid her on the bed and then proceeded to remove his T-shirt, as did Dax.

"Hang on a second," she commanded.

Both men froze.

"Isn't it more fun to…undress each other?"

Dax grinned and grabbed Clay by the shirt, dragging him closer until they stood chest to chest. "My pleasure." He grasped the hem of Clay's shirt and whipped it over his head.

Sid lay back, propped herself up on a stack of pillows and watched as Dax skimmed his hands over Clay's torso, admiring and exploring. His obvious fascination with his lover's body was as arousing as having her nipples simultaneously sucked.

Dax undid the button on Clay's jeans and fresh desire coiled in her belly. He hooked his thumbs in the waistband and peeled them down, revealing the taut ass and imposing erection she'd already become so familiar with. As the jeans reached Clay's knees, Dax paused to lick Clay's cock. His tongue ran from base to tip before taking it deeply into his mouth.

"Jesus," moaned Clay.

But the torture was short-lived. It must have been a teaser because Dax finished removing Clay's jeans and then stood before his lover again.

Unexpectedly Clay grabbed Dax by the shoulders and drew him in for a quick, hungry kiss.

Sid bit her lip. For some reason seeing the two men engaged in tongue-play always heightened her sexual awareness. She gave in to the urge to gently stroke herself.

Clay broke off the kiss, and out of the corner of his eye noticed what she was doing. "Uh-oh." He whirled Dax around so that his back was to Clay and he was facing the bed. "We're falling down on the job, man."

He ripped the T-shirt over Dax's head, reached around his waist to pop the button on his jeans. "You've got a job to do."

Dax's jeans fell to his ankles and he grinned. "Damn. It's a dirty job, but I guess somebody's gotta—" He grunted, and fell to his knees.

Clay had used his knees to unlock Dax's, and drop him to the floor.

Clay's hands roamed over Dax's chest, and then around to caress his ass and do other things that Sid couldn't quite see.

Dax's eyes closed in obvious enjoyment.

"Well?" said Clay through a grin. "What about Sid?"

Dax's eyes flew open and suddenly his hands flew out and grabbed Sid by the ankles.

"Hey!" she squealed as he pulled her to him. He tugged her closer until her feet touched the floor and her knees were hooked over the edge of the mattress.

He gripped her thong and ripped it away like it was made of tissue paper.

"Hey!" she protested. "What are you—"

Her head fell back when his mouth covered her pussy. He kissed and licked, his tongue doing sinful things to her clit and then dipping inside to taste her. She sat up in order to see him better, and was greeted by Clay's lips joining with hers. Still standing behind Dax, he broke the kiss and motioned with his eyes, asking her a silent question. She noticed that he held a small bottle of oil and was quickly coating his hands and cock with the spicy-scented lubricant.

She swallowed and nodded, watching as Clay set the bottle aside and then began working his fingers in and out of Dax's ass. At last he withdrew his fingers, parted Dax's cheeks and nudged Dax's anus with his cock. Dax groaned softly and his mouth momentarily parted from her pussy. He rested his cheek against her thigh, and she sensed him pressing himself backward.

The tip of Clay's cock eased inside slowly and then abruptly Clay grabbed Dax's hips and thrust hard. Dax grunted and his fingers dug into the covers, but the thrusts continued, hard and fast. Clay was surprisingly brutal but Dax must have liked it that way because soon his mouth rejoined with her pussy and his hands gripped her wrists, urging her to touch his hair.

She plunged her hands into his hair, reveling in the play of his tongue, and the feel of his thick mane dripping through her fingers, as Clay's thrusts increased in tempo and force.

An orgasm hovered just out of reach but then Dax slipped two fingers inside her and she fell backward onto the bed, arching her back and pushing herself against his mouth as she pulsed around him and soaked the sheets with her climax.

Clay let out a cry, and his body stiffened as he pumped himself into Dax.

A moment later he fell onto the bed beside her. "Christ," he said, studying Dax who was grinning at them from his position at the end of the bed. "That was amazing."

Sid sat up and touched Dax's face. She bent down and kissed him, tasting a blend of herself and his own unique flavor. "Maybe so, but we're not done."

"Sorry, Dax," breathed Clay, "sometimes Sid is just a little overwhelming."

"That's okay," said Dax with a waggle of his eyebrows. "I'm feeling pretty good."

"No," she whispered, not quite believing what she was about to do. She licked her lips. "I'd like to try something…different."

Dax and Clay watched as she slowly eased herself off the bed and turned her back to Dax. She smiled coyly at Clay. "I'd like to try it."

Clay moved forward and sat on the edge, his knees on either side of her. "Have you ever had anal sex before?"

She shook her head.

"Okay, then we'll take it slow."

She drew a fingernail down his chest. "Does that mean you'll help?"

He touched a breast and grinned. "I think I could be persuaded."

"Okay," said Dax, his hand stroking her bottom. "First thing you need to do is relax."

She nodded, giving herself over to their care.

"Lean toward me," said Clay his hand skimming across her breasts and down her belly.

She leaned forward until her breasts touched his chest.

His hand eased lower until he brushed through the small triangle of curls.

She nodded and parted her thighs to allow him easier access.

As he toyed with her clit, Dax grabbed the oil and began to massage it into the area around her anus.

It felt strange, but…good. She allowed herself to enjoy it.

Clay slipped a couple of fingers inside her vagina. "You're wet," he said, and she could hear the breathlessness in his voice. "God, you're wet."

"And ready," agreed Dax as he slipped one oil-slicked finger inside her ass.

Clay continued his massage of her clit and she relaxed, floating on their attention.

Dax eased another finger inside. She tensed a little, but he kissed her shoulder and she relaxed. He began to work them in and out, a little deeper each time until her body accepted each thrust easily. "Good," he whispered, his breath fluttering across her skin. "That's good."

And then, before she realized what was happening she felt a new pressure. His cock pressed against her ass and slipped inside her. Slowly. Sweetly. The pressure strange, but intriguing. He withdrew and eased inside her again, and breathless but eager, she found herself matching his rhythm.

Clay's fingers continued their massage and then she lifted her face to his and he kissed her. His fingers worked in and out of her pussy in a powerful counterpoint to Dax's thrusts.

The pressure was intense, exquisite, verging on pain, but not quite.

The blood throbbed in her clit, and pulsed through her veins, hard and fast and fierce. Growing. Building. Stealing her breath and shutting out the rest of the world. Until...

The orgasm rippled through her like an electric current. Clay's fingers ground against her, intensifying it as his tongue ravaged her mouth.

Dax's fingers dug into her hips as he made one final thrust. He moaned as she continued to come, pulsing around him and grinding her ass against him.

"Jesus," he sighed, melting over her, the hardness of his chest against her back, sandwiching her between himself and Clay. "Sweet Jesus."

"Yeah," said Clay, his hand still pressed against her pussy. "My thoughts exactly."

Sid kissed Clay's cheek. "Wow," she said softly. "That was..."

"Yeah," chuckled Dax. "It sure was."

* * * * *

Ten minutes later Sid lay in Dax and Clay's bed, Clay pressed up against her back, and Dax nestled against her front, a blanket cocooning all three in a pocket of warmth and satisfaction.

Clay kissed her shoulder. "You mentioned something about being worried about how you would...*fit* in with our relationship."

"Yeah," said Dax, his breathing slow and soft, his voice dreamy. "I remember that. I thought it was kind of a strange thing to say."

"Me too," continued Clay, "because I think you *fit* with us just perfectly."

"You know," said Sid, breathing in their scent and soaking up their love. "I think you're right."

And at that moment she knew, without a doubt, that no matter what complications they encountered, no matter what obstacles they had to overcome, they'd be able to handle it.

Together.

The End

Twilight

By
Anya Bast

Chapter One

80

It was always impressive to see, thought Dai as he and Nico mounted the top of a hill and the fourth triad tower came into view below them.

The tower rose high above the weed- and briar-choked hedges that wreathed its base. The weeds were impossible to keep at bay these days, despite the fact that darkness had grown so much that it seemed like constant twilight, and even though it was high summer, it felt like late autumn. Even now, in the gloom of the Encroaching Darkness, that tower seemed to cast a shadow.

He snapped his horse's reins and dug his heels into the beast's sides. Beside him, Nico did the same. They headed their mounts down the slope and through the gateway that led into the tower courtyard.

A black-hooded monk took their mounts and another ushered Dai and Nico into the tower. A small fire burned in the hearth, barely managing to touch the chill in the cavernous room. The floor was of solid stone, but no rushes had been laid down. The High Mages of the Vedicinn and their monks rarely succumbed to the temptation of such luxuries. A single table stood in the austere chamber, covered with texts and loose papers. Dai knew well the Vedicinn still sought ways to stave off the Encroaching Darkness, even though they all knew well it was Dai, Nico and the third member of their Sacred Triad — wherever she was — who would mean the difference between triumph and defeat.

Dai and Nico were two-thirds of a sacred triad — one of seven. The other six triads had been formed years ago and they were all waiting for the seventh to be realized. In the eyes of their elders they were failing. For years they'd searched for the woman who would complete their circle of magick. Her inclusion would form the last part of the conduit that would allow the power of all the triads to flow out and purify the binding fabric of their reality, fine-tuning it to a higher level. The formation of their triad would push back the Encroaching Darkness.

A shrunken form rose from the chair beside the table. A gnarled hand extended. The other liver-spotted hand clutched a wooden staff. "Come," said the fourth mage.

Dai and Nico walked forward and went down on their knees, touching their fingertips to their foreheads in the formal gesture of respect.

"Rise."

They rose and felt the full weight of the Fourth's gaze on them. He narrowed rheumy eyes at them. "Time is growing short," said the fourth in a voice that sounded as though it'd been broken over old stones. Timeless. Weary.

He needed to say no more.

Nico cleared his throat. His long black hair was loose and a hank of it had fallen across a dark eye. Nico was beautiful, dark and intense. It was said he could seduce anyone—man or woman. Dai knew it to be true. "We have a trace on her magick. She may be in the northern part of Carraton, and we are traveling there directly after this meeting, High Mage."

The fourth's eyes narrowed further. "I thought you told me her magick had been completely transferred to you."

"Not the entirety of it. She still has a thin thread left."

They did not know much about the one they sought, save that she was female. All the triads were of both sexes — two females and a male, or two males and a female. They also knew that years ago, some event had made their third member relinquish most of her magick. They speculated that she'd been greatly, perhaps irreparably, psychically damaged due to that unknown trauma in her past. Whatever happened had forced the magick out of her body and, as the other two sides of the triad, Dai and Nico had been forced to absorb it.

"Why have you not sensed this *thread* before now?" the fourth asked suspiciously.

His temper piqued, Dai stepped forward. It was as if the fourth thought they'd deliberately been thwarting the formation of their own triad. Even when the extra magick they carried was a heavy burden all of the time—and a nearly uncontrollable force some of the time. "We *have* sensed it over the years, High Mage, but it always moved so erratically that by the time we reached the area of its emanation, it had shifted. Now it has settled and stayed constant. We believe she has finally set up a home. I would respectfully ask your leave to be on our way immediately."

The fourth stared at Dai and he returned his gaze confidently. Dai's name was an apt one since he was like the day—friendly and full of light—but also had a temper that could grow hot as the sun.

The fourth tested that temper now.

Tense moments passed. Finally, the fourth banged his staff on the floor. "I summoned you here to impress the fact upon you that the fate of our world lies in your hands. The Vedicinn grows desperate. They search for ways to engage the magick of the triads without yours, and that will be risky. Go," the fourth barked. His face grew haggard-looking and he seemed suddenly even older than his already ancient age. "You had better find her this time."

* * * * *

Twyla dug into the hard packed earth in effort to free a hansclep root. Her nail broke to the quick and, cursing, she snatched her hand to her mouth and fell back into a sitting position. Her wooden, hand shovel had split yesterday and she sorely missed it.

It was market day in Dandre Village tomorrow. She knew she'd have to brave a trip in to buy a new one. The last time she'd gone, she'd been hassled by a local farmer. Out here in the country, women traveling alone were always suspect. The farmer, Marsten had been his name, had followed her around. Perhaps he'd thought she was a pleasure woman for hire, Twyla didn't know. All she knew was that he'd received a sharp elbow in the ribs for his trouble.

She cast around until she found a suitable branch and used it to dig. Finally the root came up. "Dinner!" she declared triumphantly to the forest at large. The root was an ugly bulbous purple mass at the moment, but cleaned up and boiled with the rest of her potatoes and an onion it would be quite delicious.

Cradling the root in her shirttails, she stood and made her way through the murky forest that she called home. She'd found a ramshackle house back in the depths of the woods. It had likely been abandoned for years and had needed many repairs. She'd set about fixing it up, and the project was nearly complete now. Smoke curled enticingly from the chimney in the distance and the thatched roof came into view. She still had things to do but it was becoming very cozy already.

Home.

She hadn't had one of those in a very long time. She'd never had a permanent one. She and her mother had always been forced to move to different villages when she'd been growing up. Never staying in one place long enough for them to settle and make friends or have any kind of stable life.

And then one day… Twyla gave her head a sharp shake. No, that didn't bear any thought at all. Better to let the past be the past.

She passed the woodpile and the hatchet she'd embedded in one of the stumps. She'd begun to line the walkway up to the door with some large, flat stones she'd found. It looked pretty that way, she thought. Yes, she planned to stay here for a while, forever if she could hold the place. She was so tired of moving.

Twyla pushed the door open and entered the snug house. It smelled of the drying herbs she'd hung from the rafters. She'd warmed some water over the fire so she could bathe. After she placed the root on the trestle table, she poured the warmed water into her hip tub. She loosed her hair from the knot on the top of her head and shook the length out. It was long, to her waist, and blood-red. She had no time or need for vanity in her life and, practically speaking, she should have hacked it off long ago. She fingered a tendril and eyed the knife on the table. *Really*, she should. It was constantly in her way and was so difficult to keep untangled. She closed her eyes as a memory overwhelmed her.

"Your hair is like rubies, darling," her mother said as she ran a brush gently through it.

Twlya inhaled. Her mother always smelled of vanilla.

"You have such pretty hair. Promise me you'll never cut it."

She opened her eyes, let go of her hair and stripped off her filthy clothing.

The water was comforting and pleasant when she lowered herself down into it and picked up the chunk of soap. She might not want to acknowledge the event that had decorated her body with a crisscrossing of thin, white scars, but she couldn't ignore them either. They traced over her breasts, her stomach, thighs and buttocks and served as an ever-constant reminder of the night she'd lost both her mother and her innocence forever. The wounds, caused by a mercilessly lashing whip, had long since healed. Of course, the far more severe wounds within her mind and her heart had never healed, and she doubted they ever would.

She finished bathing, toweled herself dry and slipped into her warm, woolen sleeping gown and slippers. After she'd prepared her stew and set it to cook over the fire, she curled up in a chair to watch the fire lick red and amber over the bottom of her cooking caldron. She considered buying a book at the market tomorrow. It was an expensive luxury, but she hadn't had a new book in a very long time. Exhaustion and relaxation gradually stole over her body and soon she found it difficult to keep eyes open.

When she awoke, early morning light filtered in through the windows and the fire had burned itself to ash. She stood and checked the caldron and found it cold, as was her cottage. Her breath showed in the crisp air. Twyla cursed under her breath as her stomach rumbled. She'd have to remake the fire for heat and for food.

She moved to pick up her kindling basket from beside the door when she saw a flash of movement outside her window. Murmuring voices met her ears. Two males. Dropping the basket, she picked up her sword that lay against the wall instead. Moving stealthily, she inched toward the door and opened it a crack.

At first, she saw nothing, then she glimpsed two men roaming around outside. One was blond and fair; the other had dark hair and eyes. They were both tall, and well built. She bit her bottom lip, assessing them. They'd be far superior to her in swordplay unless she could dodge and strike, not allowing either of them to corner her and lay their weight against her.

No…with two of them that was probably not an option.

Quickly, she turned and pulled on a pair of trews, a shirt and a pair of boots. No way would she allow herself to be cornered by two unknown males in a thin sleeping gown. Her heart pounded and nausea threatened to overwhelm her. She sat on her bed and drew deep, ragged breaths. In her mind she chanted. *Not again! Not again!* Over and over.

She wouldn't be able to stand a repeat. She simply wouldn't be able to live through it. Also, she didn't want to leave this place. She didn't want to be chased away from yet another place she desired to make a home.

Twyla opened her eyes. She had to defend herself, or die trying.

A knock on the front door scared her almost out of her skin. She ran for the window at the back of the cottage, threw it open and pulled herself and her sword out of it. Then she walked around the side of building, her sword drawn and concealed behind her back, should she need to use it.

"Who goes there?" she asked when she turned the corner.

The two men turned toward her and she nearly dropped her sword. They seemed so familiar to her. Had she met them before? And what was that fizzy sensation vibrating through her? It calmed her somehow. It felt indescribably *right*.

The blond one smiled and took a step toward her. She took a step back. He frowned and held out his hand, as though entreating a wild animal. "We won't hurt you."

Aye, she'd heard that before.

"State your business," she said.

"*You* are our business, lady. We've been searching a long time to find you."

"What trickery do you use? As far as I know, I've never met either of you before. What cause do you have here? Why have you come?"

The dark one stepped forward. "I am Nico and this is Dai. We've come to talk with you. Will you at least tell us your name?"

"I think you've no need of that information. Leave now, before I am forced to *make* you do so." She pulled the sword from behind her back. They exchanged a look, yet remained nonplussed.

Did they not think she was serious?

"Please, lady, it is urgent we talk with you," said the one who'd called himself Nico.

In response, she assumed a battle stance, her sword at the ready.

"Lady—"

She charged, flying at them both. In her mind, she reviewed her battle strategy. Strike one and then the other fast and hard, maybe she could maim them. It would make them easier to fight.

But, suddenly, she found herself at a dead standstill. Both men had their hands out, palms forward. She was paralyzed in lunging battle stance—her arms raised, intent clear on her face.

Panic, intense and complete, consumed her.

Loss of control to males.

Just like before...

Her heartbeat sped up wildly. Her breath came in short, hard gulps. Then everything went black.

Chapter Two

જી

Nico carried the young woman into her cottage and laid her on the narrow bed that lined one wall. He turned toward Dai, breathing hard and sweating, but it wasn't from lifting the woman's slight weight. It was from the hard, deep thrum of magick reverberating through him from being so near to their third, from touching her. Dai's eyes were wide and shining. Nico knew he felt it too. That extra magick within them wanted to go back to its rightful owner. Keeping it contained was a real effort.

Dai shook his head. "We have to keep it." His gaze dropped to the woman. She whimpered in her sleep as dreams set in. "At least for now."

"I know," answered Nico. He glanced at the woman. "She should sleep for a long time." Her hair flowed past her narrow shoulders like a dark red river. Her skin was so thin and pale, he could see her veins beneath it in places. Nico knew that fragility of hers was a deception. She'd almost pushed right through the magickal net they'd thrown up in front of her.

Her baggy, masculine clothing hid her body, but a man could clearly see she was sweetly shaped beneath them. Nico knew, and his cock definitely knew. He, like Dai, he was sure, had hungered for the woman the instant he scented her on the wind, the moment he'd seen her. It wasn't because she was beautiful, it was because she was their third and this triumvirate was predestined and long overdue.

Tingling sexual need tightened his body in a vise. He looked up at Dai, who held his gaze steadily. They were in accord.

"Outside?" asked Dai tersely.

Nico nodded once and they left the cottage. Once outside, he stalked to Dai, running his gaze over the other man's body as he went.

They were both well built from lives of strenuous activity, though Dai had perhaps just a little bit more bulk. Dai had been compared to a wolf by women, and Nico a large cat. The two of them together never failed to attract a woman to join them for bed play, when that was what he and Dai desired.

With his gaze, Nico traced the lines of Dai's chest and upper arms that could be seen through his shirt, and then dropped to the cock that strained against Dai's trews. Dai was every bit as aroused by the magick of encountering their third as he was. The power of their added magicks rose in them both, forcing upward and threatening to explode. It felt like a bag filling with water, the pressure forcing the seams. They needed an outlet, relief, a pinprick in the taut fabric to let just a trickle through.

Nico circled Dai with his eyes heavy-lidded, taking in the gorgeous male body that would soon be beneath him. He wanted to take Dai, and take him forcefully.

Right now.

He stood behind Dai, but didn't touch him. Instead, he allowed his body heat to radiate out into the other man's back. When Dai's breath caught, when Nico imagined his heart rate had sped up, he leaned forward and brushed his lips across Dai's nape.

"Do you want me?" Nico murmured.

"You could make water catch fire, Nico."

Nico nipped at Dai's nape, and then gently bit, tasting the salt on his warm skin. The action was a blatant show of dominant assertion. Neither one of them was naturally inclined toward submissiveness, but they took turns in deferring to the other sexually. This time Nico wanted Dai to defer and was making that clear. Telepathically he said, *you didn't answer my question.*

"Of course I do."

Nico released his hold on Dai's neck and Dai tried to turn toward him. With a low snarling noise in his throat, Nico clasped his hands to his waist and held him in place. Then he worked Dai's shirt up and over his head and ran his hands slowly down him, feeling the bunch of his muscles, the gentle rise and fall of his chest, his warm, warm skin.

Nico closed his eyes, savoring the feel of him under his hands. He dipped down and brushed across Dai's straining cock through his trews and Dai answered with a deep shudder. Nico's mouth curled up at the edges. His partner was excited by his touch.

Nico undid the trews and let them fall. Dai's cock was long and thick and heavily veined. Perfect in every way. He ran his fingers teasingly over the broad tip and then down to stroke the organ that felt so much like velvet-covered steel. Dai's body tensed and he let out a long, low groan.

With urgent lust, Nico pressed Dai to the ground beneath him, undoing his own trews as he went. He needed to be within Dai's heat. Nico needed to join himself with the man he loved, needed to feel their connection both physically and magickally. Last but not least, they needed to assuage this growing buildup of power. Nico ran his hand down the cleft of Dai's ass and then pressed a finger into his anus, eliciting groans from them both. He added another and thrust, gently widening him and relaxing his muscles.

When Dai was ready, Nico slipped the head of his cock within him, then fed the length to him inch by inch.

"Sweet—" Dai started to swear and then broke off. He shifted his weight and grasped his hard cock in his hand, stroking himself. His other hand curled into the grass beneath them. "Sweet Gods," he breathed finally.

Nico began to move, possessing the other man's body in the most satisfying of ways. The magick skittered over his skin, then, as the tension in his body grew, it began to stroke him like a hand encased with silk.

Nico reached around and took Dai's cock in hand, stroking it as he thrust behind him. Dai's body tensed in the way that Nico knew meant he was ready to climax. When Dai let out a long, low groan of satisfaction and his cock jerked in Nico's hand, Nico exploded. At the same time, the magick burst from them both, covering them over in ecstasy before dissipating into the air around them.

Relief. In so many more ways than one.

Dai allowed himself to collapse to the ground, and Nico came with him. They lay tangled together and breathing heavily for a long time. The ground and air were cold, the skies dark, but neither of them seemed able to move to go into the cottage where it was warmer. The exhaustion came partly from making love and partly from the release of the excess buildup of magick. But mostly it came from the relief of their success. For years they'd sought her, and they'd finally, *finally* found her.

The finding of their third had brought with it a powerful emotional euphoria. Joining physically was a pleasurable way of expressing it.

Neither of them had started out predisposed to men, but when the magick had built and built, sex with each other had happened in order to relieve the pressure. They'd already been good friends, but it was then they'd become good lovers. Eventually, they'd come to truly love each other in a romantic sense. Now Nico couldn't imagine life without Dai. They were two parts of a whole. Well, he amended, maybe two parts of a triad was more like it. They had one more lover to add.

At some point, they slept, but awoke to the sound of screaming. Dai and Nico jumped up and raced into the cottage.

The woman writhed on the bed, her spine snapping back in gesture of agony. Her face contorted and she cried out in her spell-drenched sleep.

Dai and Nico hurried to her bedside. "She dreams," murmured Nico.

Dai shook his head. "Those are not dreams. She suffers with memories."

She clenched the blankets in white fists and shook, screaming and crying. Finally she went limp, perspiration coating her face.

Nico began to breathe easier. Perhaps the worst was over.

That's when the words began.

Nico fell to his knees beside the bed and Dai followed. Now *they* fisted the sheets in their hands. Now they cried. Every word she uttered painted a far too clear picture of the event that had driven her magick from her and into them.

The horror was beyond all imagination.

Nico and Dai sought and found each other, as though touching would help them endure the onslaught of her words and the images they produced in their minds. She talked of the night those that pursued her and her mother had finally caught up to them. She screamed when she relived the brutal rape and murder of her mother. It had occurred right before her eyes. The woman sobbed and became unintelligible after recounting this, but Dai and Nico understood the terror that had followed, and what had happened to her. The men had done everything to her that they'd done to her mother, and more. Everything but kill her.

Finally, the woman lay still, sheened with perspiration and breathing hard. Her blood-red hair lay across her cheek in sharp contrast to the paleness of her skin. Nico reached out to brush her hair away, but Dai grabbed his wrist.

"Let her awaken on her own. Our touch, while she relives these events as she dreams, may very well make everything worse for her."

Nico nodded and began to lower his hand. Dai caught it and pulled Nico to him. For long moments, they stood by the woman's bedside, clinging to each other as her memories seared themselves into their minds. Nico squeezed his eyes shut, taking comfort in the rise and fall of Dai's chest against his own and the scent of his hair that lay against his nostrils. A mixture of fury and deep sorrow infused him. Fury at the men who had done this to her, and sorrow that he and Dai hadn't been there to protect her.

Dai pulled away, stood, and started pacing the small room. Nico watched him silently, his own emotions tightly leashed, knowing this was the fine edge of Dai's sometimes explosive temper. The last thing Dai needed now was more fuel for his emotions.

Finally Dai stopped in the center of the room and stared at Nico with a gaze made of daggers. "They destroyed her," he said in a much too soft voice. When he spoke that carefully, that softly, trouble lay ahead. A quiet Dai was a dangerous Dai.

Nico drew a breath. "We will aid her in rebuilding."

A burst of power exploded from Dai, making the glass in the cottage windows rattle and a fire begin with a poof of smoke in the hearth. "*They broke her,*" Dai repeated in a dark voice. "*Our third.* How can you be so calm?"

Nico spread his hands. "There is nothing to do now but try to heal her, Dai. The past cannot be changed, but we can help her create a tomorrow full of support and love."

Dai made fists. "We need to find them. We need to—"

"All but two are dead."

Nico whipped his head in the direction of the quiet, feminine voice. The woman sat up and pushed herself into the corner of the wall, drew her knees to her chest and wrapped her arms around them in a protective gesture.

"They made the mistake of not restraining me that night." She shrugged. "I guess they thought I was too injured to move, but I wasn't. I-I...well, let's just say I took vengeance for my mother and myself."

"How long have you been awake?" Nico asked softly.

She tipped her chin. "Long enough to know I spill my secrets when I sleep. Long enough to wonder why you think I'd want your support and especially your *love.*" She sneered the last word.

Dai moved toward her and, with wide eyes, she pressed herself against the wall . He stopped in the middle of the room. "We won't hurt you. That's the very last thing we would ever want for you. That's why I'm angry. The thought of you being"--he paused for a moment, obviously not wanting to say the word—"*abused* that way is near unbearable.

"I can take care of myself. I don't need anyone else," she snapped.

"Haven't you been lonely?" asked Dai.

"Of course I've been lonely, but lonely and safe is better than happy and endangered."

"What if you could be happy *and* safe?" asked Nico softly.

Her lower lip trembled just a bit and her eyes showed a fleeting deep vulnerability, before her features hardened. "I don't know who you are or why you've come, but I want you to leave."

Nico stood. "We're both Mages of the Triads." He waited a beat. "*You* are a mage, also. *You* are our third. That's why we've come."

"What?" Her eyes widened and she went very still.

"I'm not lying to you," said Nico. "We've been looking a very long time for you."

Her face paled. Finally, when she spoke, it was more of a shriek. "Get out! Get out now!"

Nico and Dai went for the door. Pushing her wouldn't aid them or her. She would come to them eventually. It was destined to be so. "At least tell us your name," said Dai before exiting.

Nico turned to watch her. She stood in the middle of the room, shaking nearly imperceptibly. They'd touched something within her. Something fresh and tender, and it had hurt. That was obvious. She needed time to come to terms with it.

Too bad they didn't *have* any time.

"M-my name is Twyla," she whispered, looking away from them.

Chapter Three

ജ

Twyla shut the door behind the two males and latched it. Then she leaned her head against the heavy wood and closed her eyes. Emotion jumbled around inside of her until she didn't know how she felt anymore.

There was something about them. Something that had rekindled the magick she'd had as a child, the magick that had made her and her mother outcasts in every village in which they'd tried to settle. It had flicked over her skin like a caress when she'd first seen them, then again when she'd awoken to hear them raging on about That Night. The blond one had been furious. She'd never had anyone become so upset in her defense.

She squeezed her eyes shut even tighter. They were mages. They said she was one, too, a Mage of the Triads. They were the holy people of Carraton, counterpart to the blessed ones, the Vedicinn. They lived cloistered in the Triad Towers far to the north, using their magicks for those who had need of them. Unlike witches, the mages were highly revered in their culture.

Could it possibly be?

She opened her eyes and turned away from the door. The fire still raged in the hearth where the blond one, Dai, had set it aflame with his magick. She sank into a flanking chair and studied the tendrils of flame that licked the bottom of her cooking cauldron as they warmed her stew. At least some good had come out of that encounter.

It was true that when her mother had been alive, Twyla had been full of magick. She'd had healing ability and had been able to move things with her mind. It had been what kept them outcasts. It had been why they'd been forced to move from one place to another. Twyla had always known she was different, but she never thought she was a Mage of the Triads. She and her mother had simply assumed she'd had rogue magick in their bloodline. That she'd been a witch, not a mage. A mongrel, not a purebred.

Worse, she'd been untrained. So Twyla hadn't even been able to hide her abilities. They'd just appear, sometimes at the most importune of times.

The night her mother had died, she'd rejected all the magick within her. She'd pushed all of it away from her with a supreme use of her will, blaming her magick for what had occurred. The men had tortured her and her mother because they feared her and her abilities, after all. If she hadn't been such a misfit, so strange, the men would've left them alone on That Night. Her mother would still be alive. A tear slipped down Twlya's cheek. It was her fault her mother had been murdered.

There was a deep part of her that missed her magick, that was true enough. She had to remind herself that magick only brought pain.

* * * * *

Seven days later an unnatural chill set in. Twyla stuck her head out of her cottage door and examined the darkened skies. It had been so cold and dark lately. She shivered and wrapped her cloak tighter around her throat. It had started about a year ago, but it seemed to be getting just a little darker and colder with every passing day now.

She ducked her head back in to grab her wood basket and then left the cottage. Nico and Dai had been nowhere to be seen since that first day, but yesterday, she'd started to feel their presence in the forests. It wasn't ominous or fear inspiring. On the contrary, it was a good feeling. As much as she wanted to deny it, it was a comforting sensation to know these two men were close.

That went against everything she'd become since her mother's death. It was jarring to not feel revulsion when she thought of these two men, to not want to run away as fast as possible. On the contrary, she felt drawn to them in ways she couldn't fully articulate.

It was like she had some kind of internal homing sense riveted on them. Twyla knew where they'd set up camp, more or less, because she could feel them.

She went in the opposite direction.

Her boots crunched over fallen leaves and broke twigs as she walked. Occasionally, a bird would call to another in the canopy of trees. She picked up a branch and stood, staring skyward. Not as many birds sang these days. Not as many as there should be for this time of year.

"They're upset about the strange weather."

She nearly dropped the branch at the sound of Nico's voice. Her hand clenched around it instead. She should've known they'd make themselves seen soon enough. Dropping her gaze, she narrowed her eyes at the male who leaned against a nearby tree. He wore an outfit as dark as his hair and eyes, along with a pair of sturdy boots. The fabric of his shirt stretched over a well-muscled chest and arms. She would be no match for him in a fight, that was certain. "You startled me," she said accusingly.

He inclined his head. "Forgive me." He motioned at her wood basket. "Can I help you?"

"I can gather my own wood. Save what you find for your own fire. It will be very cold once the sun goes down."

"Dai and I have much wood." He smiled. "No shelter to speak of, but a lot of wood. I have two strong arms, Twlya, I'm willing and able to help."

She stared suspiciously at him for a long moment. "All right," she said finally. "I won't turn down aid."

Nico fell into step beside her, gathering branches with one hand and bracing them to his chest with his other arm. "Have you had a little time to think on what we've told you?" he asked.

She fumbled the branch she was trying to pick up. In exasperation, she blew a tendril of hair away from her face and stood. "I don't know what I think about what you told me. Magick"—she swallowed hard and glanced away—"I don't really want a part of magick. It destroys."

His brow furrowed. "Destroys?" Then a look of understanding overtook his face. He shook his head. "Magick didn't cause what happened to you, Twyla," he said softly. "Ignorance, fear and hatred caused it."

Something flip-flopped in her stomach every time he said her name. She shook her head. "As much as I'd like to believe that... Anyway, I don't have magick anymore."

Nico turned toward her. "You do," he said empathically. "We've been keeping it for you in trust. You pushed it away that night and Dai and I absorbed it."

Confusion clouded her for a moment as her mind stuttered over the possibility. A hope she hadn't even known she'd had warred with doubt and fear. She shook her head. "What kind of game are you playing with me?"

"No games, Twyla. I can show you."

She just stared at him. Could it be possible that she could have her magick back? Tears filled her eyes. A part of her missed it deeply. No matter what manner of torture it had put her mother and herself through when she'd been a child, her magick was an intimate part of her. She couldn't deny that.

"Come. Let's go back to the cottage. I will let you peek at the power I'm keeping for you."

She nodded, only half-aware that she did it.

They reached her cottage and stacked the wood beside the hearth. When Twyla stood from piling on the last branch, Nico was staring at her intently. She took a step to the side and then back. "Will you have to touch me to do this?"

"Sometimes touching can be very nice. It can be loving and comforting. It doesn't have to be like what you've experienced."

Fear and panic rushed through her. She eyed her cutting knife that lay on a table nearby. "How *much* will you have to touch me to do this?"

"Just a little. Come here."

She stood there, frozen in place.

"Twyla, I would never hurt you. Not only that, I would kill anyone who tried." He beckoned with a hand. "I won't do anything to make you uneasy. In fact, pick up your knife there and hold it. That way, if I do something you don't like, you have a weapon."

Twyla flinched, surprised he'd suggest such a thing. She took the knife from the table and walked to him slowly.

"Hold out your hand," he commanded gently.

Carefully, she extended her hand. He reached out and took it. She jerked a little, but didn't pull away.

"Please. Try to trust me just a little," said Nico.

She drew a deep breath. "I will."

He pulled her forward until they stood just a heartbeat away from each other. Twyla could feel the heat his body generated. It emanated from him and warmed her through, chasing the chill away. The scent of him filled her—leather and some kind of spiced soap. When he pulled her the rest of the way toward him, she came without even realizing it. Suddenly, she found herself pressed up against his chest. She gasped and tried to step back, but he wound a hand to the small of her back and pressed lightly. She stopped. Awkwardly, both arms dangled at her sides, one hand weakly gripping the knife.

"Are you all right?" he asked.

His deep voice rumbled through him and into her. Her mind felt clouded by his heat, his scent and the press of his body against hers. She never would've thought she'd enjoy the closeness of a man. Never dreamed she'd... *Never*...

"Twyla?" he asked.

"I-I'm fine."

"Sure?"

She nodded.

Slowly, obviously trying not to spook her, he reached up and cupped her cheek. His hand warmed her skin, and she closed her eyes and placed her knife-free hand on his waist. He tilted her face up toward his and very gently brushed his lips across hers. She drew a sharp breath and opened her eyes.

"All right?" he asked. He sounded unsure. Like she'd bolt at any moment.

But she was just fine. Stunned, amazed...but *fine*.

"Do it again," she said with wide eyes.

He really kissed her this time. He lowered his head, pressed his lips to hers and kissed her. She closed her eyes and let herself relax, just a little, against him. The hand he kept at the small of her back felt so comforting.

That's when she felt it. Little skitters of energy over her skin. It felt so right...like it was a long-lost part of herself. Her eyes wide, she gasped, dropped the knife and backed away. *"Dear Kingdom,"* she swore. "You really do have my magick."

He nodded. "Yes."

She frowned. His eyes were hooded and his breath came fast. He looked almost as though he were in pain. "What's wrong with you?"

Nico found a chair and sat. "Do you have some water?"

She located a glass, filled it from her water jug and handed it to him. He gulped it down. Then he tipped his head back and let out a low, long groan. The sound was...interesting, almost arousing. "What's wrong?" she demanded to know.

He tipped his head forward and examined her. "Twyla, you don't know for how long and how hard we searched for you. We've been holding this extra magick and it's worn on us. To be so near you now and not to be able to...join with you. It's very taxing."

Every alarm bell within her went off. She narrowed her eyes. "What do you mean...*join*?"

He paused, watching her carefully. "I mean exactly what I said. It is part of being Triad. It is the only way to fully transfer your magick back to you and it is the only way to fulfill the prophecy. It's done by physical contact. The three of us...together. Our magick combines and fine-tunes the vibrational waves of this reality. It will chase the Encroaching Darkness away."

Her mind stuttered for the second time that morning. She sat down in a chair across from Nico and focused on the nonsexual part because it was easier. "What prophecy?"

He handed her the glass and she refilled it for him. When he was finished drinking down the water he took a breath. "I'm sure you've noticed that it's far colder and darker at this time of year than it should be, yes?"

"Of course," she snapped.

"This occurs every few thousand years. When the fabric of the Kingdom's reality begins to fray, the Mages of the Triads, under the direction of the all-wise Vedicinn, complete their circles of magick, forming a conduit that will allow the power of all the triads to flow out and purify the binding fabric of the reality, fine-tuning it to a higher level."

"The darkness will go away then?"

He nodded. "If we cannot achieve it, and achieve it soon, we will be locked in twilight forever."

She only nodded, stunned.

"You see now that finding you was very important to more people than just Dai and me." He paused and left his seat to kneel in front of her. He clasped her hand in his. "But, Twyla, you must understand that while finding you was very important in order to fulfill this prophecy, you are a part of us and our caring for you goes very deep. It goes far beyond the prophecy. You can feel that, can't you? You can feel that we're a part of you."

She pressed her lips together, fighting down sudden, uncharacteristic emotion. "Of course I can. You'd both be dead by now if I couldn't."

He smiled and stood. "All right, then. I will leave you to think more on what I've said." He turned before he went out the door. "You know where to find us, if you need us." Twyla watched him leave.

She sat in the chair for a long time, thinking. A part of her now mourned the empty cottage and absence of Nico. She wondered about Dai, the other one, and what he was like. Nico felt even, deep, and calm and Dai seemed far more volatile. Perhaps that's why Nico had come today. Then her thoughts turned to the Mages of the Triads, the Encroaching Darkness, and the prophecy. She sat transfixed within her ponderings until the wind rattled the windows and she realized she was freezing.

She stood and wrapped herself in a blanket while she made a fire and set a kettle on for hot tea. The windows rattled again under the onslaught of the cold wind and she looked southward, toward where she knew Nico and Dai were camped. She bit her lip. They were probably very cold sleeping out there without any shelter. Twyla shook her head and turned away. That was not her problem. It had been *their* choice to camp near her cottage, out in the middle of the woods.

She went about the business of the evening. Gathering and preparing food, making up her bed and organizing her laundry and the other chores she would begin in the morning.

Finally, the cottage began to warm up nicely. The windows showed frost on the outside, but between her four walls, she was snug. She poured herself a cup of tea and fished out a bit of flatbread from her stores and sat down at her little table to gnaw at it. Did Dai and Nico have enough food and fresh water? Suddenly the flatbread tasted like horse manure in her mouth. They probably had little food and were freezing out there in the middle of the woods. She let the flatbread drop to the table. "I have got to be insane," she muttered as she stood.

Twyla found her cloak and lantern, left her cottage and traveled southward.

* * * * *

Dai awoke huddled against Nico on a pallet on the floor of Twyla's cottage. He felt warm and comfortable, far different than he'd felt last night before Twyla had invited them into shelter.

He shifted his head and watched her sleep. Her black eyelashes lay like a line of soot against her pale cheeks. Desire tightened low in his stomach. He wanted her more than he'd ever wanted anyone with the exception of Nico. Nico also wanted her, but they had to go slow. It would be so easy to scare her off. Although, yesterday had been a day of great strides. Not only had she allowed Nico to kiss her, she'd invited them into the sanctuary of her home and then fallen to sleep. It showed she trusted them.

Above him, on her bed, Twlya's eyes opened and stared right into his. Her pupils dilated and she blinked. In that one unguarded second, Dai saw all the terror in her life, all the sorrow and loneliness. The realization of all the hardship she'd gone through clamped down around his heart and squeezed. It made him want to wrap her in his arms and never let her go, but she wouldn't allow that.

"Good morning," he said softly, so that he didn't wake up Nico.

She blinked, then sat up, rubbing her eyes. "Morning," she replied. Without another word, she flipped the blanket back, got up, grabbed a basket full of clothing and a couple other things, slid her shoes on and stepped outside. She'd slept fully clothed the night before—a testament to the fact that she didn't *completely* trust them yet.

After several minutes, Dai slipped out from under his blanket and followed her. Once outside, she was nowhere to be seen, so he tuned into her psychically and found her right away. Taking a deep breath of the crisp morning air, he headed down to the stream that ran a half mile from Twyla's cottage.

He heard the burbling of the stream before he reached it. Twyla knelt at the edge, splashing water on her face. The basket of clothing rested on the stream bank beside her. Not wanting to startle her, he deliberately stepped on a branch.

She glanced at him, then continued what she was doing. "You didn't have to do that. I could feel you coming down the path anyway," she muttered.

"Are you all right this morning?" Dai asked. Her moods seemed so unknowable. He felt like he was constantly dancing on the edge of her temper.

"I-I'm fine," She shot him a glance. "I'm just fine."

He waited a heartbeat and then knelt beside her. "I think not. Tell me what is troubling you."

She turned to him. "*Why* could I feel you coming down that path? Why can I sense you in ways I've never been able to sense other people before?"

"I think you know the answer to that."

She sighed, stood, and walked to the tree line. He followed. Twyla whirled on him. "What do you two want from me?" Tears stood in her eyes.

"You know the answer to that, too."

"You both want my body."

"Your body, yes. We're healthy males who have waited a long time for you. That goes without saying, but we want more than just your body."

"What, then? You want my emotion, my love, m-my *soul?*"

Dai smiled and shook his head. "Nico and I already have your soul, love. It's already intertwined with ours. We want the rest, though. Most of all, we want your love, freely given."

She stood there, looking up at him with large, tear-filled eyes. The way she looked now, she could almost fool him into thinking she was vulnerable. Maybe she was. He took a step toward her, wanting nothing more than to pull her into the circle of his arms and hold her.

"I don't have any love left to give," she whispered hoarsely and turned away from him.

He reached out and touched her shoulder. When she didn't jerk away, he pulled her to his chest and wrapped her in his arms. She let out a long, ragged sigh and relaxed against him. Closing his eyes, Dai inhaled the scent of her. His heart sang. To have her in his arms was better than all his imaginings. "You do," he murmured insistently into her hair. "Let Nico and I show you."

She turned in the circle of his embrace and tipped her face up toward his. Tears made tracks down her cheeks. "Kiss me," she whispered.

Dai kissed all her tears away, tasting the salt of them on his tongue. Then he tasted her lips. Instantly, a tendril of magick curled up his spine. He groaned and pulled her to him tightly. Her mouth was so soft and giving beneath his. Her body fit against his so perfectly. He wound one arm around her waist and put his other hand to the nape of her neck.

She made a sound of desire in her throat, and Dai slanted his mouth over hers like a starving man and feathered his tongue across her lips, asking her to open to him. Her lips parted and he swept his tongue in and touched hers. The force of his lust nearly overpowered him at the taste of her. He knew he had to handle her carefully, gently, but he had to touch her. He slipped his hand beneath her shirt at the small of her back and rubbed his thumb over her sweet, smooth skin.

Twyla moaned and pushed herself against him, tangling her tongue with his savagely. He took it as encouragement and let his hand roam her back. Trailing up her side, he reached her breast and smoothed his thumb teasingly along its underside.

She gasped and pushed him away. He'd gone too far. Twyla stood there, looking up at him apprehensively and breathing hard. She was aroused. Dai could feel just how excited that kiss had made her. His cock strained against his trews, rock-hard and all for her. His breath came fast and his heart pounded. Inwardly, he berated himself. He'd pushed her too hard, too fast. Nico never would've done that. He would've seduced her stealthily, with silky intensity, and not allowed himself to burn so hot for her.

"I-I'm sorry," he started.

She held up a hand. "No. Don't be. I just need-need a little time alone." She glanced at the stream and licked her lips. "I was going to bathe."

Dai's mouth went dry. Just the thought of her wet and nude was enough to nearly make him come in his trews. He drew a breath. "I pushed you too hard. I *am* sorry. It's just that—"

"You and Nico have been waiting a long time. Nico explained it to me."

"Yes."

"Give me a few moments to myself?"

"Of course, Twyla." He turned, still berating himself, and headed back up the path.

"Dai?" she said hesitantly.

He turned toward her and saw the barest smile curve her mouth. It stopped his heart in his chest for a moment. "I liked your kiss."

Relief poured through him. He smiled. "I'll give you some time alone."

"Thank you."

* * * * *

Twyla watched Dai leave and then nearly collapsed. She caught herself on a nearby tree trunk before her knees gave out. The kiss had seemed to touch every single part of her body and ignite it. She'd never, *never* felt that way before. The kiss had been so powerful, she'd been barely aware of the magick skittering over her skin.

Her body had responded sexually.

She'd never believed that would ever be possible. Not after what had happened. She'd expected to go to her grave having never felt lust for a man.

Carefully, she picked her way over to the water's edge and peeled off her clothes. She picked up the wedge of herbal soap she'd placed on top of her laundry and waded into the bitingly chilly water. This time when her hand passed over her breasts, they felt swollen and sensitive. She'd never noticed how her nipples pebbled in the cool water of the stream. This time when she washed between her thighs, she thought of what it would be like if Dai or Nico—not just any man, but one of them—were to touch her there. What would it be like to feel their breath on her skin, their hair brushing over her? What would it be like to feel their mouths on her body in those most sensitive of places?

Twyla explored the patch of hair that topped her sex and dipped her finger down minutely to touch herself. She'd never really thought herself as a woman until this moment. Never paid much attention to the parts of her that were female. She found a spot from which much pleasure seemed to emanate and touched it. She'd heard it called a *clit*. A frisson of delight coursed through her. Tentatively, she rubbed it, then traced downward. Her fingers stroked between her outer labia to caress the folds within. She gasped at the moisture that wept from her slit and rubbed it over her sex in long strokes that dipped her fingers inside her hot body. She circled the mouth of her vagina, spreading her juice on her engorged flesh.

Twyla dropped her other hand down to part her swollen labia, pulling her lips back to expose her sensitive clit. She touched the nub once and shivered. Twice made her moan. Gently, she teased her clit back and forth and up and down, rubbing faster and faster. The pleasure grew and grew until it exploded. Twyla keened her experience to the woods.

Opening her eyes and drawing harsh breaths, she stood in the waist high water and stared at the sandy bank in wonderment. Did her body have the ability to give her pleasure as well as provide pain and humiliation? Could it be true?

Stunned by this possibility, she waded back to the shore, dried herself and dressed. The laundry could wait for now. She wanted—no, was driven—to be in Dai and Nico's company.

She raced back up the path, but stopped when she neared the cottage. Something within her told her not to rush inside. Slowing her pace, she approached one of the windows and peered within. On the floor, amidst the blankets the two males had shared the night before, Dai and Nico lay nude, tangled and sweaty. Her body provided an instant response to the scene in front of her. The sight of two well-muscled, handsome men touching each other was enough to prime her body the same way Dai's kiss had primed her.

Dai kissed Nico savagely, then descended down his body and took Nico's thick, erect organ into his mouth. Twlya's breathing quickened as Nico's hands fisted in Dai's hair and he tipped his head back on a ragged moan, showing his Adam's apple. Even beyond the walls of the cottage, Twyla could feel the magickal pulse within as the encounter released a trickle of power.

Broad shoulders flexing as he worked, Dai pumped his mouth around Nico's erection, pushing him further toward climax. Toward that delicious sensation she'd had while she was bathing. The one she hadn't even known women *could* have. She watched Dai tease Nico with his tongue, then slip him back into his mouth.

Finally, Nico groaned and shuddered. Nico's hip jerked forward and he thrust his cock deep down Dai's throat as he came.

Then, in an act that seemed overtly dominant and aggressive, Dai flipped Nico to his stomach, parted the cheeks of his buttocks and thrust hard within. Twyla watched the two male, straining bodies work on the floor of her cottage. She watched the muscles of Dai's ass flex with every thrust into his lover's body. The sight made her even more aroused. Her nipples were hard and every breath she took brushed them against the fabric of her shirt. She was wet at the juncture of her thighs. When her breath came too fast, her heart pounded too hard, she turned away and slid down to sit on the ground.

She closed her eyes and felt sorrow. Not only was she aroused, she felt left out, she realized with a start. She could tell, by the kisses they bestowed, by the way they touched each other and talked softly to one another, that whatever Dai and Nico shared, it went beyond the physical. They cared for each other, loved each other.

For the first time since her mother had died, Twyla longed for love again. She suddenly ached for someone to share her life with. In that moment, all the years of solitude and fear pressed down upon her and she wished to be free of it.

Twyla stood and slipped back into the woods to do her laundry and give Dai and Nico some time alone.

She took her time with the clothing, despite the chill in the air, scrubbing and rinsing every article. Several times throughout the day, she felt she was being watched. It couldn't be Nico or Dai. She could sense them. She'd stop what she was doing and look around, but never saw anyone peering through the foliage at her. Shrugging it away as nerves, she went on about what she was doing.

By the time she'd finished whiling away her time, it was late afternoon. She constructed makeshift lines to dry her clothing, but feeling the chill in the air and seeing how dark the day had been, she decided they wouldn't dry there and packed them back into her basket. She'd have to dry them in the cabin, in the warmth. Picking up her basket, she headed back to her cottage.

As she neared, she saw that someone had lit a fire in the hearth. Smoke curled invitingly from the chimney. The windows showed a cheery glow within, and the smell of baked fish wafted to her on the air. Her stomach growled. She'd had nothing but a handful of berries all day long.

She pushed open the door and set the basket on the floor to the left of the door. Nico walked to her and took her hand in his. "You're freezing, Twlya. Come into the warmth and have something to eat."

"I'm fine," she grumbled. She started to pull her hand away, but he held on.

"Sit and eat," he commanded. "If you don't take care of yourself, we'll do it for you."

She mumbled something intelligible, silently pleased he cared. Dai pulled out a chair for her at the table and she sat down. Nico placed a plate in front of her, heaping with freshly caught fish and boiled potatoes. The men also served themselves and sat down with her.

They ate in silence, she not knowing what to say to them and they probably in the same situation. Finally, she laid her fork down and looked at them. "So, tell me about yourselves. If we're all so intimately entwined I think I should know you better."

Dai cleared his throat. "I'm from the Hartland Province and Nico is from Gattway. We met about ten years ago, when we were twenty. Soon after that, we realized we were part of a Sacred Triad and became involved with the Vedicinn."

She held up her hand. "No. I want to know about *you*. Not more about Sacred Triads, prophecies or the Vedicinn. What you like to *do*? What kind of families do you come from?"

Nico leaned forward and smiled. "Well, I was an only child, and Dai came from a huge family of twelve. I like fishing"—he motioned at the plate before them—"archery, and studying history. Dai enjoys anything to do with swords or a bow."

She smiled. "Tell me more."

They ended up in front of the fire, talking into the night over cups of spiced tea. Their memories danced before her eyes through verbal spells of comfort woven by their tongues. She enjoyed Dai's very first horseback ride and the tale of the first woman Nico wooed and won. She was there when Nico and Dai met for the first time and knew instantly the connection she also felt with them.

Finally, when the fire burned low and the spiced tea was all gone, she leaned back with a sigh. "But, you left something out."

"We did?" asked Nico.

She leveled her gaze at them both in turn. "You left out that you're lovers," she said softly, then looked down and away. That extra bit of connection made her feel sorrowful, perhaps because she was not a part of it.

Dai and Nico shared a look. "That's true, we did," Dai said slowly, "because we weren't sure you were ready for such information. "

"How long has it been so?" she asked.

"After we received your magick, the force of it was too strong. The only way to alleviate it was physical. At first it was only a way to relieve the pressure, but Nico and I fell in love and now it's much more than just sex. It's a way of expressing a deep emotional tie."

Nico broke in. "It's not uncommon for it to happen in a triad. In fact, I know of none in which love, both physical and emotional, is not shared by all parties."

Tears pricked her eyes and she blinked fast to prevent them from rolling down her cheeks. "I think it's beautiful and I would love to be a part of it, but I'm so damaged. I-I just don't know if I can—" she started.

"You can," said Dai in an insistent voice. "I feel it within you."

Nico inched closer to her. "Now, *you* tell us about *yourself*, my love, and don't leave anything out."

She began by talking about her mother and their life. She talked about being pursued and hunted, but also about the good things. About her mother teaching her to survive on her own, how to heal using flowers, roots and herbs. When she reached That Night, she faltered but pushed on.

Soon she was telling them everything, and sobbing violently while she did it. It was the first time she'd ever voiced the events of That Night while conscious. She told them what happened before, during and after That Night in a tearful purge that hurt, but at the same time felt good. By the time she was finished, she was in Nico's lap, limp as a rag.

Nico rocked her, running his fingers through her hair and occasionally kissing her temple as she cried out the grief and fear she'd been holding inside for so long. Finally, when she had expelled everything, her voice broke and went silent. She could hear nothing but the gentle crackle of the burning wood in the fireplace that Dai had been feeding, Nico's breathing, and the rush of the wind outside. Nico laid a lingering, emotion-filled kiss to her cheek and she let out a shuddering sigh of relief.

The last thing she remembered was being gently lifted and tucked into bed.

* * * * *

Twyla bent to pick up a smooth rock at the bank of the stream and ran her thumb over it. It was shiny and black. Not a scratch marred its surface. She slipped it into her pocket and continued her walk.

Today was a beautiful day. It was still dark, still cold—much too dark and cold for the season—but it seemed not *as* dark and cold. Or maybe it was just because her heart felt a little lighter. It had been a week since she'd had her emotional purge. In that week, she hadn't had even one nightmare. Twyla hoped she'd seen the back end of them, hoped she truly could leave the past behind...or at least learn to live with it better.

She, Nico and Dai had not talked of that night, though the memory of it hung in the air. They'd been even more solicitous to her than usual, *handling* her carefully. They were unsure of their ground now, it seemed. Afraid to touch her in any way that went beyond that which a brother might give a beloved sister. She found she missed the touches that went beyond that, missed their kisses.

She felt Nico before she saw him emerge from the woods ahead of her. He walked to the shore and sat down on the sandy beach. Her heart thumped hard in her chest and her breathing quickened. It happened every time she saw either of them.

Twyla hastened her pace and sat down beside him. She dug the rock out of her pocket. "I found this on the shoreline," she said as she pressed it into his palm.

He examined it. "It's nearly flawless. How uncommon." The lines around his eyes crinkled as he looked down at it and his black hair hung in his face.

Unable to resist, she reached up and brushed his hair away from his face in a tender gesture. When he turned his face toward her, she ran her thumb down his cheek. Dark, glimmering, naked *want* flashed in his eyes. She drew her hand back, her eyes widening. How hard was it for them to restrain themselves around her? What kind of sacrifice were they making while they waited for her?

"Nico," she breathed in a broken whisper.

He pulled away. "Forgive me. I'll go." He got up to leave.

She put a hand to his forearm. "Please, don't."

He stilled, and then sat back down.

"I had no idea," she said. "No idea how difficult it's been."

"It's-it's been hard for Dai and me, but we'll do anything for you, Twyla. Anything."

"Anything?" Her heart pounded as she curled her lips into a smile. "Then will you kiss me?"

He came toward her immediately, but then hesitated. "I don't know if I'll be able to stop—"

She rose up, closing the distance between them, and pressed her lips to his. He remained motionless for a heartbeat, and then he wrapped his arms around her and slanted his mouth across hers. His tongue swept into her mouth and stroked. A primal shiver that had nothing to do with magick shot up her spine.

With a low growl in his throat, he pressed her back into the sandy shore and feasted on her mouth. His tongue retreated and plunged into her mouth over and over in a semblance of lovemaking. Magick and desire enveloped her in a flash and her body took over for her mind. She wrapped her arms around him and kissed him back, her tongue thrusting in to mate with his.

He parted her thighs with his knee and settled himself between her legs. She gasped as she felt the press of his cock through his trews into the delicate flesh of her sex.

He pulled away. "Are you all right, Twyla?" His eyes were dark and hooded, full of unmistakable lust.

"I-I'm fine," she said in a surprised voice. She trusted Nico with everything she was, she realized. She knew both Dai and Nico would never harm her, never push her too far, never do anything she didn't completely desire.

He stroked her hair and kissed her. "I love you, Twyla, and I always have. You can trust me."

She nodded. "Yes. I do."

"Let me touch you." It was half order, half entreaty.

She nodded again. It would be touches of love, not violence, she reminded herself. He cupped her sex through her trews and she felt how damp he'd made her. With one finger, he rubbed her though the material. She gasped in pleasure.

His thumb brushed a small area of extreme sensitivity. "I could…kiss you here, love," he murmured.

She knew shock passed over her face. Twyla lifted up on her elbows and stared at him. "Would you want to do to that?"

He smiled slowly. "I want to taste you almost as much as I want to feel your heat close around my cock. You will enjoy it, I think." Instead of waiting for her reply, he slid her boots off one by one, then her trews.

Finally she was bare from the waist down both to the air and to Nico's heated gaze. He appeared consumed with the sight of her. His gaze traveled up from her feet to the patch of fiery red hair shielding her sex and back down again. Then he reached out and touched her skin, running his fingertips up and down her legs, first touching gently, then massaging. Twyla let out a pent-up breath and relaxed. Nico's strong fingers worked their way up from one foot, drawing little circles on her skin, up her calf, to the sensitive underside of her knee, to her inner thigh. He did the same on the other side. Only this time, instead of stopping at her inner thigh, he brushed her sex.

Twyla shivered in pleasure as his fingers threaded through her patch of red curls and then slipped down. He feathered over her sex, rubbing circles around the small bud that seemed to throb and grow larger at his touch. One look at his face told her he was holding back, and she was grateful for his restraint. This was the first time in her life someone had looked upon her in both love and lust. She liked the combination, but at the same time the experience was overwhelming.

All thought left her mind with a shudder when Nico lowered his mouth to her sex and drank from her center. He skated his palms over the flesh of her inner thighs and pressed her legs apart. His tongue flicked and tasted, flicked and tasted. She gasped as he licked her from her anus to her bud with one long swipe.

Twyla pressed her pelvis up toward him and dug her fingers into the shore on either side of her. Gently, he parted her folds and pressed his tongue within her and thrust. It felt hot and wet and oh, so good. "Nico," she moaned.

He made another low sound of pleasure in his throat and caressed her thighs reassuringly. He thrust again and again and pleasure built within Twyla. Then Nico moved up to her bud and laved and sucked at it relentlessly. One hand strayed to her sex and he, very slowly, slid his index finger inside her.

Twyla arched her back as pleasure exploded out from the core of her and enveloped her body. She squeezed her eyes shut and called out Nico's name as the spasms rocked her to her very center. Ah, it was very much better than when she'd brought herself to climax in the river. It was better to have Nico bring her.

A delicious, relaxing glow spread through her. Her entire body gave into it. She opened her eyes to find Nico staring down at her. She smiled, reached up, and touched his cheek. "You showed me my body can give me pleasure," she whispered with tears in her eyes.

"Ah, so much pleasure, love. So much. We've only just begun. That was merely a taste."

His eyes were bright, his breathing labored. Suddenly concerned, she pushed up into a sitting position. "What's wrong?"

He leaned in and kissed her forehead. "Nothing is wrong, love. I am happier right now than I've been in a very, very long time. I only wish Dai could've been here to share the first climax I gave you. Although maybe it's better he wasn't. Things could've gotten out of hand too quickly if he was here. Control is not his strong suit."

She glanced down and saw how his organ tented his pants. She noted how hard it was and how it pushed against his trews. Still, he held back, afraid he'd push her too far. Twyla reached down and brushed her fingertips over his erection through his trews. Nico shuddered and tried to pull her hand away.

"Please," she said. "Let me."

He hesitated and then withdrew his hand. Bowing his head in a gesture of surrender, he said, "Do your worst, lady."

Intrigued by the feel she'd had of him through the fabric, she decided to divest him of the barrier and explore. Once his boots and trews were gone, his cock sprang up wide and long and thickly veined from a mat of dark hair. Still, she wasn't satisfied. She pulled his shirt off and drank her fill of his body.

He was a glorious example of a male. She hadn't seen many in her life, but she knew Nico had to be on the extreme end of the gorgeous spectrum. Broad shoulders melded into strong arms and a muscled chest. His waist was narrow and his legs long and lightly dusted with black hair. His cock was beyond description. She never thought she'd think of a cock in those terms, as a beautiful thing. It enraptured her. How would it feel inside her? How would it feel thrust within her, as far as it could go?

Saving the best for last, Twyla set her hands to his chest. She touched his wide, flat nipples and ran her fingers through his smattering of chest hair. Nico groaned and she felt his heart speed up under her fingers. His skin felt warm under her hands and his chest was hard with muscle, yet soft, all at the same time. Taking her time, she explored every part of his body—except his cock— in complete wonder. She scattered kisses on his lips and face. When he tried to touch her, she shushed him and told him to lay still.

"You're killing me, love," he groaned. "Slaying me with your hands as well as you could with any blade."

She smiled and decided to take pity on him. Trailing her hand down his stomach, she curled her fingers around his erection and pumped.

Beneath her, Nico shuddered and his hips bucked. "Gods, yes," he hissed through a clenched jaw.

Encouraged by his response, she pumped again. Nico's body tensed. Again and again she moved her hand up and down until finally Nico groaned and pushed up. He pulled her against him and rolled her under him. She felt the press of his cock on her inner thigh, deliciously and alarmingly close to her sex and Nico let out a long groan. She felt his hot seed erupt out onto her skin as Nico pressed his mouth to her in a penetrating kiss.

Nico went still, his forehead pressed to hers. "Thank you," he murmured.

She wrapped her arms around him and kissed his temple. They stayed that way for a while, until Nico murmured something about how she must be cold, and rose. Using a little water from the stream, he cleaned his seed from her skin and helped her dress. Together, they started back toward the cottage. Nico put his arm around her shoulders and kept her warm the whole way.

When they reached the cottage, it was almost completely dark outside. Dai had started a fire, however, and the small building looked snug and inviting as they walked the pathway to the front door. Inside, Dai was sitting by the hearth with one of her precious books in his hands.

Would he know what she and Nico had done by the side of the stream?

Dai looked up and smiled at Twyla, then gave Nico a knowing look. So, he did know and had stayed away.

Twyla extricated herself from Nico's arms, went to Dai and kissed him soundly on the lips in gratitude. They were easing her into this because they had her best interests at heart. Kissing Dai was her way of thanking him.

The book thumped to the floor and Dai enclosed her in his arms and pulled her down into his lap. She ended up sitting on Dai's erection and could tell he was every bit as large at Nico. That knowledge was both arousing and slightly daunting. Finally the kiss ended.

"What was that for?" Dai asked in a thick voice. "Not that I care, really. I'm just glad you did it."

"That was simply for being here and for being one part of the triad," she answered, and then kissed him again.

Little by little, with love and understanding, perhaps she'd be ready to form the triad…and they could fulfill their duty.

"I am ready to begin this," she said, loud enough so Nico could also hear her. "But grant me control over the pace."

She watched Nico glance at Dai. They nodded. "Yes," replied Nico. He licked his lips. "Believe me, you *do* have all the control here."

Dai stood, lifting her in his arms. The sensation startled her for a moment, but then she relaxed against him. He walked her over to the bed and laid her down, then settled down beside and drew her into his arms. Nico slid in on the other side, bringing his arms around her waist and settling his cock between the cheeks of her buttocks. Enjoying the sensation of the strength of the two males surrounding her, their scent and the warmth of their bodies, she soon fell into the deepest and best sleep she'd ever had.

* * * * *

"Two crowns," countered Twyla over the bolt of soft blue fabric she wanted to possess.

The merchant's eyes narrowed. "Three."

She returned his gaze coolly. "Two crowns and two marks. That's all I'll give you for it."

They engaged in a staring contest for several moments. "Fine," the man grunted.

Twyla fished out the agreed-upon amount from her purse, handed the coins over and picked up the bolt. The man mumbled something about taking food from his kids' mouths as she walked away.

She smiled at the merchant's melodramatics and rubbed her finger across the soft material. It was an extravagance she couldn't really afford on the meager income she had from selling herbal remedies. But these days she'd begun to care more about her appearance and images of the pretty clothing had danced through her head as soon as she'd seen the material lying on the merchant's table. Carefully, she put the bolt of fabric into the large sack she carried.

She flicked a glanced at the darkened sky, barely seeing the muted sun behind the thick cloud cover. It was almost noon, time for her meeting with a man who would buy some of her herbal oils. Dithering with the fabric merchant had eaten up precious time. Happily contemplating her purchase, she turned a corner in the crowded village...and came face-to-chest with a large, smelly man.

"Excuse me," she snapped as the man's large hands gripped her shoulders in an effort to steady her.

He released her when she was balanced. She backed away. Contact with any man but Nico or Dai was still abhorrent to her. When she lifted her gaze, she saw Marsten, the farmer who'd harassed her the last time she'd come to the village. Every muscle tensed in anticipation of a confrontation.

"Ah hello," said Marsten. "I was hoping I'd see you again."

"Listen—"

He held up one chubby hand. "Hold. I merely wanted to apologize for my behavior the last time we met and offer you a gift to make peace." He smiled, showing a broken tooth. "Please? I feel so badly about what happened."

Twyla stood, staring at him. She wasn't sure how she should react.

He fished something out of his pocket and held it up to the light. A metal pendant in the shape of a crescent moon hung from his fingers. She squinted, examining it. It seemed familiar, though there was no reason for it to be so. "I bought it hoping I'd see you again."

She shook her head. "I don't want anything from you."

"Please," he said in an earnest voice. "I feel so badly about mistaking you for a whore the last time I saw you. If you don't take my offering I'll never forgive myself."

Twyla didn't care if the man ever forgave himself or not. Though she did care that it was growing late and she was going to be tardy for her meeting with the herbal oil buyer. She couldn't afford to miss it, especially after buying the bolt of fabric.

"Fine, you're forgiven," she mumbled as she snatched the cheap trinket and pushed past him. She could feel his gaze on her back as she allowed the market crowd to envelop her. Hastily, she stuffed the pendant into her pocket as the herbal oil man came into view.

The meeting with the herbal merchant went better than she expected and she was happy enough to actually be whistling by late afternoon. She crossed the village square, where the merchants were packing up their wares, and spotted Dai and Nico in front of the inn where she was supposed to meet them. She had rented her own room and Dai and Nico had gotten a room of their own. She would miss their presence as she slept, but it was one way she felt she could maintain control…and she desperately wanted to do that.

Her heart swelled with joy and love as she approached them. It was amazing how quickly they had worked their way into her soul.

Rather, they'd been there all along, she'd just had to realize it.

Dai reached out, took her bag, and then drew her into his arms. "We've missed you," he murmured as he brushed his lips across her forehead. "Did your meeting go well?"

She nodded. "Very well. What have you two been doing all day?" she asked.

"Wandering the town, mostly. Shopping a little," answered Nico. He smiled. "Arranging dinner."

"I'm starved," she answered.

They entered the darkened inn. It was crowded with many people in town for the market day. A cook fire scented the air with a combination of a roast and wood smoke. The sound of people laughing and talking assaulted her eardrums. In the background, a flutist provided music.

Nico pulled her from Dai's arms and pressed her against the wall behind her. She inhaled the scent of him as his lips came down teasingly light against her mouth. His chest pressed against her breasts. Her breath caught as a wave of lust rippled through her.

"Go upstairs to your room and don the things we've gifted you with," Nico murmured against her lips. "Then come back downstairs. We've arranged a private room to dine in this eve."

He backed away and she took a moment to catch her breath before she spoke. "But a private room? Gifts? That's all so ex—"

"Hush," commanded Dai. "Say no more. You are worth any amount to us and we would like to show you as much."

She stood looking at them, mute.

"Go," said Nico. "We'll take care of your things."

Stunned and pleased, she made her way through the throng and up the stairs. Once within her room, she found a beautiful silk green gown lying on her bed. It was a simple dress. They would've understood when buying it that flounces and lace would not be to her taste. It was elegant and well cut. Very expensive. Of that, she had no doubt. Alongside it lay underthings.

Very alluring underthings.

She fingered the delicate, practically see-through panties and the low-cut green corset with the silken, dark green ties. Lace-topped sheer stockings that would come up about midthigh lay on the bed's red coverlet, along with a pair of gorgeous ladylike shoes with high heels.

Never in her life had she ever worn shoes like that! She'd fall flat on her face.

She picked a shoe up to examine it and remembered the bolt of blue fabric, the frivolous nicety she'd bought in order to be more attractive to Dai and Nico. Aye, she wanted them to think her beautiful. Therefore, she'd risk falling on her face.

She set the shoe down and turned to see that the bathtub had been filled. Delicate lavender petals floated on the top of the water. Thick towels and a creamy-looking bar of soap lay on a chair alongside the wide tub. Her gaze caught on objects laid out to the right, on the dressing table. She walked over and examined the articles. There were two gossamer, green clips for her hair, each in the shape of a dragonfly, a filigreed gold necklace also in the shape of a dragonfly and made of expensive jade, and a bottle of perfume.

Feeling pampered, she smiled as she divested herself of her clothing. It all felt very strange, but she would enjoy it all the same. She pinned her hair up, since the thick length would take all night to dry if it became wet, and sank into the warm, comforting water. She scrubbed her skin until she glowed, then toweled herself off and anointed her body with the spicy-scented perfume behind her knees, between her breasts, and behind her ears. She inhaled and sighed. They'd known exactly the kind of scent she'd like best.

The silken stockings felt heavenly as she slid them on. The panties and corset felt odd. She struggled drawing the ties of the corset up, and considered calling one of the inn's serving girls to help her. In the end, not accustomed to having help, she managed it herself, though it took a good while. Finally, she slipped into the shoes and teetered to the full-length mirror to have a look.

Dear Kingdom…she truly *was* a woman.

The shoes showed off her long, shapely, silk-stocking-clad legs. She actually did have shapely legs. She'd never known that before! The sheer panties allowed enticing glimpses of the red hair covering her mound, and completely revealed the cheeks of her buttocks when she twisted around to look at her back. The corset cinched her already small waist and forced her breasts up to overflowing at the very low-cut top, making the edges of her dusky nipples show.

Her entire body responded at the sight of herself in the mirror. Her nipples hardened and her sex grew damp. She looked womanly, alluring. She looked like a woman who wanted sex. This had likely been Nico and Dai's plan, to draw her into her own body's natural needs and desires.

She wanted Nico and Dai's hands on her. She wanted their mouths exploring. She wanted their cocks slipping inside her, giving her pleasure as she, in turn, gave them pleasure. Her breath came faster as the images filled her mind.

Experimentally, she reached up and ran a finger over the part of one partially revealed nipple and felt a frisson of lust go through her. She reached her other hand down and parted her legs, running the pad of one index finger over her swollen bud. It responded instantly to the stimulation, making her gasp. Twyla forced her hands away from her body. She would save her responses for Dai and Nico.

She turned from the mirror and donned the gown. The material slithered down over her body and came to rest flawlessly on her person. The size was perfect. Finally, she carefully put on the jewelry, brushed her hair out and pinned it up on each side with the dragonfly hair clips. Then, taking a deep breath, she left the room and went downstairs.

Twlya tried to ignore the attention she received from the men in the room. It both pleased her and made her uneasy. She asked a barmaid where to find the private room where Dai and Nico awaited her and then went there.

"Oh, sweet Gods," breathed Dai, as she closed the door behind her. "I knew you'd look beautiful in that gown, but I never thought — sweet Gods."

She felt herself flush and glanced away.

Both Dai and Nico stood. Nico walked toward her, his eyes bright as he took her in from head to toe. He took her hand and whispered in her ear, "You are beyond stunning."

"Thank you," she mumbled.

Dai came to her other side and gently pressed her between himself and Nico. He kissed her cheek and then her earlobe. "You're lovely, Twyla," he murmured. She could feel the heat from both their bodies caress her skin and warm her. She shivered. It was a safe sensation to be enclosed by the bodies of these two men. It was not threatening. Indeed, it was nothing but comforting and arousing.

She turned and tipped her head up to Dai. He took the invitation and kissed her. Behind her, Nico shuddered in pleasure, put his hands on her waist and laid a kiss on the skin of her shoulder. Dai's tongue swept into her mouth and she savored the taste of him. He twined his arms around her waist, tangling with Nico's.

Finally, Nico pulled away. He sat and then patted his lap, "Please sit. Consider me your chair for the evening."

She glanced at an empty chair, knowing she had the choice, but decided to take him up on his offer. His arms enveloped her as she sat down and she felt the rise in his trews where he'd grown hard for her. Her body answered swiftly and she felt her panties grow wet.

The table held all kinds of culinary delights, thick slabs of bread and creamy butter, roasted pork and a tossed salad and fruits and vegetables of all varieties. Dai pulled a bench near them and straddled it. Then he reached across the table and piled a plate with various samples of the dishes and set it in front of her.

She speared a bit of pork with her fork and closed her eyes as the sweet, perfectly prepared meat filled her mouth. It'd been so long since she'd had a hearty meal like this. Mostly she only ate what she could grow or glean from the forest. It wasn't exactly a balanced diet.

After chewing and swallowing, she opened her eyes and realized with a blush that both Nico and Dai had been watching her intensely. She speared a bit more and brought it to Dai's mouth. He took it, all the while keeping his gaze locked with hers.

That gave Nico the idea of feeding her. He fed her a couple more pieces of meat, and two green collevege spears. Finally, he picked up a thick, plump strawberry and set it to her lips. For a moment, she wondered how they'd been able to grow it. Her strawberries had been scrawny and late this season. But once the sweet taste of the berry filled her mouth, she stopped wondering. In fact, she stopped thinking altogether.

Both men's gazes were riveted on her lips as she took bites of the fruit, on her face as she tipped her head back and groaned her approval at the flavor.

Nico's hands rubbed her thighs and her breath caught. She chewed the strawberry slowly and swallowed, wanting him to go farther than that, but unsure of how to communicate the desire. As if reading her mind, his hand slipped down her leg to the edge of her gown and traveled beneath it.

Nico leaned forward and kissed her ear lobe. "All right?" he murmured.

She closed her eyes momentarily and nodded.

"Mmmm…good," he purred.

He trailed his hand up her leg, bringing her gown with it. When he reached her upper thigh, his hands veered toward her sex and he brushed his finger lightly over her bud. She shuddered at the blatant tease.

"Do you know how much I want you out of this gown, my love?" he whispered into her ear. He kissed her earlobe and then bit it gently. She let out a soft moan. "I want you out of it so I can see your luscious body in those underthings we bought. Did you know Dai and I had to…ease…ourselves this afternoon just thinking about how you'd look in them?"

Dai trailed his fingers up her calf and fingered the edge of the top of her stocking. Her sex swelled and she grew wetter. Her breasts felt heavy and her nipples hardened. They rubbed against the top of the corset with every breath she took. "T-take the gown off," she answered in a breathless whisper.

"Our pleasure."

Together, Dai and Nico drew the dress gently over her head and off. Then Dai sat back on his bench and looked strained, like he almost had to sit on his hands to keep from touching her further. Had they agreed to let Nico take the lead? It was likely so. Twyla could well imagine that they may have thought Dai too intense for her at this moment...and they may have been right.

Or not. Her body's demands seemed to be growing with every breath she took. It was an odd sensation to have her body rule her mind, negate any and all fear she held within. And, yet, it was not only lust that she felt. Something within her desired her to join body and soul with these men, to give them everything of herself that she possibly could.

She heard two male groans fill the air. They were both staring intently at her. She was now dressed in nothing but the heels, stockings, see-through panties and revealing corset. The plump of her breasts swelled over the top of her corset and the air caressed her reddened, erect nipples.

Nico moved his chair back and shifted her so that she had her back to his chest. Dai positioned himself directly in front of her.

Dai leaned forward and positioned her left leg so that her inner knee was hooked over Nico's knee and her calf trailed down Nico's shin. Then Dai cupped the ankle of her other leg in one strong hand. He brought her still-shoed foot to rest on the bench that he straddled. Her toe just barely rubbed at his straining erection with every movement she made.

In this position, she was completely spread and open to him. It made her feel vulnerable, but deliciously so. His gaze focused on her swollen sex, which the panties she wore did not fully cover. Gently, he massaged the muscles of her calf, very slowly working his way higher. The sight of her leg, clad in the stocking, the sexy shoe, and Dai's large hand moving up over her skin made her breath come faster. Dai paused and rotated his thumb in little circles on the sensitive flesh near the back of her knee. It sent little frissons of pleasure through her.

One of Nico's hands moved from her waist slowly up to cup her breast. He ran a finger over the pump of one, rubbing along the exposed part of her nipple. Another moan filled the air and she realized it was hers.

"Your breasts tempt me," Nico murmured near her ear. His chest braced and warmed her back. He rubbed over her nipple again, stiffening it impossibly harder. Dai circled his thumb around and around on the back of her knee—as if he massaged the sensitive bud between her thighs. Her clit pulsed at the dual sensations and she tipped her head back and panted, giving in to a near climax.

Nico pulled at the string of her corset and she felt it loosen. At the same time, Dai moved higher on her leg, to her mid thigh, and continued to draw those little circles on the sensitive flesh there. Her panties were sopping wet by now, her sex plumped and pulsing and ready for attention. She realized she'd spread her legs wider for Dai, with that very wish foremost in her mind. All she wanted was for him to touch her there where she was most needy. He continued those little, concentrated circles around and around, higher and higher. It was as though he touched her clit.

"We can smell your desire," crooned Nico in a strained voice. "We can see your chest rising and falling, hear the thump of your heart as you grow more aroused. Your lust is our aphrodisiac, my love. Let's drive it higher."

Her corset loosened further and then fell away, leaving her in only her shoes, stockings and panties. Her breasts felt full and her nipples stood erect, like two suckable small cherries. The motion of Dai's hand faltered at the sight, then steadied. He moved up higher and ran his finger along the top of her stocking, then went higher still, caressing the soft skin where her inner thigh met her pussy.

Nico brought his hands up her rib cage agonizingly slowly until he cupped both breasts in his hands. His thumbs flicked skillfully over her nipples, back and forth until her back arched and she let out a small moan. In the same instant, Dai pushed aside the wet slip of material shielding her pussy. With one finger, he trailed over her labia, then sank into the wet depths of her and thrust slowly in and out. With his thumb, he rubbed her clit. Dai groaned low at the feel of her.

Powerful pleasure washed over her. Her back bowed again and her hips bucked. Dai and Nico didn't let up on the erotic ministrations to her body. Dai continued the dual act of finger-fucking her and rubbing at her clit. Nico continued caressing her breasts, teasing the reddened, sensitive nipples. The sheer wonderfulness of having so many erogenous zones stimulated at the same time drove her to climax. Her body tensed as the waves of pleasure consumed her. She felt the muscles of her pussy convulse and contract around Dai's pistoning fingers. A rush of liquid lubricated her passage. When it had subsided, she was left shaking and yet even hungrier for them.

She struggled to stand. Shakily, she stood in the middle of the room watching them, seeing the hunger for her in their eyes. She watched how their cocks strained against the material of their trews. They held themselves back. They were afraid to spook her, but, oh, how clear it was that they wanted her. She realized something.

She held power here.

Dai and Nico were hers. She trusted them completely to never do anything she did not wish. They would not do anything unless they had her permission. She held their leashes in her hand. She could hold their leashes as tightly or as loosely as she wished. It was her call.

Perhaps she'd let up a little this evening. She craved a loving she had invited of her own free will and here were two beloved, trusted males willing and able to give her just what she wanted.

With more confidence than she had just a moment before, she walked to the center of the room and felt their hot gazes follow her. She turned and cleared some of the plates away so she could halfway sit on the table. The position provided them with a view of her wet pussy. She cupped her breast in one hand and rubbed the nipple with her other hand.

Their bodies tensed visibly and they sat forward, watching her movements. Her other hand trailed down to her pussy to rub at her clit. It was even now growing aroused again. Their eyes followed every flick of her finger against the bud. It grew large and sensitive once again.

She tipped her head back and sighed. She could make herself peak right now just by doing this. Instead, she caught their gaze both in turn. "What were your arrangements for the evening? One of you must've agreed to hold back."

Dai swallowed hard. "I did."

She nodded. It was as she'd presumed. Dai was too intense, too uncontrolled. They had not wished to scare her with his sexual aggressiveness. She shifted her gaze to the man beside him. "Nico," she said softly. "Come here."

Nico stood and walked toward her. His eyes were heavy lidded and dark. The pupils were dilated, revealing his arousal. He enveloped her in his arms and she felt the delicious press of his hard chest against her bare breasts. One of his hands rubbed at her lower back. His finger teased the band of her panties. With his other hand, he cupped the nape of her neck and tilted her head to the side. She felt his lips press against the sensitive flesh of her throat and his teeth nip territorially at the place where her shoulder met her neck.

"Grant me permission to take the lead," he whispered in his velvet voice.

She swallowed hard and nodded. Glancing down, she found her hands grasping fistfuls of his shirt, wanting it off.

He untangled her fingers and removed his shirt. "All right?" he asked.

"More than all right," she murmured as she proceeded to explore his chest, tracing every delectable bulge and biceps with questing fingers. He was magnificent.

Suddenly, he grasped her wrists, firmly yet gently, and placed them on either side of her on the table. "Please, you're driving me insane. I need to keep my control."

He dropped to his knees in front of her and drew a nipple into his mouth. Her back arched and she whimpered at the sensation of his warm tongue drawing circles around the erect tip and the gentle suction he exerted on it.

She noted that Dai had dropped his trews and now caressed his thick, hard cock in one hand as he watched them. Having Dai's gaze on them as they engaged in this erotic act only fanned the flames of her desire higher.

She'd wondered if the memories of the past would rise up to smother her once she began these acts with Nico and Dai. But *this* was so different from that. There really was no comparison. *This* was about love and caring. *This* was about shared, mutual pleasure. It had absolutely nothing to do with what happened to her so many years ago, though they were both carnal acts.

Nico's hand slipped down her back to her waist. He slipped his thumb under the thin silk waistband of her panties and pulled down. The small slip of material slithered easily down her legs and she stepped out of them.

He switched his oral attention to her other breast and moved his hand ever so slowly up her inner thigh to her sex.

Gently, he traced circles around her swollen clit until she moaned and tossed her head. "Please, I need —"

She didn't even have to finish the sentence. Nico's hands grasped her waist and lifted her up to sit on the table. He pulled her so her buttocks were just at the very edge and her legs dangled over the side. She reached for the buckle of his trews but he was faster. He undid them, kicking off his boots at the same time, and slid them off.

She sucked in a breath of awe as she reached out to stroke the thick length of him. He tipped his head back and groaned, making his Adam's apple vibrate. She couldn't wait to feel what it would be like to have that massive cock within her.

Nico tipped his head forward and studied her with predatory calculation, as if deciding the best way to take her. Finally, he slid a hand to the small of her back and closed the distance between them. His mouth came down on hers as his finger slipped within her. She moaned and squirmed, but he held her fast. He thrust a few times, until he had her panting, and then added a second finger. Patiently he worked her with his hand, widening her entrance large enough to take the considerable girth of his cock.

Her hips bucked forward of their own accord and she grasped the edge of the table as he finger-fucked her. Finally, his hand left her and she felt the wide, silken head of his cock press against her. Little by little, he thrust within, backed out and thrust again. Bit by glorious bit, he fed her every inch of his rock-hard erection. She grabbed his upper arms as he embraced her and sank her teeth into his shoulder. It felt so exquisite to be filled, possessed by a man she loved and trusted. Her body felt completely his, utterly and totally a part of him.

"Ah yes," he hissed as he seated himself to the hilt within her.

He placed a hand beneath one of her silk-stocking-clad knees, the other he braced on the edge of the table and he began to thrust in and out of her. She felt every vein of him rubbing in lovely friction against the inner walls of her passage. Every groan of pleasure he made excited her further. She looked down between them and saw the thick, ridged length of his cock plunging in and out of her body.

It pushed her over the edge.

Her climax hit her hard. The muscles of her sex pulsed and contracted around his length and she felt a flood of moisture release from between her thighs. Nico took her in a hard kiss, consuming all her cries and whimpers of passion. He didn't stop shafting her and once her climax had passed another began instantly to build.

Nico's body jerked and shuddered. He thrust into her as far as he could and came. He groaned loudly and she felt his seed bathe her within. She held him close, scattering kisses over his face and throat as he passed his moments of ecstasy. He shook when it was finished.

"I love you, Twyla," Nico murmured into her ear.

"As I love you," she whispered, answering from her heart.

With one last mind-numbing kiss, Nico slipped from her body, revealing Dai, still sitting on the bench, still caressing his painfully hard-looking cock. She wanted Dai within her, she realized suddenly. She wanted to connect with him as she'd connected with Nico. She loved them both. She wanted to take each of them into her.

"Dai," she said softly. "You need release. Come here."

He stood and kicked his trews off the rest of the way. "You must be absolutely certain, Twyla. I won't coax and seduce climaxes from you like Nico, I'll pull them from your body. I won't be able to hold myself back."

170

"Come," she said softly. "Come here."

He stalked to her and drew her hard into his arms. His mouth came down on her lips and his tongue slipped within. He tasted hot and slightly angry, instead of cool and mysterious like Nico.

"So sweet," he murmured. "So incredibly sweet." He fell to his knees, coaxed her thighs to part and licked up her pussy.

She jerked, surprised by the action. His tongue swirled around the opening to her passage and circled her clit. Her hands clenched around the edges of the table and she fought a scream of anxious, confused pleasure rising in her throat. All the while he dipped his tongue within her, sucked on her clit like it was a piece of candy. He was unrelenting, unstoppable. Dai drew her labia into his mouth. He made noises like she was the best thing he'd ever tasted.

"Dai," she gasped urgently. It sounded like a plea for him to stop to her own ears. Was that what she wanted? He was like a whirlwind, enveloping her body. Sensations assaulted her mind and for a moment she fought them. Then something within her relaxed. She remembered that she trusted Dai not to hurt her and decided to give her body over to his care. He wanted her pleasure, nothing more, nothing less.

She gave in to it, gave in to the force of him. She cried out as pure pleasure suffused her body, this time without the confusion or the anxiousness. It danced her to the razor edge of another climax.

Finally, when she was panting and almost clawing the table, he stood and kissed her deep. He pulled away and set his forehead to hers. "Turn around, love. I will take you from behind."

Her breath caught at the note of control in his voice, the look of ownership in his eyes. She turned and grasped the edge of the table. She felt his strong hands on her hips as he pulled her toward him. With one foot, he coaxed her still-shoed feet further apart. Then he ran a hand up the back of one thigh and flicked his fingers minutely over her wet, sex-swollen pussy. He pressed his cock within her. He wasn't as gentle as Nico. It was a good thing she'd been prepared before she'd taken Dai. He thrust within her to the maximum, until she felt like she'd be spilt right up the center, and then started shafting her. He pushed himself within her as far as she could take him.

Instantly, a climax ripped through her. With every thrust Dai made, he rubbed some spot of sensitivity, a bundle of nerves hidden deep within her. It was almost unbearably good. Since she was lubricated thoroughly now, Dai picked up the pace.

As he thrust, he gently circled the opening to her nether hole. It surprised her at first, but she realized quickly that it was a powerful erogenous zone. When Dai slipped a finger within, she came hard once more. Her loud cries and moans filled the small room.

He drew two more climaxes from her before he finally released his seed within her. She realized one of them may have impregnated her and the possibility bought a fast flush of joy.

She leaned down and rested her flushed cheek on the smooth wood of the table. "Tomorrow, I'll be ready. Tomorrow I'll take both of you," she murmured.

Chapter Four

Twyla fingered the pendant Marsten had gifted her with as she sat in front of the hearth in her cottage. The day had dawned in twilight as every day had for a long time. Though today the twilight would be lifted. This morning, Dai and Nico had traveled out to prepare the circle in which the final ritual of the final Sacred Triad would be performed. This afternoon, it would be finished.

Deep in thought and caught in a review of her life, Twyla turned the pendant over and over between her fingers. It was a silver crescent with a small red jewel at the top. The pendant seemed so familiar to her for some reason, but why?

She frowned as a flash of this pendant entered her mind's eye. A flash of the piece of jewelry on someone's throat. Her mother's laughter rang through her head, making her tighten her grip on the piece of metal until she drew blood from her palm with the sharp edge.

She closed her eyes as a flash of the pendant assaulted her again. This time the piece of jewelry was smeared with flour. The scent of bread baking and the feel of a warm fire filled her senses. The image widened and steadied into a full shot of her mother's face as she baked in the kitchen of their three-room cottage. She laughed and joked as she rolled out bread dough. The lantern light flickered on the pendant she wore around her throat.

"Oh sweet..." Twyla breathed and pain and memory assaulted her. She'd forgotten so much about her life before That Night in an effort to protect herself. How had Marsten obtained her mother's pendant?

She cried out and fell to her knees in front of the fireplace as more memories rose up. She'd pushed them far back into the recesses of her mind, but with the pendant in her hand, they rushed back.

Marsten's laughing face on that long ago night entered her mind. Gods, she'd driven their faces so far from her mind, she simply hadn't recognized him.

Marsten as he ripped the pendant from around her mother's throat as she screamed in agony.

Marsten dropping his trews and…

Blinded by tears and emotions, she crawled across the floor toward the door. She let the pendant drop from her fingers as she moved. She needed air. She needed space. She needed to be anywhere but where she was right now.

By the time she reached the door she felt like a wild animal. As the memories and feelings that she'd forgotten out of a sense of self-preservation filled her mind, they stripped away her humanity. They reduced her to a savage thing, bent only on her own survival, wanting nothing more than to escape, to run, to hide somewhere alone and lick her wounds. These memories she did not need. She did not want them. Maybe if she ran hard enough, she could outrun them.

Twyla pulled the door of the cottage open, feeling as though someone held her head under the rushing water of the river, and ran, trying not to drown.

Branches ripped at her clothing and at her face as she bolted blindly through the woods. A log tripped her and she went sprawling on her chest, knocking the air from her lungs. Pausing not more than a heartbeat, she jerked to her feet and ran on.

Dai and Nico followed her. She could feel them behind her. She wanted to stop for them, but she couldn't. She was unfit for them, an unfit partner for their triad. She was damaged, dirty. They needed someone cleaner, better than she.

"Twyla!" someone yelled behind her. She ran faster.

As she entered a clearing, something hard hit her from the side, bringing her down and sprawling her in the soft grass. Through her tears, she had glimpses of Dai's face. "No," she keened as she fought and kicked and bit. Still, Dai wouldn't let her go.

She felt wild. She clawed at the ground in a frenzy to get free of him, to bolt into the forest and never look back. The part of her that was still Twyla wanted to stay, but the twisted part...that part wanted to run and run and never return.

Finally...success. She bolted to her feet and toward the thick forest. Dai and Nico shouted and ran after her. They grabbed her at the same time and in a tumble of arms and legs, wrestled her to the ground. She ended up facedown in the grass, struggling, yet restrained by two powerful male bodies. It took the two of them to keep her from fleeing. It was as if this sudden fear she had made her stronger than normal, stronger than was natural. The part of her that was still Twyla was grateful for Dai and Nico. Happy they could control her. She wanted, *needed*, them to do so.

Dai ended up between her spread legs, pinning her down with his hips. The mound of his flaccid cock pressed against her buttocks through the fabric of her skirt. She felt exposed and vulnerable in this position. She felt how she'd felt on the night of her rape. It made her claw the ground and scream and cry.

Nico grabbed her arms and held them down. "Calm," he yelled. "Please, Twyla. It's us. It's us. We won't hurt you. Never hurt you. We're only trying to prevent you from hurting yourself. Hush now," he said over and over.

Inexplicable animalistic lust tore through her. Her pussy was sopping wet, so ready to be taken. It's all she wanted. All she could think about. Using the little space she had to move, she spread her legs as far as she could and positioned herself against Dai's cock and rubbed her hot sex against him. His body tensed and she felt his cock grow hard.

"Twyla," Dai said in a warning voice. "Don't do that."

She made a frustrated, animal-like sound and wiggled her hips, deliberately trying to push him over the edge. She just wanted him inside her. She wanted to be filled, taken, subdued and controlled. Sex was the only thing that could ground her now.

Dai snaked his hand around her hip and pulled her shirt up. He thrust his hand down the front of her skirt. His fingers found her wet sex through the material of her undergarment. He let out a sound that was like a growl of anticipation. "You're ready for a cock, love. Do you know that? Do you want me, Twyla? Is that what you want?"

She nodded and dug her fingers into the earth at the feel of him touching her. Couldn't he see that's all she wanted?

He moved the scrap of material aside and slicked his fingers through the cream she'd made for him. She shuddered when he found her opening and pressed two of his thick fingers inside her. Her hips jerked involuntarily as he started thrusting in and out of her. *Oh yes. Sweet Kingdom, yes*, she chanted in her mind. She pushed up further, so she was fully on her knees and he let her. He pushed his knees forward, forcing her thighs apart as far as they would go. In this position, she was completely vulnerable to him. Completely at his mercy. It was like before, when she'd been taken against her will, but yet completely not. She *wanted* this.

She needed it.

She needed this memory of Dai and Nico to overlay and consume the bad memory from her past.

"Yes, I want you. Both of you," she rasped. "Let's do this now."

Dai thrust his fingers within her hard and fast and she arched her back at the sensation. She couldn't speak anymore. She could barely think.

"You're sure?" Nico said somewhere near her ear.

She nodded. "Please," she whimpered.

"Not here, love," said Nico. "If we're going to do this, it must be in the circle."

She shook her head. "No. Here. Here." But they were lifting her, carrying her. Dai held her in his arms and when she fought him, he gave her over to Nico, who slung her over his shoulder and let her beat his back with her fists. Her hair hung loose and long over her head, brushing the ground as they bore her to the circle.

It was a large clearing that thrummed with power. It should have calmed her, but did not. A blanket had been spread in the center. Nico put her to her feet on the blanket and crushed her to his chest. "Hush, Twyla," he crooned as she cried into his chest. "What's the matter, love? What's wrong?"

She pulled away from him without a word and began to undress him. "Please. I need to feel you, both of you. Please, I need your skin against mine. Please, please," she said over and over. "Now."

Nico gently withdrew her hands from him, swept her off her feet and laid her onto the blanket. "That you will get, love."

She turned over on her stomach, offering her ass up to the both of them. "Please," she cried out.

Nico pulled her skirt up to her waist and ripped her undergarments at the seams to get them off her. Soon, she was naked and exposed from the waist down. Her ass was in the air, offered up like a juicy bit of fruit to their gazes and their touch. Someone groaned at the sight of her. She thought it was Dai.

Twyla closed her eyes, listening to the rustle of clothing being taken off.

Twyla didn't know how Dai had gotten his pants off, but soon she felt the press of the wide, thick head of his shaft pressing into her. Bit by bit, he worked his shaft into her. She was so wet, that despite his size, he slid in easily. He stayed embedded in her to the hilt and groaned low and long. Then he grabbed her hips and started to thrust. The pace started slow and she wanted him to go faster, harder. Digging her palms into the grass and grunting, she pushed back against him, making every thrust as deep as she could make it. Her vision swam as the pleasure of it filled her. This was the ultimate possession of Dai over her. She wanted to be possessed by him.

Taking the hint, he picked up the pace. He pulled back and slammed into her over and over. She clawed the ground, giving in to the ecstasy of it. Her orgasm hit her hard, rolling her eyes back into her head. "Ah yes, Dai, yes!" she screamed.

He pulled free of her body without coming, and pulled her up against him, letting his hand tangle through her hair and stroke down her tear-stained cheeks. "Is that better, love? Do you feel calmer now?"

She fisted his shirt in her hands and shook her head. "No. More. *More.* I need both of you. I want to feel both of you. Please."

He lowered her back to the blanket and came down on her right side.

Nico lowered himself to his knees on the other side of her and stroked his hands over her body, over her breasts and between her legs to graze her swollen, needy pussy. She shuddered. At the same time, Dai slipped a hand to the nape of her neck and rubbed with strong fingers. She sighed as the tension left her body in a whoosh.

Her hands sought and found Dai's cock, still wet from her own juices. His hips jerked as she ran her fingers over it, teasing him, trying to push him past the limits she knew he had. Nico was harder to push, but Dai...he was easy. On the other side, she found Nico's cock and let her fingers curl around the shaft. She pumped them at the same time, relishing the dual groans that filled the air and the lovely sensation of both their cocks in her hands at once.

Dai's mouth came down on hers and she closed her eyes, allowing him to part her lips and stroke his tongue into her mouth. He pulled her against him and her breasts brushed the rough hair of his chest. Her body felt heavy with desire. Nico spread her labial lips and Dai rubbed his finger through her folds. Her hips thrust up involuntarily.

"Ah," Dai murmured against her lips. "I love the way you feel, Twyla." He slipped a finger into her, then another and pumped her with them, while Nico stroked her clit.

"You're so wet and slick," Nico growled near her ear. "I want you so very much, love."

She closed her eyes and let her head fall back. Her pussy gripped Dai's fingers. Nico pulled away for a moment and came back to find her nether hole. He'd coated his hand in some kind of lubricant. With a finger, he stroked around her anus and then slipped inside. She let out a low moan and tossed her head from side-to-side as both orifices were pleasured simultaneously. In and out, they thrust relentlessly, widening her pussy and her anus to take their cocks.

"I will take you here," purred Nico as he thrust extra hard into her ass. She groaned.

"And I will take you here," murmured Dai as he thrust in and out of her pussy. "At the same time. Are you ready for that?"

Those dark words poured over her, lighting a fire in her lower belly. Her climax built slow and intense. It wouldn't be long before she exploded. She nodded.

A second finger was added to her nether passage and the fingers pistoned in and out of her, driving her crazy. Her moans filled the clearing and her back arched, thrusting her breasts into the air, her nipples hard and demanding attention. Dai's head came down to her breast to capture and lave over a nipple. He licked it with the flat of his tongue and then nipped at her gently. The little bit of pain combined with the incredible amount of pleasure tilted her over the edge. She screamed as she came, her vaginal muscles clenching and releasing as she poured out her hot juice over Dai's hand.

"Mmmm…yes," Nico murmured into her ear. "You are relaxed and wet and ready for us. First, I want a feel of your pussy around me."

Twyla watched as Nico settled himself between her thighs and guided his cock within her. Her fingers grasped his forearms as he gave her all those luscious inches slowly, then pulled almost the full way out and slid in again. She arched her back and moaned as he took her at a pace slow enough to blow her mind. Nico leaned down over her and kissed her cheeks and her mouth, telling her how beautiful she was, how much they both loved her.

Tears coursed down her cheeks and Dai leaned over her and tenderly kissed them away. Their love felt like a palpable thing, like a velvet blanket wrapping around her, warming her through. If love was an energy, Dai and Nico emanated it now in totality. The sensation made her heart swell with deep emotion, made her see the world so differently. No longer was it a place of anger and hatred. No longer was it a world where she was made to run and hide from those who wished her harm. Her reality was suddenly filled with the bright light of belonging and mutual caring.

She was loved.

That knowledge transformed everything.

Nico pulled out without coming and Dai took his place. He restrained himself, shafting her slow and easy, just as Nico had. After bringing her to orgasm once again, they switched off, Nico taking Dai's place and loving her gently and slowly once more. Twyla felt like she'd explode from the sensation of it and the love they seemed to fill her with.

Finally, Dai leaned backward to lie on the blanket and Nico helped to position her so that she straddled Dai, her swollen pussy just brushing the head of his cock. She pushed her hips down, trying to slip him within her. Nico and Dai's hands went to her hips and together they guided her movements until his cock slid within.

And in, and in, and in… Soon she was seated on his pelvis, with the entire thick length of his cock thrust up within her as far as it would go.

"Yes," she breathed as his length and width filled her. She closed her eyes and pressed down, pushing him within to the hilt. It felt right to have him inside her. It would feel even better to have them both possessing her in tandem.

Dai groaned and closed his eyes. He brushed her hair back from her shoulders. "Ah Twyla. You feel so delicious around me. I'll never grow tired of your beautiful body."

Nico covered her back, scattering kisses on her shoulders and the nape of her neck. His warm flesh teased her sensitive body. He touched her buttocks with a lubricated hand. "Are you sure?" he murmured.

She dropped her head down to kiss Dai, which brought her ass up enough to give Nico access. "Fill me," she panted. "Fill me up with both of you. Fill me up with love. Fill me to cover over the memory of terror and replace it with one of pleasure and passion. *Fill me, Nico.*"

Nico pressed a finger into her anus, then two, widening her. She bit her lip at the feel of her muscles stretching to accommodate the invasion. At the same time, Dai lifted her up just a bit to give himself room to move. He thrust his cock in and out of her so slowly she thought she'd die.

"Does it hurt?" asked Nico.

She shook her head. There was a slight pain, but it was actually arousing. It made the pleasure so much more pronounced. Nico's cock pressed at her nether hole, circled it, and then entered. She gasped and almost pulled away. Both Dai and Nico held her hips in place.

"It is just the head that will hurt, love," Nico murmured. "Once we get past the crown, it will not pain you much. On the contrary, there will be only pleasure." He pushed the rest of the way in and, indeed, it was true it was not so painful when it was the shaft that breached and stretched the tight muscles of her anus.

She moaned as the men started to love her slowly…so very, very slowly, both attuned to the other's pace. Dai watched her face carefully, monitoring the play of emotion and pleasure.

Nico brushed his lips across the crown of her head and then dropped his mouth to her bare shoulder. "Are you all right, love?" he murmured.

Magick skittered across her skin, trying to find a way in. It brushed over her breasts and thighs, making her shiver. That, combined with the gentle, mind-blowing glide of the cocks of the two men she loved was enough to set her teeth into her bottom lip. She whimpered in pleasure and nodded.

Dai shifted his hips a little so the tip of his cock paid special attention to the spot within her that felt so very good when it was rubbed. "So sweet, so tight," groaned Dai. "You are perfection, Twyla."

She released her lip. "Do you feel that? The magick?"

Nico kissed the curve of her shoulder. "Yes, love. It's your magick trying to return to you. If you allow it in, we can complete this ritual. Your magick needs to be home before it can join with ours."

"Allow it, Twyla," murmured Dai.

She closed her eyes, concentrating on the magick smoothing its way over her skin. The image came unbidden. Perhaps it was instinct. Either way, she imagined a door in the center of her chest. She opened the door and pushed out all of the fear and terror and rage and let her magick flow into her. She gasped as it filled her up, settling around her heart and infusing her mind with powerful intelligence. It felt silky, warm and comforting. Twyla opened her eyes, knowing she'd finally regained the part of her that had been lost. The part that had been stolen from her so long ago on a dark night when hatred had reigned.

Dai and Nico both groaned loud and low. "Thank the Gods," Dai murmured.

"Good girl, love," said Nico as he dropped a kiss to her ear. "Now, are you ready?"

"For what?"

They didn't answer her. Instead, their pace quickened. Faster and harder they thrust. Twyla curled her fingers into the blanket on either side of Dai and hung on. They shafted her in tandem now, each perfectly attuned to the other's movements, driving her toward another climax that would shatter her world. Twyla felt a scream building in her throat.

Being so filled this way, having Dai pistoning in and out of her pussy, and Nico filling her anus, it was almost too much to take. Too much sensation for her body to handle at one time. It was heaven and it was hell all at once.

She dropped her head down on a moan. Her hair fell over Dai's shoulder. He put his mouth to her ear. "You're so hot, Twyla. You're so hot and sweet and tight. We're so close. We just need to hear you cry out your pleasure. Come for us, my love...my beauty. Scream out your climax."

Her climax ripped through her and she screamed. Waves of intense pleasure racked her body, making her knees go weak and blackening her vision. It stole all her thought, her muscle control and almost stole her consciousness.

Dai groaned as he released a hot jet of come into her. Nico did likewise, thrusting as far into her as he could and letting loose.

Twyla's head snapped back as a thread of her magick exploded upward from her chest, drawing another scream from her. Dai and Nico also cried out as their magick left them. She could feel it around them, curling through the air and snaking around each other as the tendrils melded. She couldn't see it, but she could sense it with everything she was. The threads of magicks were like three great and powerful beasts scenting each other and deciding to mate.

Finally, the magick sped straight upward. Nico and Dai moved, toppling them all onto the blankets in a tangle. They watched as the magick seemed to explode in a brilliant flash of white in the sky above them. The grayness over their heads broke and light poured through it. The crack grew larger and larger until the entire sky was consumed with daylight.

"Sweet..." Twyla breathed. "Sweet Kingdom."

"Finally our magick had joined with the magicks of the other triads," said Nico. He breathed out slowly. "It's done."

Together, they stayed on the blanket for a long while, kissing and holding each other, murmuring words of love and commitment in the bright daylight of noon.

Epilogue

ॐ

Twyla pulled her silk-lined cloak about her shoulders and allowed her footman to open the door of her black and gold carriage and help her out. She stepped on the cobblestone street of Middleton, a city near to the one where she, Dai and Nico now lived. It had taken her three months to track Marsten down. He'd fled Dandre Village when he'd discovered she was part of a Sacred Triad.

But she would not be denied closure, and he would not escape retribution.

His rooms lay above a cookshop in one of the seedier parts of the city. The city's inhabitants eyed her black and gold carriage drawn by six perfectly black horses, curiously. Twyla felt at home in an environment like this, but she realized the poor, bedraggled residents of this neighborhood likely didn't get many visitors as well-heeled as herself.

Nico and Dai had fought to accompany her, but she'd been firm in her resolve to do this on her own. After all, it wasn't like she was powerless. Her magick had returned to her in full and then some.

With a look toward the blue sunlit sky, she entered the building and walked up the stairs to Marsten's room. Steeling herself to again lay her gaze on one of the men who'd killed her mother, she raised her hand and sent a blast of magick against the wooden door. It flew off the hinges, and a draft of fetid air from Marsten's flat hit her square in the face. She turned her face away and coughed.

Marsten sat at a long table eating a stew. He wore a grimy tunic and sat with one hand to his mouth, frozen with shock, his eyes wide. He started to stand. "Hey, you can't—"

She shot her hand in his direction, firing a quick blast of power that sat him back down in his chair. Marsten *oomfed* as his breath left him.

"Stay," she commanded.

Marsten squinted up at her. His angry gaze traced up from her silk slippers to the burgundy gown to the expensive jewels that glittered at her ears, throat and wrists. His gaze settled on her face. Fear shot through his mud-colored eyes. "T-the pendant, that was a just a little joke, milady. I never meant any harm."

"Silence!" Her magickally enhanced voice boomed throughout the room. Rage ripped through her and she fought to control it. Rage and magick did not mix. That was one of the many lessons she'd learned in her recent magickal studies.

Marsten's mouth snapped shut with an audible click.

"I suppose you meant no harm the night you raped and killed my mother, also." She stepped toward him, looking him up and down. "I came here today in order to prevent you from hurting any other women. I will also be searching out the other participant from that night who still lives. Now, listen carefully, because I don't want to waste any more time on you than I must."

Marsten looked at her with wide eyes. She could taste his fear on her tongue. Twyla didn't enjoy it, and she didn't want it. All she wanted was to get on with this business so she could go home to the ones who loved her.

She raised her hand and closed her eyes, feeling the magick within her bubbling to the surface. It tickled her palm as it radiated out, seeking and finding its focus.

"You and your mother were not the first," Marsten yelled. "You were not the first women I forced that way. You won't be the last, either." He laughed. "Dirty whores! You *all* like it in the end, anyway. No matter what we do to you, you still —" He gasped and looked down at his crotch, where her magick was fulfilling its purpose. About now, he should've been feeling his cock shrivel.

Marsten shrieked. He stood up, causing the chair to fall backward, and retreated to the far corner of the room to cower. But he wouldn't be able to prevent her magick from completing its task.

The magickal stream ceased and retreated into her body. "*I* was the last. Marsten. Your days of seeking pleasure from the terror of women are over." She raised an eyebrow. "Indeed, you will not be able to seek your pleasure in any fashion again, ever."

She turned and walked out the door, leaving Marsten to yell and cry behind her as he realized she'd wasted his member.

Happy to have that unpleasant business completed, her heart light, knowing that other women were now protected from the fate she'd endured, she walked back down to her carriage that would take her back to the men who loved her.

About the Author

ॐ

Anya Bast writes erotic fantasy and paranormal romance. Primarily, she writes happily-ever-afters with lots of steamy sex. After all, how can you have a happily-ever-after WITHOUT lots of sex?

Anya welcomes mail from readers. You can write to her c/o Ellora's Cave Publishing at 1056 Home Avenue, Akron OH 44310-3502.

Also by Anya Bast

ॐ

A Change of Season

Autumn Pleasures: The Union

Blood of an Angel

Blood of the Damned

Blood of the Raven

Blood of The Rose

Ellora's Cavemen: Tales from the Temple III (*anthology*)

Ordinary Charm

Spring Pleasures: The Transformation

Summer Pleasures: The Capture

Water Crystal

Winter Pleasures: The Training

Pirate's Booty

By
Ashley Ladd

જી

Chapter One

🔊

Spaceship alarms sliced through Princess Melena Androkova's luscious daydreams, jerking her alert with a rude start. A force field shimmered to life around her as she jabbed at her earring communicator. "Admiral, status report!"

Her pulse racing, she swore under her breath when the com emitted ominous sounds of taser blast. "Georges? Who's attacking? Why are we under siege?" This was a diplomatic mission to cement the treaty between Neteera and the neighboring planet of Teeran Hauft. Hostilities had ceased and both planets were relieved at the promise of lasting peace. Unless... Was Teeran Hauft luring them into a trap?

"Pirates...Your...Highness. They've taken over the ship! You must hurry to the escape pod." Normally charming and serene, the admiral's voice came halting and breathless.

Alarmed, her heart stopped for infinitesimal moments. *"Pirates..."*

No! Her mission would not be thwarted by a renegade band of miserable pirates. This couldn't be happening.

When the craft lurched and screeched alarmingly, the force field winked out.

"Warning. Warning. Abandon ship. Destruction is imminent. Proceed to the life pod." The whiny computerized warning repeated ad nauseum throughout the transport.

Melena held her hand over her mouth as she made her way through the smoky corridors, but she still couldn't suppress the coughs niggling at the back of her throat.

"Going our way, Blondie?" A tall cinnamon-colored pirate twirled a long microbraid around his fingers before lunging and grabbing her around the middle. He dragged her against his rock-hard frame. His scintillating gaze that devoured her was none too friendly as his long braids swayed about their bodies.

His fierce, dangerous strength stole her breath. Tamping down her fear and fury, Melena jabbed a well-placed elbow at her attacker's groin.

With a litheness that betrayed great virility, he caught her wrist as easily as if he held a butterwasp's wing. Then he pressed the tip of a taser gun to her throat, its pointy nose pressing against her delicate flesh. "No messing with the precious cargo, honey."

The brilliant flash of his latinum teeth reflected off the titanium walls, and she swallowed a growl. Her blood pressure soaring, she grunted. "I don't take kindly to being hijacked and kidnapped. How dare you threaten our divine mission!" Seething, her chest heaved. Screams of outrage gurgled in her throat and she couldn't remember when she'd been so livid.

The man had the audacity to fill her ear with his guttural laughter.

"How dare I? How dare a pirate anything? How dare you flaunt this expensive bauble before me and not expect my mouth to water?"

To her mortification, he wrapped his vile fingers around her sacred amulet and yanked it off. Mustering all her courage, she hiked her chin high. "Return it at once!"

The pirate pushed the gun deeper against her flesh. "I wonder, are you really so brave or just tremendously foolhardy?"

"Your Highness..." Georges rounded the corner, wheezing. He cut off his own greeting and pulled up short when he spied her captor.

"*Your Highness?* Daresay I have the Princess of Neteera in my clutches? What treasure indeed. You'll fetch a pretty ransom, Blondie." The pirate smoothed a lock of her hair between his calloused fingers.

Melena swallowed hard, recoiling at his vile touch. "My father doesn't negotiate with terrorists and kidnappers."

"You'd best pray he does for the sake of your pretty little neck."

"If you lay one grubby finger on her..." Georges' love for her was no secret, although forbidden, for he was not of noble blood but of lower military lineage. Regardless, her sire, the King of Neteera, had betrothed her to the Prince of Teeran Hauft in the hopes of fostering a lasting peace between the long-warring planets.

The pirate snarled and dangled her amulet just out of her grasp.

Without warning, another series of explosions rocked the ship. Flames spurted. Sparks flew. The jolt loosened the pirate's grip and knocked the taser from his hand.

She might die this day, but at least the infidel would accompany her on the journey to the dead side. Unleashing the dormant wildcat scratching to get out, she clawed at his eyes. "The hottest fires of hell are too good for you, *pirate*."

Profanities tumbling from his lips, the man loosed her so fast she stumbled backward, flailing. The scoundrel squinted. "You'll be sorry..."

Georges grabbed her around her waist and thrust her behind him protectively. "Stay back and let me do my job."

Although Melena knew the truth in his words, her heart rebelled.

Mere seconds later, Georges sailed through the air. His head hit the bulkhead with a thunderous crash, and unconscious, he slid to the floor.

Before she could catch her breath, a second pirate beamed into the hallway and hauled her into his arms.

"Bastard!" She thrashed about to no avail. To her chagrin, the newly arrived pirate held her in his iron grip. Never before had she felt so impotent.

"Tsk, tsk. Zarod, do you hear that? Her Highness has such a diplomatic tongue." The newcomer's long mustache bounced upward as insane challenge sizzled in his ebony eyes.

The ship went into final countdown, its mechanical voice tinny, devoid of emotion. "Self-destruct has been activated. All hands abandon ship. Proceed to the life pod. Ninety seconds. Eighty-nine seconds…"

"Unhand me!" Preferring death over defilement, she kicked and pummeled him with all her might.

"Shut up or I'll give you your wish, and you can go to Hades with your ship." Zarod flipped open a communicator and barked into it, "Beam us aboard. We have a little surprise."

Only static answered.

Zarod scowled deeply. "Where are you? I said *now!*"

Faint words wove in and out of the static. "We're…hurt. Crippled…Can't…Fare thee well."

"Goodbye?" Keir swore and his grip tightened on her arms.

A black hole could fit inside Zarod's snarl. "They wouldn't dare leave us on an exploding ship!"

Melena tried to draw back even further lest she be sucked into the deadly void.

"They could and they did, mate." Keir said, adding, "Don't worry. When we catch up with them, there'll be hell to pay."

Zarod nodded sharply and shook his taser in the air. He muttered a frightening curse.

"Thirty seconds. Twenty-nine…" the ship's countdown continued.

Melena placed a well-aimed kick at Keir's ankles while he was distracted and jabbed her elbow into his ribs so that he dropped her as he doubled over.

Free at last, she darted away.

But Zarod made a lunge for her and grabbed her around her middle and tossed her over his shoulder.

She clawed, bit, and pulled his hair but the giant pirate seemed impervious to pain.

Zarod ordered, "Keir, help me carry this termagant." Together, they held her kicking, writhing body and dragged her to the life pod.

Zarod swore loudly and punched the wall. "I still can't believe those lousy traitors took off without us."

"Never trust a pirate, mate." Keir said with a lopsided grin. "Except for me."

"I'll put a voodoo curse on them! If I ever get my hands on them…" Zarod's face almost turned purple and his eyes bulged.

"You won't unless we get out of harm's way. *Now!*" Her captors hurtled the ship into light speed. Zarod tumbled backward on top of her, his weight nearly suffocating.

Swallowing the bile that bubbled in her throat, she shoved away the brute. "What do you think you're doing?"

"Saving your ungrateful lily-white ass, *princess*."

"Princess" was muttered with more derision than she'd ever heard it uttered, even by the most antagonistic government officials. Biting back her own foul curses, she rose gingerly and massaged her sore muscles until she realized the pair held her under inscrutable regard. Shifting to a more gracefully royal pose, she treated them to her haughtiest gaze. "What about my crew? We can't just leave them to die."

The one called Keir tented his brows and slanted his head at the view monitor. "Looks like several pods followed us out. If I were in your glass slippers, I'd worry about your own dubious plight."

She bit back a sigh of relief, not wishing them to see how genuinely she cared for her shipmates. Emotional displays would only weaken her position. Pirates would jump on any perceived weakness. The greedy bastards only cared about booty—in its many forms. She did her best to suppress a shudder and, as casually as she could, tugged up her drooping neckline, hoping they were only interested in her material riches. "Return me to Neteera at once and I promise clemency."

The pirates exchanged wickedly mirthful glances and broke into riotous laughter. Zarod held his stomach as he doubled over. "*You* promise. And what will your daddy, the King, have to say about it? Besides, what will we get for our valiant efforts?"

They'd take her seriously when they found themselves in the king's taser sights! "If you harm me, it's a sure wager he'll have you castrated." Then skewered and beheaded. She shuddered and resisted the urge to hug herself. Her sire would avenge his only child in the ancient ways, inflicting as much pain and torture as humanly possible. A throwback to barbaric times, her father thrived on vengeance.

Blinding light blurred her vision. Moments later, the escape vessel rocked furiously from the vehemence of the explosion, knocking her off her feet again, this time into the lap of the acerbic-tongued Keir.

When his despicable arms steadied her, burning her flesh, she jumped to her feet so fast her head spun. Seething, pointing to the ship with a trembling finger, she hissed, "See what you've done? That wasn't merely one of the royal fleet, that ship carried emissaries to prevent interplanetary war. If I'm not immediately delivered to my betrothed, Prince Gallakin of Teeran Hauft, the blood of innocent millions will stain your hands."

Keir bolted out of the captain's chair, his unruly hair swirling around him in his haste. "Bloody hell... Better tell that to the hunk of space junk headed dead for us."

Melena's gaze darted to the heart-stopping scene rapidly monopolizing the space display. Her breath froze in her constricted throat. "What space junk?"

"Debris from your killer craft." A sinister scowl marred Zarod's high brow as his fingers flew over the control panel. "Better put your head between your knees and pray."

The coarse sentiment barely fazed her as she focused on the impending doom. She had been lifting fervent prayers to her goddess since she'd first laid eyes on the pirates.

"Hard astern!" Keir warned.

Screwing up his face, the pirate grunted. "I know what I'm do —"

A deafening explosion chopped off his words as their craft hurtled out of control, pitching them around the compartment.

Melena landed against the unrelenting wall so hard her skull made a horrible cracking sound. Searing pain slashed her temples and then blessed darkness shrouded her.

Chapter Two

ॐ

With smoke tickling his nostrils, Zarod awoke with a start. Fighting off the fog that veiled his brain, he leapt to his feet to meet the danger head-on, but his bones felt like they were splintering, and his muscles protested so he staggered to his knees in agony. "What happened?" he asked, as disorienting vistas flashed before his eyes.

An ordinary raid…

An extraordinary find…the Princess of Neteera and her mouthwatering dowry…

An exploding ship and then a hurtling spacecraft…

And then?

And then he had no clue as his world had gone pitch-black. No rays of recollection filtered through, until now.

Oh God! Keir…

His love…

Where was he? Was he hurt? If anything happened to him…

His gut twisted sharply. He had to find him.

"Keir?" His vision clearing with each passing second, he grimaced at the wreckage that swallowed them. Tearing through twisted scraps of metal and smoldering circuitry, he searched for the man who claimed his heart and soul.

Weak coughing made him pivot on his heel. No words had ever sounded so sweet to Zarod's ears as Keir's muttered curses.

"Over here, mate. Lend me a hand. My leg's pinned under this mother…"

With three huge strides, Zarod was at Keir's side, heaving the heavy bulkhead off the trapped leg. When Keir rose shakily to his feet, Zarod put a restraining hand on his wrist. "Not so fast, Kee. Let me see if anything's broken." Gingerly, he ran his fingers up and down the mottled flesh, relieved when he found no sign of serious injury.

"What's the verdict? Think I'll live?"

Keir tossed him the saucy grin that never failed to melt Zarod's heart. When he patted Keir on the shoulder a thrill of electricity tingled through him. "Only another seventy-odd years."

Squinting, Keir peered around him pointedly. "Where's our *friend*? She okay?"

Guilt struck Zarod square in the chest. All his thoughts had been centered on the man's fate and none on their distinguished *guest*. Of course, spoiled, hellcat princesses didn't rank high on his priority list. Not that he took responsibility for many wenches, much less a *princess*. He didn't cherish the sensation. This was supposed to be a simple ransom to strike easy plunder. The princess of the richest planet within a hundred sectors, she was a rare find. Her people would relinquish opulent treasure beyond his wildest dreams for her safe return.

If they could return her safely.

Judging by this mutilated mess, chances were slim to nil.

If she were still breathing.

"I was too busy ensuring your safety to find out," he spat out, not wishing to show his chagrin.

Keir quirked his lips and shook his head. "My white knight."

Always and forever. He'd do anything for Keir, even lay down his life. "She can't have gone far." Unless she'd been disintegrated…

They sifted through the rubble, checking beneath the fragments sufficiently large to hide an entire body. Just when he'd started giving his disintegration theory more credence, weak mewling reached his ears. Barely audible, whispery soft, it was like a small animal's whimpering from beyond the perimeter of the wreckage.

Zarod cocked his head and listened intently, focusing on the direction. When the sound echoed again, he turned in its direction. He tapped his companion on the shoulder and pointed to the rugged brush a few feet away. "Over there."

Half buried in lush bushes, the princess sprawled awkwardly.

His heart lurching into his throat, he glanced sidelong at Keir. "Do we dare move her?" Violent growls rose from over the ridge no more than a couple kilometers away, and uneasiness prickled down his spine. He'd only heard such vicious animal noises on B'Lan Yoshique and the memory made his flesh crawl.

Keir shuddered and jerked his thumb in the direction of the fearsome noise. "It'll be a long wait for the medics and I don't fancy being the main course," Keir said with deadly sarcasm.

Nor did Zarod. His gaze raked the surrounding inhospitable countryside, taking in the harsh scrub. No trace of civilization or shelter met his hopeful gaze and he grunted. "Any brilliant ideas?"

"Wait here with Her Highness while I scout things out." Keir swaggered off with his mouthwatering devil-may-care gait.

Zarod's heart rose in his throat when someone—or something—let out a bloodcurdling screech. *Holy!* "Be careful."

Keir winked. "You know me—an extremely cautious fellow." Without another word, he crept away, his form merging with the lengthening shadows.

The princess stirred, lifting a groggy gaze. She licked her swollen, cracked lips achingly slow as if pained to do so. She lifted her head fractionally but it lolled back. "Father? Prince Gallakin?"

Not quite…

"Save your strength, Blondie. You crash-landed harder than the rest of us."

Squinting, she struggled to a sitting position. Then her eyes widened in her angelic face, her scorn impossible to miss. "You! Pirate." Her nostrils flared as she recoiled. "Keep your distance."

Zarod bowed and backed away as commanded, not wishing to be any closer to the hostile woman than she did to him. The desolation of this place chained the arrogant wildcat to him, without him having to get close enough to risk life and limb. "As you wish."

Breathing heavily, she struggled to her feet, never taking away her wary gaze. "Where is this place?"

He tilted up his head toward the sky. "It has to be either Lukopth or Beincasa, one of the uninhabited planets in this system capable of sustaining life. Or maybe one of the many moons surrounding these systems. Could even be an asteroid."

Great. Just great. An asteroid? No one would think to look for them on a hunk of space rubble. She just glared, lifting her regal chin higher, the glint in her eyes growing steelier. "In other words, we're lost."

"Marooned," Keir said too cheerfully, as he loped back. "Stranded," he enunciated. "There's a cozy little cave about five hundred meters to the southwest where we can camp for the night."

"Camp? Cave?" Her lips twisted. "Us? Me with the two of you? Intolerable! I won't hear of it. My fiancé would be livid."

Keir's lips turned up in the mischievous way that lit Zarod's heart.

"Be our guest. Make your own camp. Fend off those howling creatures by your lonesome. Who are we, lowly pirates, to stop you?" He turned to Zarod and crooked his head in the direction where the cave was purported to be. "I suggest we hoof it before one of those *friendly beasts* beats us to our high-class accommodations."

Good, if the princess didn't join them for the night, he could spend it in the comforting circle of Keir's strong arms.

As if on cue, ferocious growls resounded in the air.

The sound reverberated chillingly through him but he masked his features so the woman wouldn't read his fear.

Shudders racked the princess and she squared her shoulders as she glanced furtively around the shadowy wasteland. "I suppose I can band together with you for *one* night. Tomorrow, we'll survey the area for assistance. Have you tried our communications to see if you can contact anyone?"

"We were too busy saving your *ungrateful* royal ass," Keir said with a chuckle as he swept off his hat and bowed low.

"You mean that melted pile of rubbish that used to be our communications?" Zarod shook his head at the imperial airhead. Had she no concept of the real world? Of course not. The Princess of Neteera had obviously been coddled since birth. She seemed to hold no concept of the real world. He'd be surprised if she knew how to lace her own shoes.

Melena thrust out her chest and snorted in a very unprincesslike way that Zarod found amusing. Glaring down her long imperious nose at each of them in turn, she said disdainfully, "You're just protecting your investment. I don't delude myself. You're not the savior, white knight types."

Keir's mouth curved into a wicked grin as he twirled his handlebar mustache. "Pray tell, what *type* are we?"

"*Pirates*." Her word rang out like a taser blast as if that answered everything. Clamping small fists on narrow hips, she appeared more shrewish than regal.

The extreme prejudice coloring her voice grated on Zarod's nerves. It was his turn to hold his chin high. "Many pirates are good men."

A snort escaped her lips. "Kidnapping, marauding pirates?"

If Her Highness didn't drop the prima donna act very quickly, he would turn into a *murderous* pirate. Hands clenching and unclenching at his sides, he shot a commiserating glance to his partner, pleading with him to turn the conversation before his blood pressure rose to dangerous levels.

"Temper, temper. For better or worse, we're stuck here together. We could be on our own for quite awhile so let's play nicely." Keir crooked his finger before he turned on his boot heel. "This way."

Zarod forced himself not to bare his teeth and to swallow the growl rumbling in his chest. The only thing wanted to play with this insufferable woman was jailer and prisoner. Then he could lock her up and hide the key. Maybe he wouldn't have to suffer more of her caustic comments.

* * * * *

Was the pirate rabid? Feral?

Just in case, Melena took a step back physically, as well as verbally. She highly doubted he was up to date on his rabies vaccine.

Pivoting on her heel, she scurried to catch up to Keir. Although on the quirky, even possibly insane, side, he was much friendlier. Plus the one called Zarod had been the one to abduct her, so the majority of her hard feelings were directed his way. Perhaps Keir had just been trying to save her neck as by the time he'd shown up, the ship was preparing to explode. Not that she entertained any great love—or trust—for pirates, but paradoxically, her safety depended on these two tonight.

Safety?

And who was supposed to safeguard her from her most improbable *protectors*?

Exhausted and dispirited after the day's events, her mind was soup. As if it wasn't subject to enough torment already because she was being forced to marry that crusty prince for diplomatic purposes, now she had to deal with near death, kidnapping, wild animals, and being marooned with two such *friendly* gentlemen.

She'd give anything to relinquish her crown. If she were an ordinary woman, none of this would be happening. She wouldn't have to make the utmost sacrifice for her planet, indeed for the galaxy, and marry a foreigner she didn't love. And no one would dream of kidnapping or ransoming her.

Chattel.

That's all she was. Her dreams, desires and needs didn't matter. With privilege came responsibility. She'd heard that phrase so much from her father, she gagged every time it popped into her mind. Right now, with sharp brambles tearing her impractical robes and scraping her legs, she really failed to see where the privilege part came. Her royal silk slippers had not been intended to replace sturdy hiking boots for such rough, rocky terrain. Of course, she had dressed with a royal wedding in mind, not a spacecraft crash and camp-out.

More of the creatures bayed, shooting shivers down her spine. She did her best to suppress the shudders just as she'd been doing since her first meeting with Zarod. In her experience, showing fear never helped. People, like animals, pounced on it, preying on the weak.

Checking out the neighborhood, she asked, "Just how much further 'til we reach this safe shelter? They sound hungry." Starved, to be more precise.

At mention of the final word, her stomach responded with an embarrassing growl. She shuffled her feet, hoping they hadn't heard. "And just what are we to do for food?"

Keir pulled up so short she bounced against his back and sprawled on her derriere. He turned and treated her to a snooty stare. "This is no time to sit on our duffs and take a break. There's no telling what manner of beast will come out after dark."

Scrunching up her nose, she mumbled wryly, "That never occurred to me." As if the raucous animals would let her forget it for a second. They had landed on wild animal world.

Large hands grabbed her under her arms from behind, and she started to squeal and just as quickly swallowed it when she realized they belonged to Zarod. Serious heat seeped into her from him, catching her off-guard. Shaking herself from the trance, she tried to wrench away and spat out with more force than she intended to, "Stop manhandling me. I can stand on my own."

Ignoring her, Zarod set her on her feet and patted her behind. "We're in no mood to deal with a spoiled brat. Either work with us or strike out on your own."

Spoiled brat?

She was the least-spoiled member of royalty she knew. Her father had insisted she grow up strong and independent. That didn't preclude her being treated with respect and common courtesy, however. His disrespect of her would have earned him a hanging on Neteera. She straightened her spine and lifted her chin high. "Treat me like an equal and we'll get along much better."

Keir rolled his eyes while Zarod's chest shook and his eyes crinkled with mirth. He seemed to be stifling a laugh.

Ah, he'd just been teasing. She was entirely too gullible. She had to stop taking herself so seriously.

"As an equal, you'll have to pull your own weight while we're on this little paradise vacation. Cook. Clean. Sew."

Teasing or not, she arched her brow. Not that she was above manual labor, but to be relegated to ancient woman's work, to even joke about it? Who were the barbaric ones now? "I'm capable of standing guard and constructing shelter, not merely cooking and cleaning."

His gaze penetrating with sizzling challenge, Zarod got up in her face. "And hunting hostile yeti? *Skinning* them."

Nodding emphatically, she crossed her arms over her chest and took a step away from him to break the spell of sensuality that had briefly held her in its grasp. She had almost lost herself in the depths of those intense eyes but she wasn't crazy enough to allow that. Still, she felt slightly disoriented, slightly dazed and shook herself mentally to bring herself back to reality. "I can do anything you can do — better. Does that mean you can't cook, clean and sew?"

Keir clapped his hands sharply. "While this battle of the sexes might prove quite amusing in some other venue, daylight's almost gone. Pirates learn from an early age how to take care of our needs. Now, are we going to move it on out, or just wait here to be nabbed as takeout victuals?"

His analogy turned her stomach and a whisper of dread coursed through her. Of course, she had no desire to become something's bedtime snack. The pirates would probably prove poisonous, but that would only provide momentary satisfaction.

Smiling sweetly, she gestured for him to resume the lead. "We're waiting. What's stopping you?"

Keir squared his shoulders and marched ahead like a drill sergeant. "Snap to it, soldiers. No telling how fast their suns set."

She cocked her head and examined the amber celestial bodies. The first sun melted on the horizon while the second shimmered mistily amongst heavy cloud cover. Gloomy, spooky, this world wasn't the least bit welcoming. She should be grateful the atmosphere was breathable and the temperatures tepid. They could have landed on acid world or lava central. So, why didn't she feel very grateful?

Chapter Three

ഔ

Luckily, the cave was unoccupied, as they were forced to make it home, sweet home for several weeks while they scavenged for materials to erect an adequate refuge.

Keir chafed that they had to share it with Her Highness as that meant he and Zarod had no privacy. He ached for his lover's caresses, for the warmth of his touch. But they weren't into voyeurism and he didn't think Her Highness would take kindly to their relationship. Although sexual enlightenment had come to most sectors of the galaxy in the twenty-seventh century, Neteera was well known for its prudishness. Homosexuality was considered a crime on her planet, punishable by death.

Then again, just about everything was punishable by impalement on her home planet. Her father was the king of backwardness. Keir still hadn't pegged her. She was quite the enigma, sweet and funny one minute, imperiously starchy the next.

They ventured out in a pair, leaving one to guard the cave at all times. For that purpose, they maintained a good stock of firewood and kept a campfire going day and night, as the native creatures seemed most intimidated by flame. Gathering firewood wasted a big bulk of their day. Scrounging for food and constructing a more solid shelter took up the remainder of their time. They hadn't had much chance to search for civilization and thus hadn't ventured very far afield.

"Finally!" Zarod wiped perspiration from his brow and stood back with a glint of pride in his eyes as he regarded their new home. "It's not the palatial castle, but I imagine Her Highness will prefer this to the cave."

Keir surely would. Their new digs provided the much longed-for privacy. His body ached to feel Zarod's touch, to know his kisses, and to have him inside again. It felt like eons since they'd been together. Tonight, they would feast on more than food.

The princess wandered out of the cave clad in a skimpy bikini top and skirt fashioned from the remnants of her royal gown. He much preferred the cavewoman look than the stodgy royal fashion that was a constant reminder of her elevated station. Dressed in this manner, he was far better able to relate to her.

Her long blonde hair swept high into a ponytail that bounced down to the small of her back, she sashayed up to them. Nodding with pride, she circled it. "It's ready to be christened."

Keir wiped the grit from his hands down the length of his dungarees. Braiding his beard as he often did to keep it from tangling or catching on fire, he gleamed with pride at their work. "Sure thing. It's feast time."

Zarod's sultry, smoldering gaze caught his, sending definite invitation for a private banquet. Licking his lips with the tip of his tongue, his message was unmistakable.

Quivering with lust, Keir nodded back almost imperceptibly. How he longed for sunset when the princess would retire to bed so they could, as well.

"I prepared a most special dish for the occasion." Excitement glowed in Melena's turquoise eyes, making them more beautiful than he'd noted before, stealing his breath.

Taken aback at the thought, he mentally retreated. What was he doing noticing the princess's eyes? Zarod's milk chocolaty ones were the only eyes he had a right to drown in. Chastising himself, he turned his gaze on his lover. He had no desire, no need, to cruise anyone else. He had already found his soul mate.

* * * * *

Keir wished for romantic music, scented candles, and rose petals for his first night in Zarod's arms on Planet Paradise. After such a long, excruciating fast, this night would be a magical celebration of love, a feast for their souls. They'd have to settle for the special treat he'd rigged up— and, of course, each other.

As long as they had one another, nothing else truly mattered. Still, he was excited to see Zarod's reaction to his surprise.

Opening his arms wide, he could feel the love infusing him, the sudden driving desire.

"I've missed you so." Zarod walked into his embrace and captured his lips in a tender, provocative kiss.

Against his lips, Keir murmured, "I've never left." And he never would. Their souls were entwined so that nothing and no one could separate them.

Feathering kisses along his jaw, Zarod's lips grew more fervent, his breathing more ragged. Ravenous, they feasted upon each other as if they'd been starved many long months.

"Promise me we'll never abduct another wench. We've paid too dear a price." Off- balance from the smoldering kiss they'd just shared, Keir unbuttoned Zarod's shirt, revealing his very muscular, furry chest that never failed to send shivers down his spine and all the way to his toes. The man was built like a god and he was so blessed to be his chosen one.

Zarod trembled beneath his ministrations and placed his large hand over his heart. "I hereby solemnly swear. That had to be the absolute worst idea I ever had. Slap me if I ever have such a boneheaded notion again."

Breathless, excitement thrumming through his veins, Keir shoved aside the bothersome material of the shirt so his lips could cherish the exquisite living canvas.

"Didn't you say something about a *surprise*?" Zarod quivered against him and his cock twitched enticingly inside his tight breeches.

Keir's own cock bulged in response and he rubbed his groin wantonly against his lover's. Moaning loudly, he slid his eager hand under the rim of Zarod's waistband and unsnapped the pants to loosen his exquisite treasures. "In good time, mate. Anticipation sweetens the pleasure."

His own anticipation certainly soared as Zarod's callused hands roamed his length.

Keir's knees almost buckled when Zarod licked and nibbled his way down his body. When he started to wobble, the gentle giant scooped him into his arms and cradled him against his warm chest. Reverently, Zarod laid him on the soft bed of wooly pelts, then stretched out beside him. "I think I'd have died if anything had happened to you."

As touchingly, lovingly sentimental as his lover's words were, they troubled him. Sliding a finger under Zarod's chin, he forced Zarod to meet his stern gaze. "Promise you'll go on if anything happens to me. You're strong and beautiful and you'll live for both of us."

Zarod paled under his swarthy complexion. "Don't talk that way. You'll jinx yourself…"

Keir shushed him by putting his fingers against the beloved lips. Unlike his mate, he didn't believe in curses, voodoo or the occult. Sometimes, he wondered how such a pragmatic soul as he fit so perfectly with such a superstitious one. Over their many years together, he'd learned to accept the inexplicable and enjoy life's surprises.

Ashley Ladd

"I'm not going to curse myself. Just promise me." He held firmly onto Zarod's broad shoulders, willing him to acquiesce, not merely to give lip service to his wishes.

"Promise, but let's not be so maudlin. I'm not ready to mourn you yet."

"Believe me, I'm in no hurry to die myself, so no worries."

A sunny smile dissipated the storm clouds brewing in Zarod's eyes. "No worries."

To completely get Zarod's mind off the dangers facing them, he deemed it time to reveal his present. Standing, he reached high and cranked back the skylight he'd fashioned in the ceiling from pieces of the ship's wreckage. Stardust shimmered over them as they were bathed in the moon's golden glow. "Voila! You like?"

Nodding, open-mouthed, Zarod stared at the heavens with awe. "Stupendous. I wish I had something special to give you."

Keir returned to the side of the bed and divested himself of his clothing. He lowered himself beside Zarod and cupped his lover's cheeks between his hands and kissed him tenderly, savoring his lips. "You give me yourself daily. That's all I need or want. You're my fondest desire."

Zarod rolled onto his side and stroked Keir's pulsing cock, gently at first and then with more fervor.

Moaning with delight, Keir gave himself up to the incredible sensations, desire simmering in his gut. Returning the favor, he caressed Zarod's rod, running his fingertips up and down the long shaft.

Quivers racked his body as Zarod licked his chest, paying special attention to his nipples. When a finger slid along the crack of his butt, he shivered. How he wished they had lubricant, for his body quaked for release and being sucked off wasn't what he craved. He yearned for good, rough frolicking and fucking.

Zarod released him and he shivered from the chilly air that settled on the formerly warmed flesh, and looked askance at him.

A wicked grin dawned across Zarod's face as he reached for a carved-out wooden bowl filled with a jellylike, fruit-scented substance. "I made lubricant from native berries."

Trills of anticipation shot through Keir as he scooped two fingers into the silky gel to test its consistency. Slick and creamy, it felt perfect. "And you said you had nothing for me. This is so extraordinarily special. No wonder I love you so very much."

Zarod beamed. Huskily, he murmured as he scooped a goodly amount into his hand. "Care to test it?"

Keir nodded and stood on his knees, giving Zarod better access to lubricate his throbbing cock. God, his hands felt wonderful stroking up and down its straining length. Much more of this and he wouldn't be able to block the floodgates.

With great restraint, he held himself back. "Turn around. Get on your knees," he said huskily to Zarod as he helped him turn, his hungry hands kneading Zarod's firm buttocks.

"Fuck me now," Zarod pleaded, his muscles cording.

Oh yeah!

He liked to draw out the pleasure, to tease, to make Zarod beg for it so he slid the tip of his cock along Zarod's butt, then along the slit.

"Tease." Zarod pushed against him, his balls hanging heavy, his juices slicking Keir's cock rubbing deliciously against him.

"How bad do you want it?"

"Desperately. Now! Before I flip you over and pound my rod into you."

"Promises. Promises." From experience, Keir knew Zarod was serious. Greedy, wanting to be fucked almost as much as he wanted to fuck Zarod's rosy ass, he entered his lover with a powerful lunge that made Zarod scream and moan in ecstasy.

Oh God! Keir cherished their privacy and dreaded interruptions. All he wanted to do was to fuck Zarod all night, every night. "Shush! Her Highness will hear us."

Slamming his butt against him in the ancient dance, Zarod asked between pants, "Why do you care? Blondie's a big girl. Surely, she can handle knowing about our relationship. And if she can't, that's her problem. We've never hidden our love before. Why should we now?"

Keir didn't like his reaction or the fact that it worried him. He loved Zarod and only Zarod. Although he was developing a surprising fondness for the princess, he'd never based a friendship on lies before. Zarod was right, she should know. They could be stranded here for a very long time.

Angry at himself over his confusion, trying to empty his mind, he pounded harder into the sexy ass as his balls slapped against Zarod's firm buttocks. Wild, abandoned sex had always cleared his mind of everything else before. So, why not this time?

Climbing on higher and higher swells of bliss, teetering on the brink of ecstasy, he surfed the wave. As quivering waves of rapture captured him, he slipped into a mindless frenzy.

Frantic pounding on the metal door startled him.

"Hold on, I'll rescue you. Stand back, I'm going to blast down the door."

"Don't! We're fine!" Wrenching out of Zarod's ass, his cock raging with fire, he flung muffled curses around as he threw himself down to the mattress. "Cover yourself with the blanket! I should never have given her one of our tasers," he hissed. Frustrated beyond belief, his erection died an extremely miserable death.

Zarod growled as he tumbled to the floor and rolled onto his back. "I don't believe this. You *are* worried about what Miss Priss thinks."

"Not in the way you think." Keir hoped he wasn't lying to himself. Unfortunately, he wasn't convinced.

"What about what I think?"

Keir opened his mouth to reassure Zarod, but was cut short by fracturing metal as a hole blasted through the door and a wild-eyed Melena rushed through, with a burst of chill air. Staring open-mouthed at the demented wench, he tugged the covering more modestly over his naked form.

Melena stopped dead in the center of the room, her forehead pinched beneath her riotously disarrayed hair. "Where are the vermin? It sounded like they were mauling you."

"Not in here," Zarod said dryly, eyeing the party crasher with frank appraisal.

Keir adopted a cavalier attitude to throw her off their trail. "You must've had a bad nightmare. Or maybe you heard noises outside."

She shook her head, her gaze shifting back and forth as if seeking apparitions in the shadowy crevices of the boxlike room. "I don't think so. I was wide-awake."

"Maybe she's delusional," Zarod whispered in an aside to Keir, his mouth twisted in mimicry of a smile, his eyes dark and heavy-lidded. "You know how the royals interbreed their insanity."

Melena struck an annoyed pose and instilled an edge of defensiveness in her voice. "I heard that, and you can speak directly to me, if you don't mind. I'm not feeble-minded."

The cynicism in Her Highness's voice made him flinch. "Go get your beauty sleep, princess. Tomorrow's going to be a long day. We've got a door to replace." Keir stifled a fake yawn and waved her away.

Shuffling her feet, shifting her gaze, she hesitated in their room several moments longer. Rubbing her arms as if she were freezing, she spoke in a small, hesitant voice. "Do you think I can sleep in here with you? Non-sexually, I mean. Just for tonight. Those noises gave me the willies and I can't stand the thought of going back into my dark chamber alone."

Turning a darkly dangerous gaze on the woman, his voice a rich milk chocolate to the ears, raw sensuality oozed from Zarod. "What makes you think it's less dangerous in here with us, Blondie? We're the scourges of the universe who kidnapped you."

Keir simultaneously longed to kick him and kiss him senseless. Zarod's jealousy wasn't any more fetching now than it had been on T'Laun. How many times did he have to assure the guy he was the only man in the world for him? His heart went out to Melena, so small and hesitant. He couldn't send her into exile. But besides Zarod's mockery, there was the little matter of their nakedness he didn't want her to discover.

So, why was his cock flexing back to life at the thought of the princess seeing him in all his naked glory?

He didn't dare examine the reasons, especially not this moment while perched so precariously on top of such an explosive powder keg.

Zarod seemed in no mood to take prisoners. He was shooting off his mouth before thinking.

Finally Keir said, "Step out of the room for a few and give us a moment to get decent."

Her blonde brows knitted and she gave them an odd look. "Oo-kay."

The moment her backside disappeared from the circle of moonlight that provided the only illumination in the hut, Zarod swore under his breath. "I'm not getting dressed just to satisfy Blondie's tender sensibilities. She'll be perfectly safe in the other room. It's not like she's in a separate hut. Nothing will happen to her."

Keir swallowed a sigh and rose to his feet. He retrieved his pants and stepped into them, tugged them up around his waist and fastened them. Glaring at the dolt, he said, "Fine! I had mistaken you for someone with a heart. I'll just have to go into her room since you don't want her in here."

Zarod's eyes narrowed dangerously, challenge gleaming in them. "You wouldn't dare."

Keir shrugged into his shirt and began to button it. Then he snatched his blanket off the floor and slung it over his shoulder. "Just watch me." With his head held high, he marched away with nary a look back at the fuming pirate. Zarod could stew in his own misery for all he cared.

* * * * *

Seething, Zarod stared at the traitor's retreating back. Fuming, his gut tearing apart with jealousy, he flung a boot across the room. "That's it, desert me for Blondie."

When the boot sailed by Keir's back and slammed into the far wall, he froze. But then he shook his head and disappeared into the shadows.

Cursing the traitor, Zarod lay back on the bed in a huff. His heart ripped to shreds, he was bleeding to death internally.

How could the pirate choose the woman over him? How could he let the wench interrupt their lovemaking and not even show the slightest dismay?

Furious, he punched the blanket, forgetting it covered a hard floor. Pain slammed into his hand and shot up his arm. Grimacing, cursing his stupidity, he waved the injured member in the air.

He lay awake for many hours not finding the silvery moonlight in the least bit consoling. Alone in his misery, the moons looked as cold and forlorn as he felt. They looked as cut off from companionship as he was.

Fitful dreams plagued him through the night as he tossed and turned. Nightmares of Keir with Her Royal Highness tortured him. Several times, he woke up in a cold sweat, fighting the covers, usually losing.

What felt like only seconds later but must have been several hours, as sunbeams danced across Zarod's scorched eyelids, he heard Keir's sarcastic voice ripple across him. "Still sulking?"

Squinting open one aching eyelid against the relentless glare, Zarod frowned at the turncoat who dangled his boot in front of his face. Snatching it from Keir's hand, he threw it against the other wall. "I suppose you and Blondie got it on over there?"

Keir bent over and massaged his forehead with a sigh. "I merely provided comfort, I didn't *sleep* with her."

"I needed comfort, too. Last night was our first night together in ages and you left me hanging. I had to jack myself off after you deserted me." The memory seared him and his cock still ached as he'd pumped it so hard in his fury, he'd made himself sore.

"I wasn't leaving you. I was just being human…"

His soul singing, Zarod relaxed and tied his heavy braids at the nape of his neck. Forcing himself to take a deep breath, he quipped, "Oh, right. A good-hearted *pirate*. Next you'll tell me you're buttering her up so her daddy won't impale you."

Locking gazes with him, Keir squatted and rubbed his knuckles along Zarod's cheek. "As you so like to tell me, many pirates are *good* men. I'm one of them. I don't discriminate against females."

"Congratulations, mate. Once again you win the award for understanding and compassion." Zarod wished he was half the man his mate was and reminded himself how very blessed he was to have his love.

Chapter Four

ဆာ

After dressing and making his way outside, Zarod looked around for Keir. Shaking off the fog that shrouded his thoughts, he tucked his thumbs in his belt loops and regarded the twin suns quizzically. They had arisen on a killer of a new day and he vowed to make a fresh start with Blondie.

If only the woman wasn't so outright exasperating, he might actually be able to tolerate her. Her privileged existence had come to an end—at least to a screeching hiatus.

Instead, he found the reason for his soul-searching. Fascinated by her activity, Zarod felt a bemused smile tug at his lips.

She was single-handedly repairing the hole in the door. Melting the surrounding metal with her taser, she used the most innovative technique he'd ever seen.

Intrigued by her ingenuity, he watched stealthily, not wishing her to notice his presence. He had to give her credit. She was pretty darned good for a woman, a royal at that.

Expecting the heavy work to have worn her out, he was surprised when she ventured back outside. She finished whittling a new arrow that she added to her growing handmade quiver, collected wild berries and roots, baited traps for wild game, and then strolled to the lagoon.

Expecting super princess to fashion a fishing pole or even to dive for fish using her bare hands, he was surprised when she stripped before his eyes, revealing the body of a goddess.

His breath suddenly caught in his throat at the willowy sensuality of her svelte form as he felt himself being drawn into her warmth.

Bloody hell. What was happening to him? He'd never been attracted to a woman before.

Of course, he appreciated a fine, fit physique, as much as anyone. That's all it was. An appreciation of art.

When she waded into the gently lapping water up to the juncture of her legs where it licked her pussy, he was held mesmerized, wondering what it would be like to lap her luscious fruits. When she waded in further so the murky depths rose around her slender waist and her blonde silky hair floated around her lush, pert breasts, his cock flexed.

Frowning, he regarded the burgeoning bulge in his breeches, chafing at their tightness. "Whoa! Down, boy," he ordered, a mass of confusion. "Even if women turned you on, she's way out of your league. At least she thinks so."

The lecture did naught to stop the blood pounding furiously through his veins. He still felt inexplicably vulnerable, as if a freighter raced toward him, and he was too paralyzed to move out of its way.

She must be a siren, luring unsuspecting men to their doom. He'd been unsuspecting all right. Never would he have thought himself vulnerable to her charms.

Captivated, he couldn't tear his gaze from her, as if the siren had cast a magical spell. Who said the princess wasn't magical? He watched her closely for signs of sorcery.

A dreamy expression dawning over her heart-shaped face, she squeezed the tips of her nipples, and licked her lips erotically as she rinsed herself.

Her fingertips danced down her belly, to her wiry curls, then dipped mouthwateringly lower. Whimpering softly, she ran her fingertip in concentric circles over her clit.

Sizzling!

Searing heat flooded his body.

Her moans grew louder, more insistent, and she delved her finger into her pussy. Rocking back and forth, she seemed to really be getting off on her hand. Pure ecstasy washed across her face. Any moment, her juices would mingle with the river.

He no longer cared that his seed seeped unashamedly from his cock or that every nerve in his body was burning with a wild, suffocating need. God help him, but he was horny for the wench. Raw, animal passion surged through him and unable to stand the tight pants a moment longer before they broke his stiff rod, he tore them off.

Stroking himself, he stifled his moans so as not to scare the unsuspecting nymph. A yearning to bury his cock inside that luscious pussy assailed him, made all the more sweetly erotic by being so wickedly forbidden. As wave upon glorious wave of rapture flooded him, he became remotely aware of danger dancing in the wind.

Too late, he noticed the small animals pricking their ears, then fleeing. Too late, he recognized the raunchy stench of the dangerous mammoths that terrorized this world. Only when a ferocious growl ripped through the glen and the monster lunged at the princess, did the clues bring enlightenment.

There was no time to tug on his pants or even to wrap them around his nudity. He dove into the water and grabbed her a split second before the giant, deadly paw swiped the empty space where she had stood petrified mere moments before.

He swam like mad but her weight anchored him down. When the creature grabbed his foot, dragging him underwater, he released her, hoping she could swim to safety.

Unprepared to go underwater, he hadn't taken a breath. Wrestling with the creature, its horrific nails scratching his arms and torso, he fought heroically.

Dazedly aware of blood oozing into the water, he started to lose consciousness. The fight seeped out and blackness overcame him.

* * * * *

Fear catapulted through her. With a sudden, savage burst of anger, Melena cursed her lack of judgment at skinny-dipping alone. The life-and-death struggle was her fault.

Her wildly independent streak had not only landed her in trouble but put Zarod in mortal danger. So what if the warm suns and warm water felt heavenly on her bare skin? So what if the desire to cleanse herself in this paradisiacal lagoon lured her? Her sexual desires had demanded to be appeased, and it wasn't a crime to do so.

Regardless, letting down her guard had been a stupid thing to do.

Brainless, dim-witted, and thick!

Getting on her hands and knees, she groped about for her taser. But it wasn't where she'd left it, hidden under her carefully folded clothing. It looked as if wild animals had thrashed about in her things.

"Stop your hiding or I'll have you melted." Threats worked for her father, although truly, they weren't her style. "Please! I don't have time to play games."

She rose to her feet and when her foot hit something metal, she spun. Sunlight glinted on her taser that lay half-hidden amongst a pile of damp, moldy leaves.

Thanking the goddess, she snatched it up. Aiming it at the ugly mongrel, she prayed the pirate didn't get in the way. "Take this, you filthy sloth."

But when she squeezed the trigger, nothing came out. Not even a hum. Ugh! She throttled an incensed scream rising in her throat. She shouldn't have wasted its energy building the new door. "Great! You wait 'til now to need a recharge."

Furious, without so much as a bow and arrow, much less a taser, she hurled the projectile at the ogre. In the future, she vowed to carry her bow at all times.

When the gun cracked its skull, the monster howled and released the man. Baring filthy fangs, it advanced menacingly.

"Yikes!" Scared witless, she grabbed rocks and sticks and flung them with a fury born of desperation. An excellent marksman, her aim was true and she felled the beast.

Losing no time, she dove underwater to retrieve her would-be savior, grimacing at the irony. The water helped buoy him up, but he was harder to drag once they reached dry ground. She pumped his chest and performed resuscitation until he coughed and water gurgled out of his mouth.

Breathless, gasping for air, she lay on her back, thoroughly exhausted. As she regained her equilibrium, sanity trickled back. She was naked, lying beside a naked, extremely tantalizing pirate.

She knew why she was naked, but why was he? *Hmm…*

Considering how he'd teased her unmercifully, he couldn't have been following her—watching her. He'd probably not seen her, and like her had decided to bathe. Only after the creature had made its presence known had he spied her.

Feeling a treacherous sense of relief that Zarod's breathing returned to a semblance of normalcy, she screamed for Keir to help her carry him to safety.

* * * * *

Weeks had passed since they'd been stranded, and Melena studied Keir under the veil of her thick lashes as he worked tirelessly to provide food and enhance their shelter. A puzzle, he didn't fit the mold for a pirate she had built up in her mind, despite his outward appearance.

He was an honorable, decent man. He hadn't been forced to provide a separate space for her nor was he forced to hunt for her food now, but he did. In general, he had turned out to be a nice man. They both were.

If she was ever to fall in love with one…

Love?

No, no, no, no way!

The Princess of Neteera couldn't possibly fall in love with a lowly, scroungy pirate, no matter how sexy or how nice he was.

Utterly unthinkable!

Besides, she was betrothed to the Prince of Teeran Hauft. They were virtually married. This illegal line of thought, these alien stirrings, were completely, disgracefully disloyal. Although she hadn't chosen him to be her husband, didn't want him as her mate, she had taken a solemn oath.

And her word was platinum.

No matter what, she had pledged her loyalty and she couldn't let him, her father, or her people down.

Not that Keir entertained the least inkling that she couldn't stop watching him, or she quivered whenever he came within fifty feet. He had no notion he'd visited her very erotic dreams every night for weeks.

She frowned. In fact, both men had been perfect gentlemen and neither had threatened her honor. Not that she wasn't happy, but that went against everything she'd ever heard about pirates, everything she'd been raised to believe without question. The dirty scourges didn't only plunder monetary treasure but a woman's treasures, and they'd not laid one finger on her, not even the night she'd begged Keir to stay with her.

The pair was a puzzle indeed. Especially Keir.

Keir laughed at her jokes. He stood closer than necessary whenever circumstance threw them together. His eyes twinkled with stardust when he thought she didn't see him regarding her. And she could swear he quivered whenever they happened to touch.

Zarod regarded her with a smoldering sensuality that sent tantalizing thrills straight to her core. More often than not, his darkly magnetic gaze sent her senses spinning out of control.

What if they were stranded here forever? What if they were never rescued? The niggling thoughts grew louder each time the suns rose and she scratched tick marks on her tree trunk. Fifty-two excruciating days, and no sign of civilization or a rescue team. Fifty-two days of eating the horrid smoked meat and the fruit and berries they'd been able to harvest. Fifty-two days with only her own hand to satisfy her needs.

Keir's warm breath tickled the vulnerable nape of her neck. "Something troubling you, princess?"

Her hand grasped her throat in shocked alarm. "I have a name. Would it hurt you so terribly to use it?" She exhaled slowly as she turned to find him barely kissing distance away. Lifting her lashes slowly, she gazed up at him. Not as tall as his colleague, he was the perfect height for her, his nose level with the top of her head. His lips rested at her eye level and from this distance, they looked ideal, too. Usually she couldn't see them for his full beard, but at this distance, she could see them very clearly.

"Melena." Keir caressed her name as no other had before him. It rolled off his tongue like the richest Synkethian milk chocolate.

Enthralled by his dark, sultry voice, a minute gasp escaped her lips. Craving him with a need that was beyond all logic and reason, a twinge resounded between her legs. It might not hurt him terribly to use her given name, but apparently it made her ache. Too late to take back her foolish request.

Realizing she stared as if he was her last supper, she cursed silently and forced herself to act nonchalant. She was chained by a thousand different prisons and had no right to quiver at his nearness or devour his lips with her gaze. It was too late to act as if everything was sunny when she probably looked as if she were about to go nova, so she confessed to the partial truth. At least he wouldn't hear the wobble of a lie in her voice. "What if we're never rescued?"

Swallowing the lump in her throat, she swept her gaze wide in an all-encompassing arc around the glade where they'd moved their camp. Lifting her chin high, she tried to sound confident, but her voice emerged sounding strangled. "What if we spend the rest of our days on this planet, completely alone except for the three of us?"

Keir raised his hand as if to stroke away the stray wisps of hair from her heated face, but it hovered midair and then dropped limply to his side. "We have to be optimistic. We can't give up hope."

If it were only the two of them, she and Keir, it could be paradise. She would gladly lose herself in their own private rapture. But three? She worried her bottom lip between her teeth. Someone would be the odd man out and that spelled trouble.

Uncomfortable with the force of her building physical need, she camouflaged it with a sarcastic chuckle. "Why?

Shouldn't they have found us by now if they were searching? My people must think me dead from the explosion. They may not have launched any missions of rescue."

Keir slid a finger under her chin and forced her to look him square in the eye. His were murky pools that she could happily drown in given half the chance. "Because we'll go crazy if we give up. Because you're much stronger than that. We're not just going to lie down and die…"

The creatures picked that moment to roar in chorus. Thunder seemed to shake the ground as a herd of wild animals hurtled out of control.

"Look out!" Keir grabbed her to him tightly and they dove to the ground and he rolled several times over, crushing her between him and the rocky terrain.

Dust and dirt flew into her mouth and coated her face. Hacking and choking, she spluttered, 'Those creatures almost stampeded us. If not for you…" She stared in disbelief at the stocky, furry carnivores still dashing past in a mad frenzy. Awed, she mumbled, "You saved my life."

Keir smiled down at her tenderly. "I just have quicker reflexes, having lived on the edge all my days."

Affection curled in her stomach as Keir blushed adorably and veiled his incredibly emotional eyes with the thickest set of lashes she'd ever seen on a man. Nestling closer to her savior, she was in no hurry to move out of the circle of his very warm, very safe arms. She rubbed her cheek against his chest, reveling in his strong heart beating against her. "You're entirely too modest. Many of my guards would have frozen in such a situation. You're quite a man."

Glazed pride flowed through Keir's eyes. Almost as quickly, he blinked it away. "Anyone would have done it. I'm sure you'd have done it for me soon as you had time to react."

Most certainly…as she'd have done for either of her fellow castaways. But she wasn't a pirate.

There was that hateful word again. *Pirate.*

What exactly was a pirate? She'd had a lot of time to ponder that dilemma over the past several weeks. He'd wrecked her preconceived notions. She supposed there was such a thing as a good pirate. Keir and Zarod were her proof.

"You're very special and I won't believe otherwise, no matter how modest you are." He was so refreshing. Most men would have strutted their accomplishments before her to gain favor of one kind or another. This man wouldn't dream of it.

Unless he saw no need because he secretly believed they would spend their future here. No one cared, so why should she?

She had a captive audience. He'd played rescuer to her twice now, and still he hadn't so much as kissed her. Time for the fairy tale to change and the damsel to kiss the handsome, if reticent, hero.

So, why didn't he kiss her? This was the opportune moment. The hero always chose a romantic moment like this to kiss the heroine.

It was a shame to let such a beautiful moment slip away. Reaching up, she strained her body against his and slashed her lips over his. His lips intoxicated her and she longed for more so she moved her lips over his and curled her arms around his neck, pulling down his head.

Sweetly, his lips moved against hers, tentatively at first, and then with more zeal. Against her lips, he murmured, "You know I've never kissed a princess before."

Urgent need building, she arched up to kiss him again. Laughter bubbling to her lips, she smiled against his. "Then we're even. I've never kissed a pirate. Looks like I've really been missing something extraordinary."

"Same here." He dipped his head lower and plundered her lips, stealing her breath. His hands explored her breasts, then roamed lower to the swell of her hips, making her heart palpitate.

She opened her mouth wider, eager to surrender completely. Entwining her hands in his beautiful hair, she clung to him with an abandon she'd never felt before, ready to grant his every desire.

Then another rumble broke through the smoky haze, and clouded her good sense. At first, she couldn't identify it, then a pair of booted feet stomped in front of her face and their owner cleared his throat again.

Squinting up, she stared into Zarod's pinched, belligerent features. His feet at parade rest, his fists balled up on his hips, his brows knitted together, he was the most fearsome warrior she'd ever gazed upon.

"What's going on here?" The slight breeze tossed Zarod's braids, pushing several across his dangerously narrowed eyes.

Keir pulled away from her so fast, she reeled back, bumping her head on the hard ground. Bemused, she wondered why Keir looked so spooked. It wasn't as if they'd been caught naked, in the act of making love. Perhaps in a few more minutes, if not for the untimely interruption…

Angry at Zarod's bad timing, she scowled. "I was just showing my gratitude to Keir for saving my life."

Zarod's countenance darkened and growling, he marched up to her. "You didn't show me such gratitude when I saved your life."

Keir's shocked glance bounced back and forth between them. As if an afterthought, Keir stretched out a hand and hoisted her up. But his touch was very sterile, very cold, as if they'd never shared jokes, much less such feverish kisses.

Zarod must be jealous. Guilt niggled. Was it her fault a rift existed between the captain and his mate? Both men apparently wanted her but only one could win.

Or was she dreaming this evening? Most of her dreams were deliriously happy. In her naughtiest, darkest fantasies, the three of them lived happily ever after…

Shocked, shaking herself, she pulled short her extremely wayward musings.

The three of them…

But who else would ever know? It was just the three of them against a harsh, uncaring universe.

What of her fiancé? Most certainly she owed him her allegiance.

But she wasn't cut out for abstinence. Not when her blood simmered at just the thought of the very virile men bedding down in the chamber next to hers.

She knew without a doubt that she wouldn't turn either man away should he steal into her chamber some sultry night. Both were incredibly fine male specimens. Both made her blood boil.

Problem solved!

What a weight lifted off her shoulders. The men would just have to share her. Surely, they would find that far preferable to one of them becoming a monk.

Squirming, her thoughts made her hot. Her pussy tingled and her juices flowed. If their cocks were half as luscious as the rest of their awesome bodies, she'd be the luckiest woman throughout eternity. The thought of two huge cocks fucking her made her quake.

So hot, she longed to strip right here and ravage them. It took all her control to rein in her wild emotions.

This would work so much better if she led them to believe a ménage was their choice, that they had overwhelmed her with their raw sexual magnetism into being so lustful she'd fulfill their every desire.

Exploring her wanton fantasies with climbing anticipation, she had to bite down on a sneaky smile.

Soon, heaven would be hers.

Chapter Five

𝒮𝒪

Jealousy, hot and raw, slammed into Zarod, reeling him backward. But it wasn't a straightforward, simple jealousy at finding his lover succumbing to the siren's charms. As much as that sliced his heart to shreds, he could understand it.

With every fiber of his being, he'd wanted to haul Melena out of Keir's arms and kiss her senseless while conversely he'd wanted to tear Keir from her arms and bed him.

Nuts!

Noodling the crazy problem, he pronounced himself certifiable.

Exile on this rock had affected him. In turmoil, he rounded on Keir who knew better than to cheat. "You lied." Seething, sickened at the betrayal, he didn't think he could feel much worse if he'd caught them making love. A few moments later and he most assuredly would have.

Keir's gestures screamed impatience as he marched up to him, opened his mouth and then shut it without uttering a word. Ruddier than normal, the pirate's face was almost scarlet. Even the tips of his ears were turning purple. "*She* kissed *me*, in case you didn't hear."

He'd heard but it didn't change anything. "Incidental. You were kissing her back." He almost choked on the force of his fury and damned his hateful jealousy.

Melena stepped between them. "Tempers, gentlemen. Screaming accusations won't solve anything. Let's discuss this calmly and rationally."

No longer in the mood for her touch, for tenderness of any sort, Zarod gritted his teeth. "I tried discussing it, but it doesn't work with a thick-headed numbskull who's telling bald-faced lies."

Keir's muscles tensed and his hands fisted. "I've never lied to you. I would never lie to you and I don't appreciate your unfounded accusations."

Zarod gaped in disbelief. "I just caught you rutting around like a pair of cats."

"Fine! Believe the worst if it makes you feel better. But stay out of my face." Keir spun on his boot heel to march off.

Melena grasped his wrist tightly and held it. "Gentlemen! We can't afford to divide ranks. It's just the three of us against this hostile world. We need one another to survive."

Zarod snarled as guilt flooded her lovely, pleading eyes. He wasn't sure this wretched existence merited survival.

Melena bit her lips. "Look. I know this is an extremely awkward situation, two men and only one woman."

Zarod narrowed his eyes. She didn't know the half of it.

"Ideally, there should be another female so we could pair off in couples, but it's highly unlikely another will just drop out of the sky…"

Her words hung heavy on the stagnant air, shocking him. Blinking, he stared, his stunned expression most certainly mimicking that of Keir's. Chancing a glimpse at his estranged mate, he confirmed his suspicions. Keir felt just as astonished.

Unable to keep the inner devil in check, he drawled, "You mean boy-girl, boy-girl? Or boy-boy, girl-girl?"

It was Melena's turn to blink, which she did profusely. Slowly, questions dawned in her widening eyes.

Keir slung him a disgusted look. "Always the delicate, thoughtful one, aren't you, mate?"

Zarod had always taken perverse pleasure in shock value. Besides, he was tired of pussyfooting around, hiding his true identity. "If 'delicate' is another term for 'lying', no, I'm not delicate. I'm honest."

He threw out the challenge for Keir to own up and reveal the truth. Even if he chose the siren over him, the woman deserved to know the whole truth first. No lasting, honest relationship could thrive on lies. Whether she knew it or not, he was doing her a favor by lancing their festering secret.

Melena's gaze slid from him to Keir, then back. Wringing her hands together, gazing unblinkingly into his eyes, she asked, "Boy-boy? You mean you...and *him*..." She tilted her sunny head at Keir with emphasis. "You mean you weren't jealous over *me*. You were jealous over *him*?"

A twinge of sadness struck him that he and his honesty were the source of the pain shining in her eyes. Yet, the alternative, lying, was unpalatable. Commiserating with her, well acquainted with jealousy and heartache, he nodded somberly. "Yes. We've been a couple for several years."

The pain multiplied in her expressive eyes. Veiling her lashes, she bent her head and seemed to find her feet extremely fascinating. "I've been so blind, so unperceptive. No wonder you didn't ravage me. I thought you were both such gentlemen. I thought..."

Sniffing back tears pooling in her beautiful eyes, she gave them both piteous looks. Ineffectually swiping at the tears sliding down her cheeks with her fingertips, she choked back a sob. "It doesn't matter what I thought. I never would have meddled in the middle had I known."

Zarod scowled, knowing that as the truthful one, his way would have been far kinder had Keir gone along. He tossed an I-told-you-so glance at the lying cheat. "I hope you're happy now."

*   *   *   *   *

Detesting weak women who cried in front of others, Melena turned her back on the happy couple and left the scene of the crime. Her heart breaking, she replayed the events since crash-landing on this inhospitable place.

All the clues fell into place. If she'd had her eyes and ears open, she should have picked up on them.

The secret glances the pirates exchanged all the time.

Their excessively "gentlemanly" behavior.

They shared a room even though she had a private suite…

Oh yeah. She had been blind and deaf.

That night she thought they were being attacked inside their new dwelling hadn't been an attack at all. They'd been screaming in bed, probably in ecstasy and definitely not in terror.

"Oh goddess! I've been so obtuse. Why didn't you let me see? Why'd you let me fall so desperately in love with him?"

No answer boomed down from the heavens. The goddess probably couldn't find her on this lost planet at the end of the universe, either. She was well and truly alone.

Keir's heart belonged to Zarod and Zarod's to Keir. No one wanted her heart, not even her official fiancé. By now, he'd most assuredly wed another diplomatic gem — probably her cousin Kinyo who'd had a greedy eye on her crown for as long as she could recall. Not that she truly cared beyond hoping it sealed peace in their quadrant. Maybe fate had stepped in and made a real love match for him. That would make two happy couples and still leave her odd woman out.

"Melena!" Keir's anguished voice prodded her forward faster, deeper into the glen and off the known path.

Unable to look upon him without choking up, she preferred her own company until she got a grip on her gushing emotions. The dense brush provided the privacy she so desperately craved.

She did her best to drown out Keir's voice but had about as much luck as she did drowning the fiery ache in her heart. Finally, his voice dimmed and then faded. If only the throbbing ache inside would dull.

She walked for hours, dizzy from going in circles in her mind. The only thing that made sense was that she was a fool—the home-wrecking other woman—uh, person.

No wonder love triangles had such scandalous reputations. Protected, locked in a glass cage most of her life, she'd never dreamed she'd get sucked into one. And never one so impossible. She was surprised when the first sun began to set. It must have been hours since she'd last eaten, but she didn't feel the least bit hungry. As if her stomach read her mind, it grumbled rudely.

"Oh, hush up." Food didn't sound appetizing. Nothing did right now except maybe fine, aged, amber wine so she could forget the pain in its golden depths. If she could, she'd swim in it.

But what good would that do her? So, she'd still be heartbroken, foolish *and* drunk. *And lost.*

She retraced her steps as best as she could but she always passed the same lichen-covered tree. When the second sun sunk low in the sky and the dim light cast eerie shadows all about her, she admitted she was well and truly lost.

Rubbing her arms briskly against the merciless chill wind, she chuckled wryly, "Well, guess I'll get my wish never to see those blasted pirates again."

On the one hand, she had no desire to see their faces. But as the only other humans on this rock, she longed for their companionship. Totally platonic, of course. She was no home-wrecker. Nor did she want her heart completely ripped from her chest and shattered. It was battered enough from their sweet encounters. Obviously, she'd read too much into the men's friendship.

Never before had she grown so close to any man. Of course, she'd never been permitted such access to any man, in order to develop a serious attachment. Her father had kept her on the mantel like a prized, but oft-ignored, porcelain doll. Everyone looked. Most admired. But only the foolhardy dared touch. Everyone was scared to leave a smudge on her pristine countenance, most of all herself.

How ironic! She scrunched her nose. When she finally broke free from her gilded chains and kissed the handsome man of her choosing instead of some stuffy prince, he turned into a frog. He belonged to someone else. His heart was already taken. The best she could hope for was friendship, maybe a few stolen kisses.

But she wouldn't be content to sneak around behind Zarod's back, to steal moments here and there. She longed for a real, committed relationship, something she'd never been destined for. At least with Prince Gallakin, there'd been a slim hope they could have grown to love one another, to have a family.

As long as they were marooned on this boulder floating in space, she stood no chance of achieving her dearest desires. Devoid of love and sex, she would dry up and turn to dust. One touch from this most inappropriate man had set her aflame.

The forest grew eerier as the light faded and the night creatures began their ferocious rumblings. It was suicide to ramble about in the dark, most probably straight into the fearsome creature's ravenous maw, so she hunkered down in a mangrove and pulled large palm-type leaves over her as makeshift blankets. Unless forced to flee, she wouldn't budge until both suns climbed high in the sky.

* * * * *

Zarod was going out of his mind with worry. A basically levelheaded soul, Melena knew how very perilous the outdoors became after dark. He figured she'd sulk for a while but return in time to observe safety precautions. He'd almost forgotten she was an illogical woman with legendary capacity to drive men wild with worry, as well as desire.

Disheveled and sullen, Keir dragged into camp. "I lost her trail. Did she show up yet?"

"No." Zarod still nursed hard feelings toward the man. Unfortunately, they had to team up to find the princess, to survive, so he bit down on the growl rising in his throat. Steeling himself against Keir's magical touch, he stuck out his hand to shake on it. "Cease-fire? Let's find our princess and bring her home."

Keir regarded him suspiciously at first and then with a ray of hope flickering across his brightening gaze. "Does this mean we're back to normal?"

Zarod withdrew his hand and pulled himself up to his full height. "We're *talking* and banding together to find the lost member of our group. That's all I can deal with right now."

Keir pursed his lips and clapped his shoulder. "We'll find her and then set things right."

Too bad he didn't share Keir's optimism. Trust was so very easy to lose but took a long time to build, and even longer to be rebuilt. Unable to promise, he just grunted.

Truthfully, he hoped it could be done, particularly if they were destined to live out their lives here.

"We'll cover more ground if we split up. She was headed southwest. I'll take this path. You take that one." Keir pointed him at the less-traveled path.

"Be careful." Despite his anger, concern filled him. By venturing out in the dark, they risked becoming the beast's fast-food meal.

Keir turned and flashed a tremulous smile. "For what it's worth, I love you."

The words "I love you" stuck in Zarod's throat but they reverberated in his tattered heart. "Good luck. Send the signal if you find her."

Keir clicked his heels and saluted sharply. "Will do."

The creatures began howling in earnest, sending shivers up his spine. "They're having a God-damned convention." When they got the princess back to safety, the first thing he was going to do was to spank her royal fanny.

Quivers chased away the shivers. He grew steamy at the thought of putting his hands all over her cute behind. Try as hard as he could, he couldn't erase the erotic vision.

* * * * *

Keir stumbled upon a pack of the hairy beasts. Cursing his bad luck, he hid in the bushes, hoping the wind didn't shift so they could pick up his scent. Of course, it would be amazing if they could smell anything over their horrible stench. Nothing, not even the Kolekas on Seti IV, smelled so horribly disgusting.

Keir's muscles kinked under the strain of sitting rigidly still. Finally, the herd moved on and he breathed a sigh of relief.

He followed her trail with the aid of the dim moonlight, and this time, he picked up the clues he'd missed before. But when he came full circle without finding her, he swore. Where could she have gone? Unless something picked her up.

Too horrible to contemplate, he focused on what he wanted to say once he found her. What he wanted to do.

Emotions battled inside him. He wanted to yell at her all the while he longed to kiss her senseless. He wanted to take her in his arms and never let her go. Fat chance she'd let him now. Zarod, either.

If things kept up like this, they'd be the most dejected souls in the cosmos. They couldn't go on without speaking, without looking at one another, without working together to survive. How mad would he go if they exiled him?

The clouds shifted, letting silvery moonlight shower down on the forest. And there before him stood Melena bathed in the ethereal light, like an angel.

Blinking, he thought he was dreaming. Or perhaps it was her ghost…

No! His breath stuck in his chest as he stared at the lovely, if disheveled, vision. He might be a little warped, but she couldn't be a ghost. He couldn't have lost her.

Still, he wasn't sure.

Moonbeams shimmered around her, casting an eerie glow. Afraid to spook her into fleeing again, he smiled gently and held out his hand for her to take. "I'm sorry, Melena. I never meant for you to find out that way, for anything to grow between us…"

Her eyes incredibly wide in her waiflike face, her gaze drank him in. Her lips moved but no sound came out at first.

Then she spoke so low he had to take a step forward to hear her.

"So, I imagined your feelings for me? I misread you..."

She blinked back the moisture making her eyes glassy. She gulped and gazed heavenward as if searching for answers. "Goddess, but I'm a fool. I truly believed you returned my feelings. How could I be so wrong?"

Pure heartache gleamed in the gaze she turned on him, breaking his severely bruised heart. He closed the gap between them and brushed the tears from her pale cheeks with his thumbs. Gazing down upon her lovely face, he closed his eyes and let his heart speak. "You didn't misread me."

Surprise flickered across her face and she scrutinized him closely, but didn't flinch from his touch. The tip of her pink tongue peeked out and traced her lips. "But Zarod... I thought you loved him?"

Keir searched his heart even as he was compelled to kiss the tears from her cheeks. "I do."

She drew back a pace, misgiving shielding her eyes again. "I don't understand. How can you love him *and* love me?"

Keir sighed and pulled her against him, heart to heart. Stroking her silky hair that cascaded over her shoulders like a polished waterfall of honey, he gentled her as he would a wild colt. Against her soft, warm cheek, he murmured, "I don't understand it, either. I only know I love you desperately." On a long shuddering breath, he also admitted, "And I love him desperately. I want you both, I need you with all my heart and soul."

Trembling, she leaned against him and her arms crept around his waist. Her ear against his hammering heart, she murmured, "Do you know how impossible this is? I'm not a magician. I can't slice you down the middle and keep half." A ragged sigh rushed out in a whoosh as she ventured on. "Nor can I just give you up—not as long as we're constantly thrown together here."

Her hands clenched his shirt and her voice lowered another decibel. "How am I supposed to lie alone in my bed night after night listening to you making love with him? Please explain it. Or will you take mercy on me and build a separate hut across the compound so at least I don't have to hear your lovemaking?"

She was right. This was totally impossible. If only he could go back to the beginning and take it all back... First and foremost, they wouldn't board her ship. But even if they had, he wouldn't allow tender feelings for her to develop. He'd remain cold and aloof and keep contact minimal.

But, of course, he couldn't travel back in time any more than he could get them off this world or change his heart. Even if he went back in time, he'd surely fall in love with this adorable woman again no matter how pristine his intentions.

Heat flared in places it had no business flaring, and his breath caught in his throat every time he gazed upon her loveliness. This was his—their—destiny.

His heart bursting with love, he cradled her against him, rocking gently back on his heels, he vowed to make this right for all of them. "I won't let that happen. Promise."

"If only you could." A quaver rang in her voice and his shirt became damp again.

Cursing this damned situation, he lifted her chin gently to prove how much he meant it. Damn. He could get lost in the depths of her amazing eyes. Lowering his head, he tasted of her lips.

She remained frigid at first but as he poured all his love into his caress, she began to move against him and then parted her mouth. They drank deeply of one another, losing track of time and their surroundings.

Then footsteps broke through the heady fog, moments before a discreet cough sounded mere feet away. "This is getting to be a bad habit," Zarod drawled, his countenance stormy.

Gasping, Melena tore herself from Keir's arms and jumped back, the feral gleam returning to her eyes. "Impossible, you mean."

"You could have at least let me know she was safe." With a dangerous glint in his eyes, Zarod shoved Keir so he stumbled back into a bush.

"So I was relieved to find her, things got out of hand. I'm human." Incensed, gnashing his teeth, Keir bounded to his feet. They circled each other warily before he shoved Zarod.

The other man stumbled back a couple of paces and steadied himself against a giant oak tree. "You make too lightly of this. You always have an excuse. At least, you could have sent the signal, instead of letting me go out of my mind with worry."

Zarod made a valid point. He should have been more sensitive to his feelings. It's just that his senses were so full of Melena. "You're right, mate. I should have sent the signal. It was wrong of me not to."

Annoyance and relief warring in his eyes, Zarod blushed and shoveled his fingers through his hair. "I should spank first you, then her, for worrying me to death." He glanced about him nervously. "And for endangering yourselves making out in the open like this. If I didn't know better, I'd think someone was manipulating you with the black magic."

Melena tilted her chin impishly, exposing the inviting ivory column of her throat and chuckled dryly. "Spank me? No one's ever spanked me."

"Too bad, Blondie. You might find you like it. Maybe you wouldn't be so spoiled…"

"Spoiled?" She wiggled her brows.

"You heard right. Palaces. Servants. Oceans of latinum. Everything your spoiled little heart desires."

Keir folded his arms across his chest and tried to stifle the laughter bubbling up. When Melena blinked back more tears, his amusement faded and he swore silently.

"Believe me, I don't get everything my heart desires. Not nearly so." Melena shielded her gaze with her sooty lashes as bright splotches blossomed on her cheeks.

The creatures picked that moment to roar and shake the ground.

"Let's continue this back at the ranch." Keir scanned the shadows for signs of company. He held his hand out to the princess, willing her to take it. "You must be chilled."

She nodded and slipped her hand in his. Then she held out the other to Zarod with a dare lighting her eyes. Tilting up her lips to his, she quipped, "What do you say we kiss and make up?"

"Make peace, not war?" Zarod slid a sidelong glance at Keir and lifted a challenging brow. He bent low and slashed his lips against Melena's, and then, without warning, he pulled her into his arms and drank his fill.

Awed, bemused, and entirely, powerfully jealous, Keir just stared, feeling the odd man out. Melena was right, this was impossible. How were they going to get past this?

Chapter Six

ॐ

"So, we're here. Home, sweet home." Trying to contain her nervous fidgeting, Melena curled her fingers and dug her ragged, very unprincesslike nails into her palms. The sharp sting helped to keep her grounded in reality. With all the testosterone flying about the tiny chamber, it was most difficult to keep her wits.

Zarod flexed his fingers and his naughty gaze raked over them. "I still say you both deserve a sound spanking. You, Blondie, for running away and endangering all of us, and you for not signaling me when you found her."

Flushed, Keir bolted upright. "I was too busy..."

Zarod's brow shot up. "Making out. I saw," he said wryly.

"You're the one with the spanking fetish," Keir drawled.

Violently coughing, Melena almost choked. Clutching her throat, she tried to clear her strangled airway.

Keir thumped her on the back as his eyes filled with a protective sparkle. "You going to live?"

Zarod cracked a broad, devilish grin. "Obviously, Blondie has no fetishes. I bet she has no wild fantasies, either."

Rounding on her tempting tormentor, Melena stood toe to toe with him, craning her neck to gaze up at him. "I have fantasies. Why does everyone insist on treating me like some emotionless china doll? Melena has a brain. Melena has feelings. Melena craves love like every other person."

"Melena talks about herself in the third person." Zarod laughed uproariously, holding his stomach and doubling over.

Annoyance boiled over and she gritted her teeth. His teasing had gotten out of hand and she wanted to wipe the smirk off his handsome face. He might have trouble getting serious, but she was dead serious about it. "Stop patronizing me. I'm so tired of being labeled and pigeonholed."

Zarod stroked his chin as if in deep thought, and then his smile turned wistfully apologetic. "Princesses don't corner the market on being misunderstood. Try being a pirate. *A kidnapping, marauding pirate.*"

Judge not lest ye be judged. The ominous words tolled through her head. Biting her tongue, she recalled her earlier unfair accusations. She'd been myopic. His plight had never occurred to her, and she felt rotten. "Touché."

"So let's just be *people*, plain and ordinary. No princesses. No pirates. Let's start over." Keir unbraided his beard and began combing it out. When he hit a snag, he winced.

"Here, let me help." She'd been dying to sift her fingers through his silky beard but hadn't dared. Now she trembled with anticipation as she knelt by his side.

Keir shot a triumphant gaze to Zarod as he lifted his chin to her. "Go easy on me, darlin'. Let your fingers work their special magic."

Ooh! The double-entendre in his ruggedly sexy voice made her quiver with an all-consuming lust. How she wished!

"Plain, ordinary people." Zarod nodded and joined them on the bed. He kneaded her shoulders with his strong, warm hands. Pressing against her back, his heat seeping into her, his hot lips seared her sensitive ear lobe. "Truce, darlin'?"

Barely able to drag in a breath her chest was so full of warm, tingly emotions, she nodded. "Truce."

"What are they?"

Breathless, on fire, she could scarcely speak. "They?"

"Your most sinfully sexy fantasies. Your most dearly held desires." Zarod nibbled her ear and then dipped his tongue into the canal, making her shiver.

"'Fess up, darlin'." Keir ran a sensual fingertip over her lower lip. "Everyone has them and you allege to be as human as the rest of us."

She quivered with lust, remembering her recurring fantasy to be sandwiched between the two pirates, to be fucked by both simultaneously until she begged for mercy. But it was one thing to dream and quite another to speak it aloud, especially to this dodgy pair. "You first."

Zarod bit her ear harder. "Uh-uh. We asked you first."

Caught off-guard, she yelped. The pressure of his hands held her in place when she would have moved away.

Keir leaned forward and replaced his fingers with his tongue. "Go on," he murmured against her lips. "We're extremely unshockable."

Would they be repulsed or turned on by her most erotic, carnal fantasy? Closing her eyes against the rush of heavy sensations bombarding her, she tasted Keir's scrumptious lips before revealing herself.

Behind her, Zarod licked his way to the nape of her neck to an erogenous zone she hadn't known existed, sending tremors of delight cascading through her. His hands grew bolder as well, creeping around to her front, grazing the slope of her breasts.

Feverish, already well on the way to realizing her fantasy, she wondered if they were mind readers. "This.

Making love to both of you at once. Being ravished by you, having your big, juicy cocks fuck me at the same time."

She opened her eyes and stared dreamily into Keir's eyes as Zarod kneaded the tightening buds of her aching nipples. "Are you scandalized?"

Rapture flooded her as Zarod's hands adored her. Moaning against Keir's mouth, she plundered his lips and drank deeply.

Keir drew back and gazed at her. "Not at all. Just disappointed."

Huh? Taken aback, she blinked. Saddened she repeated dumbly, "Disappointed?"

Keir nodded emphatically and his devilish dimple came out to play. "That you didn't let us in on it a long time ago. We would have invited you into our bed and feasted on you."

Overjoyed, on fire, she squirmed, eager to enact her most cherished desires. To be feasted on by two such scrumptious men... *Yum!* "And I on you."

She wondered if their cocks had different flavors, different scents. If they would both fit inside her at once?

She yearned to find out. In heat, her pussy quivering, she purred. "It's sweltering in here. Do we really, truly need all these clothes on?"

"If you insist." Keir tugged off her skirt as Zarod lifted her shirt over her head and tossed it to the end of the bed.

Then Keir tore off his breeches, releasing a long velvety, throbbing shaft that glistened with his juices.

Her mouth watered and her juices flowed, lubricating her pussy. Longing to touch his enticing cock, she lifted a hesitant hand. "So hot." So luscious. She yearned to feel it pounding into her, the rougher the better.

Zarod kicked off his pants and slid his very thick, pulsing cock down her spine and along the crack of her behind to her anus. One hand curled around her waist while the other skimmed her side down to her pussy and delved inside her slit. "Oh yeah. You're ready for us."

Us. Melena trembled, still marveling that her most cherished fantasy was being acted out.

Keir rubbed his cock over her stomach and then brushed against her pussy. "I know you want two cocks at once, but let us lubricate ourselves first."

A giant mass of quivers, she nodded. She had never yearned for anything more in her life than to be filled by not just one, but two giant cocks. Ravenous as she was, she could make the ultimate sacrifice of being filled by one cock at a time—to start.

Keir laid her gently but masterfully on her back and spread her legs wide. Plunging inside, he groaned in ecstasy. "You're so very wet. So extremely tight."

"You're so incredibly large."

Keir clasped her hand in his, squeezing it. "You're absolutely fantastic. We'll get so addicted, we'll never want to get out of bed."

Keir filled her completely. Her pleasure increased exponentially with each stroke.

The most wonderful sensations beyond her wildest imagination flooded her, as if she'd never made love before.

As Keir's rhythm increased, her fever raged out of control. Her heart was so very full, she was amazed it didn't pop out of her chest. Flexing her inner walls, she milked his seed greedily, only now remembering they weren't using any form of birth control.

Oh no! Unprotected, she could conceive.

But her worry evaporated almost instantaneously. She wanted babies. Lots of them. They had no birth control here and she had no intention of abstaining from sex or love. Now that she'd tasted it, she was addicted. She craved more cock, more mind-numbing kisses, but most of all, more of this exhilaratingly glorious emotion called love.

Zarod brought his cock to her lips and prodded it against her teeth. His eyes were full of rascally promise. "Suck on me, darlin'."

Eager for her first taste, she feathered a kiss over the so-enticing tip. "So salty." Truly an enigma, his cock was so very hard and soft all at once.

"You like?" Zarod swiveled his hips in front of her face so his magnificent braids danced around his waist.

"I *love* it," she murmured huskily. She licked her way down the top and up the velvety underside. Opening her mouth wide, she took him deep inside. More luscious than ice cream.

She almost swooned. Two glorious cocks fucked her. Two virile men ached for her, cherished her, and were treating her like a goddess. No prince could compare to her two sexy pirates.

Losing herself in the sensations, she gave in to every wanton desire. Too soon, the fireworks consumed her, each explosion more thrilling than the last.

Clinging to Keir, she milked him for every last drop of his precious seed.

Breathing heavily, Keir pulled out inch by excruciating inch. He kissed her beaded nipple and then lay beside her, gazing dreamily. "You're a fast learner."

"I have excellent teachers."

Zarod quivered and shot his seed deep inside her. Then he gathered her into his arms and stroked her back. "*Lovers.*"

"Lovers…" she repeated dreamily as they held each other for countless moments, perfectly in tune.

Sometime later, Zarod asked huskily, punctuating each word with kisses over her nipples, "Ready for round two?"

Her greedy pussy tingled and she nodded in eagerness. For so long she'd dreamed of this moment and now that her wanton ménage was reality, it was exceptionally better.

"I've been ready for just about forever. Love me."

"I'll never stop."

"*We'll* never stop," Keir corrected.

She hoped he wasn't making promises he couldn't keep. Charmers both, they knew all the pretty endearments to murmur in her ear. Lovers, they had all the right moves. But were they sincere in a forever kind of way?

Forever…

It seemed they were trapped in this goddess-forsaken place evermore.

Trapped?

How could her own private paradise fantasy be a trap? The royal palace had been her cage. Here she knew boundless freedom and joy beyond her wildest imagination. Here she could follow her heart.

Bereft without a big cock to complete her, she wrapped her fingers around Zarod's thick rod and tugged it gently toward her pussy. "Love me."

"You can talk dirty to us, you know." Zarod's voice filled with warmth. "Climb on top of me and he'll get behind you for the fuck of your life. I'm rested up and ready for more loving."

Up, he certainly was. Extremely erect and succulently turgid.

She straddled Zarod and hovered over his large knob. Gyrating her hips, she rubbed it with her velvety lips.

"Now who's the tease?" Zarod regarded her quizzically.

Melena couldn't hold out. She slid down its hot length. She was so very full. He was so extremely wonderful. He completed her to perfection.

"My turn. It'll be tight, but that's the best way." Keir eased himself inside from the rear and then stroked with a rough tenderness that stole her breath.

The two cocks drove her to a frenzy, rocking her. Only a thin membrane separated them, and together they thrilled her, fulfilling her most decadent, stimulating fantasies.

Mindless with rapture, she absorbed their seed. Sated at last, wrapped in their dizzying earthy scent, she dozed off snuggled between them.

When she awoke, chill air brushed her flesh. The men had relinquished her. Holding their memories close, she hugged herself.

Hearing them close by, she rolled onto her side to witness a very sensual, spine-tingling kiss as Zarod mounted Keir. Her mouth watered and her pussy tingled as Zarod's beautiful cock thrust into Keir's well-sculpted ass. First the head and then the shaft disappeared from her view, then it pulled out almost to the tip. Rosy red blood pumped through it furiously as it plunged back in.

Keir's cock was full and erect as well, hanging heavily between his legs. Droplets of his juice clung invitingly to the tip.

Insatiable, she yearned for more. Relief flooded her. Instead of being jealous of their union, she was so hot from the sight, she was ready to come again.

Zarod caressed Keir's balls so tenderly, Keir moaned. "Oh yes!" With a final thrust, Zarod held Keir's ass firmly and quivered uncontrollably.

Writhing, her legs spread wide, Melena massaged her clit until she joined her lovers in exquisite ecstasy.

Chapter Seven

๛

They made love morning, afternoon and night.

Melena was always hot, perpetually ready to make love. She stopped wearing her undergarments and often shunned her top, especially when she wanted to signal the men she was hot for them, which was the majority of the time.

She patted her still-flat belly in blissful awe. In a few short months, her stomach would be swollen with her baby, and after the child was born, she would have to practice modesty for his or her sake. For now, however, she wanted to enjoy complete freedom.

Maternal instincts cocooning her, she tended a garden. No longer would they have to brave inclement weather to gather nuts and berries. She had also started a fish farm and raised some small animals. Her child would never know starvation.

On the sly, she sewed infant- and toddler-sized garments. She hid them in her trunk until such time as she felt the men were prepared to hear the happy news they were to be fathers.

At least, she hoped they'd be happy. They'd never broached the subject of babies or parenthood. But both were bright, perceptive men who surely realized they were virile and of breeding age and had no birth control at their disposal. As much as they had filled her with their seed, it was inevitable it would take root.

They *shouldn't* be surprised, but that didn't mean they wouldn't be surprised or unhappy. After all, they were men.

Then there was the little matter of not knowing which man had actually fathered the child. Since both fucked her daily, she couldn't pinpoint a precise day.

Not that she cared. She loved both men with all her heart and soul. The three were a family. They would both make fantastic fathers. The biology made no difference.

"Good hunting today," Keir said as he unloaded the day's kill by the smoking hut where they cured the meat and tanned the hides.

Turned on by his sultry voice, she wiggled her ass in the air. The skirt bunched around her waist, revealing her treasures.

Primitive growls rose in Keir's throat. "Is this an invitation?"

She purred as she tossed a come-hither look over her shoulder. "You know you have an open invitation. At least, you should know by now."

He tore off his pants and plunged into her. "You grow more beautiful daily. You're positively glowing."

His cock was so thick and hard, she screamed in ecstasy. "Of course I glow. I'm the luckiest woman in the universe." Silently, she added, expectant mothers always glow.

* * * * *

Keir loved fucking Melena. He couldn't get his fill. She was such a sensual siren. She was also an enigma, especially when keeping mum about her condition.

He recognized the signs of impending motherhood. He'd be blind not to. The heightened nurturing and nesting instincts. The burgeoning lushness of her body, especially her swelling breasts. The way she glowed. Her increased appetites.

He wanted her to feel free to confide in him, so he dropped hints to let her know he was okay with her pregnancy without stealing her joy in making the announcement. He couldn't wait to hold their baby. He and Zarod had longed to become parents but never dreamed it could be this special. They'd discussed hiring a surrogate, and that would have meant the birth mother wouldn't be a permanent part of their child's life.

Fate had had a much better plan in waiting. Being marooned was the best thing that had ever happened to them.

"Harder!" Melena screamed, grinding her hips against his. "Faster!"

Gratefully, he complied, his cock driving incredibly deep.

Panting heavily, Zarod loped up. When he stopped just short of them, he held his gut. "Several space ships just landed over the ridge."

On the brink of orgasm, Keir swore. He couldn't close the floodgates now if he tried. Quivering from the rapture, holding Melena's butt firmly, he drilled her as his seed gushed forth and spasms racked his body.

Moaning, the wanton minx ground her hips against his and tried to stifle her screams.

Zarod disappeared inside the hut and reappeared seconds later with Melena's discarded undergarments and a modest robe. As he helped her dress, he snarled at Keir. "Get dressed, fool. We could have visitors any minute."

* * * * *

Appalled, praying the visitors didn't include her father, she gasped. Rushing to pull up her panties, she struggled to breathe. Pulling in too much air, she feared she'd hyperventilate and hurt the baby.

Settle down, princess.

"Thank God, they haven't killed her. We're just in time." Georges' relieved voice reverberated through her as if in a nightmare. Her former admiral looked ragged and gaunt.

A twinge of guilt assailed her. Had her disappearance affected him so?

To her horror, her father marched into their encampment while Keir's breeches were still around his knees and his cock hung heavy and dripping with their juices. Worse, her chest was still bare as Zarod held out the gown for her to shrug into.

His face turning purple, his lips thinning to the point of disappearing, her sire exploded in a murderous rage. "Melena Marguerite Amelia Androkova, what is the meaning of this indignity? Why are you in this disgraceful state of undress?"

Before she could move her stunned lips, he turned on the men. "This is far worse than death. The scurvy bandits ravaged her. We caught them in the act."

Pointing at Keir, then Zarod, the King commanded, "Apprehend the criminals. Impaling will be too good for the likes of them. Perhaps we should let the royal tigers *toy* with them in the arena."

To Melena he said with only a minimal softening of tone, "For God's sake, cover yourself properly and distance yourself from them."

Pain and concern blended in Georges' expressive eyes. Separating himself from the royal guard, he crossed to her side and draped her modestly with his cape. "The nightmare's over, Your Highness. You're going home."

Home. The cold, barren palace had never been a home. A gilded prison was too generous a description. "*This* is my *home.*"

Her father jutted out his imperial chin. "Your *place* is with your betrothed on Teeran Hauft. Your duty lies in fostering peace in the galaxy."

Place. Duty. Disgustingly cold words that sickened her stomach, and brimmed with guilt.

The creatures began their nightly rumblings as the first sun hovered on the horizon. "On second thought, chain the brigands to the trees and let the beasts feast on them," the king said, sadistic glee flashing in his eyes.

Her heart broke into shards and she tore away from the admiral. Fighting her way to her lovers' sides, she stood in solidarity with them. "No! I won't let you harm them. You'll have to kill me to get to them."

Stealing a taser from the closest guard, she shielded the now-chained men and directed her weapon at the royal brigade, daring them to take one step forward.

All the blood drained from her father's pinched face, aging him a good twenty years. "For the goddess' sake, stand down, daughter. You can't seriously wish to protect your abductors."

"They've brainwashed her," Georges said, offense ringing in his voice. "She's not herself."

Turning a sympathetic gaze on the admiral, she smiled softly. None of this was his fault. She still held a lot of brotherly affection for the man. "On the contrary, I'm finally free to be myself. Gloriously, wonderfully, free."

Georges blanched. "You can't possibly know what you're saying."

Keir lifted his chin defiantly, exuding a more regal air than any member of her family had ever displayed. "She's an amazingly independent, intelligent woman. Give her the credit that's due her."

Pride flooded her. Never had she loved him more than in that instant. She smiled her gratitude and was overjoyed her child would have such a magnificent father.

Zarod snarled, pulling on his chains. "They're begging for me to cast voodoo spells. They'll pay dearly for hurting you."

Her smile widened impishly as she pretended to enjoy his suggestion. When the guards fidgeted, she almost laughed aloud.

Zarod spat at the king's booted feet. "I can shrink their hideous heads if you like. Put them on pointy sticks."

One of the guards wobbled, all blood draining from his milky-white face.

The king marched over to them and glared hatefully at the superstitious man. "Not if you're dangling from the end of a stick, pirate. Your damned soul will forever drift in Purgatory."

"Haunting you." Zarod's darkened eyes narrowed.

"Down, boy," Keir said, shaking his head ever so slightly. "You're not scoring points."

"Why should I want to?"

The king sighed heavily. "Just leave them here and be done with them. I tire of their sarcastic mouths."

"No!" Panicked, Melena gripped the weapon more fiercely and waved it menacingly. She had no choice but to admit the truth about the baby. "You can't kill the father of my child." With high emphasis, she added, "*The royal heir.*"

She glanced at Zarod and Keir, praying the fathers wouldn't hate her for such a blatantly insensitive announcement. She prayed the reality of his grandchild, a royal heir, would soften her father.

A flash of bewilderment flashed across Zarod's face but not Keir's.

The king's features contorted and his gaze darkened dangerously. "How could you disgrace the throne by consorting with a... a pirate?"

Grief rimmed Georges' eyes. "No," he said in a shocked whisper. "I was never good enough for you, but a pirate is?"

Furious at the slur, she thrust out her jaw. "They're *good* men."

"Which one's the father?" Hatred gleamed in the king's eyes.

Why did it matter? She loved both men with all her heart. Pity swelled in her for the lovelorn soldier. Evading Georges' question she said, "Love can't be forced."

"Love?" the king bellowed. "You're not in your right mind. We'll have to pray Prince Gallakin will still accept you in such outrageously soiled condition."

Soiled? She was in the most glorious, wonderful condition of her life. Melena bristled at the blithe assumptions, the horrid insults. "I'm not joining with Gallakin. I'm staying with the father of my child."

Her father exploded. "You can't keep this child! You can't give birth to a pirate's spawn."

Hurt, infuriated, she approached her father with grim determination and acute disappointment. "I will never abort my child. Nor will I give it up for adoption. He's part of me. And he's your grandchild."

"No *pirate* spawn is an heir of mine. He will never ascend to the throne."

Insulted, her heart broke that her father could disown her child so callously, even though the throne meant nothing to her. Squaring her shoulders, sucking in her breath, her gaze dueled with his. "Nor will I. I renounce my claim to the throne."

The king's nostrils flared. "You would let our people down? Your family?"

Keir's lips curled up sardonically. "Like her family let her down? Not just now, but always?"

"Stay out of this, *pirate*. No one wants to hear from you." The king turned his back on Keir as if he was of no more significance than a bug to squish under his boot heel.

Melena stood straighter and prouder. She sliced the men's bonds with a taser blast. "I value their opinion. How dare you barge into our home, bully us around, and insult us? You're out of your jurisdiction. You are not king of this land."

"*You're* my jurisdiction, *daughter*."

"We're a package deal—the baby, myself and these men. You can't have me without accepting them." Challenging her father risked great loss, but then if he was so insensitive, so inflexible, what was she losing? She'd never had his love, only the great burden of being his sole heir. Her cousins would kill for the chance to take the throne. Royal blood ran through their veins, so they could take her place.

"No one threatens me. Not criminals. Not even you. Until you wake up and divorce yourself from these anchors, you're dead to me and to our people. I'm young enough to produce another heir."

Her covetous cousins would be so very disappointed. Pity.

Regret washed through her that yet another child would be subjected to a cold, loveless childhood. But she couldn't control her father now any more than in the past.

"Will you tell our people I died?" Amazingly, Melena wasn't troubled by the notion.

"As of this moment, Princess Melena Marguerite Amelia Androkova is officially deceased." He pierced his guards with a steady gaze. "No one is to speak of this or her name from this moment forward. We will leave one ship, fully equipped with fuel and supplies. Put it in the report as destroyed upon landing."

His expression devoid of any trace of emotion, his gaze carefully avoiding Melena's, Georges nodded and bowed. "Yes, sire."

The king pursed his lips and shook his head. "I hope you won't come to regret your decision. Anyone can be a parent. Not everyone can be a monarch."

Unflinchingly, she stared him in the eye. "Not everyone can be a parent." Fortunately, her child would be blessed with three loving, involved parents who would always support him. That was worth so very much more than all the glittering treasure and intoxicating power her father possessed.

The king arched his bushy gray brows. "If that is your final decision?"

She smiled at her men, hoping they still wanted her and her baby after her sacrifice. Whether they did or did not, she would have her child.

The king pivoted on his heel and marched into the glen, surrounded by his men.

Georges glanced over his shoulder, seeking out her gaze. Stopping, he turned and saluted her.

She saluted her old friend Georges, as she also symbolically saluted a goodbye to her former life. Amazingly, her heart felt incredibly, wonderfully lighter.

"Are you okay?" Keir asked, tucking her hair behind her ear tenderly.

She searched his eyes for signs of joy and acceptance, or conversely, condescension. Then she turned and studied Zarod in a like manner. "That depends…"

"On?" Zarod spread his palm over her belly, awe dawning in his expression.

Hope flared and she covered his hand with hers. "On whether you want to be fathers. On whether you still want me now that you're free to leave and do anything, go anywhere, be anything you desire."

The men hugged her fiercely to them and Keir gave her a stern look. "Brat. What makes you think we wouldn't want you—or our precious child?"

Melena looked down at her stomach. "I can't tell you which one is the father."

Keir tilted up her head, forcing her to look into his soulfully tender eyes. "You think that matters? We love you. We love *our* child."

Zarod nodded. "We couldn't be happier."

"But the ransom? And I have no dowry now."

Zarod shushed her with a finger to her lips. "We have the best treasure of all—you and our baby."

Keir added, "Kidnapping you was the best thing we ever did."

Zarod shook his head. "No. Loving each other is."

Her heart swelled with love for her pirates, and she thanked the goddess for watching out for her. "You didn't kidnap me. You set me free."

About the Author

$\mathcal{EO}$

Whether it's strolling through the worst slums of the Third World to serve the poor in her day job, marching in the Mardis Gras parade representing the US Air Force, falling off horses in the middle of riding competitions (while she's trying to impress a really handsome real-life hero), or spending unforgettable romantic afternoons on the sun-kissed Florida beaches, Ashley Ladd lives for romance and adventure.

Wanting it all, Ashley is not content to sit back and watch life pass her by. Her lifelong quest is to find the perfect hero, run faster than a speeding locomotive, stop speeding bullets, fly through the heavens—*oops*, that's her *really* top top secret identity. Like herself, her heroines often do crazy things like fall off horses at the worst possible moment leaving no choice but to laugh at themselves as they blunder their way through this, or far-distant, crazy mixed-up worlds. In the end, dreams come true, the handsome hero falls madly in love with the heroine, and all is right with the universe, crazy as it may be.

In reality, Ashley Ladd lives in South Florida with her husband, five children, and beloved pets. She loves the water, animals (especially cats), and playing on the computer. She's been told she has a wicked sense of humor and often incorporates humor and adventure into her books. She also adores very spicy romance, which she weaves into her stories. She loves receiving email from her fans at Chinara@aol.com and she also invites you to visit her cyber home at: www.ashleyladd.com.

Ashley Ladd welcomes mail from readers. You can write to her c/o Ellora's Cave Publishing at 1056 Home Avenue, Akron OH 44310-3502.

Also by Ashley Ladd

ຂ

American Beauty

Blessed Be

Carbon Copy

Civil Affairs

Price of Fame

Purrfect Justice

Sex Kittens (*anthology*)

Why an electronic book?

We live in the Information Age — an exciting time in the history of human civilization in which technology rules supreme and continues to progress in leaps and bounds every minute of every hour of every day. For a multitude of reasons, more and more avid literary fans are opting to purchase e-books instead of paperbacks. The question to those not yet initiated to the world of electronic reading is simply: *why?*

1. *Price.* An electronic title at Ellora's Cave Publishing and Cerridwen Press runs anywhere from 40-75% less than the cover price of the <u>exact same title</u> in paperback format. Why? Cold mathematics. It is less expensive to publish an e-book than it is to publish a paperback, so the savings are passed along to the consumer.

2. *Space.* Running out of room to house your paperback books? That is one worry you will never have with electronic novels. For a low one-time cost, you can purchase a handheld computer designed specifically for e-reading purposes. Many e-readers are larger than the average handheld, giving you plenty of screen room. Better yet, hundreds of titles can be stored within your new library — a single microchip. (Please note that Ellora's Cave and Cerridwen Press does not endorse any specific brands. You can check our website at www.ellorascave.com or

www.cerridwenpress.com for customer recommendations we make available to new consumers.)

3. *Mobility*. Because your new library now consists of only a microchip, your entire cache of books can be taken with you wherever you go.

4. *Personal preferences are accounted for*. Are the words you are currently reading too small? Too large? Too...**ANNOYING**? Paperback books cannot be modified according to personal preferences, but e-books can.

5. *Instant gratification*. Is it the middle of the night and all the bookstores are closed? Are you tired of waiting days—sometimes weeks—for online and offline bookstores to ship the novels you bought? Ellora's Cave Publishing sells instantaneous downloads 24 hours a day, 7 days a week, 365 days a year. Our e-book delivery system is 100% automated, meaning your order is filled as soon as you pay for it.

Those are a few of the top reasons why electronic novels are displacing paperbacks for many an avid reader. As always, Ellora's Cave and Cerridwen Press welcomes your questions and comments. We invite you to email us at service@ellorascave.com, service@cerridwenpress.com or write to us directly at: 1056 Home Ave. Akron OH 44310-3502.